# PURSES
# and
# POISON

Books by Dorothy Howell

HANDBAGS AND HOMICIDE

PURSES AND POISON

Published by Kensington Publishing Corporation

# PURSES
# and
# POISON

## Dorothy Howell

KENSINGTON BOOKS
http://www.kensingtonbooks.com

KENSINGTON BOOKS are published by

Kensington Publishing Corp.
119 West 40th Street
New York, NY 10018

All Kensington titles, imprints, and distributed lines are available at special quantity discounts for bulk purchases for sales promotion, premiums, fund-raising, educational, or institutional use.

Special book excerpts or customized printings can also be created to fit specific needs. For details, write or phone the office of the Kensington Special Sales Manager: Attn. Special Sales Department. Kensington Publishing Corp., 119 West 40th Street, New York, NY 10018. Phone: 1-800-221-2647.

Kensington and the K logo Reg. U.S. Pat. & TM Off.

Library of Congress Catalog Number: 2009923862

ISBN-13: 978-0-7582-2376-0
ISBN-10: 0-7582-2376-5

First Hardcover Printing: July 2009

10  9  8  7  6  5  4  3  2  1

Printed in the United States of America

*To David, Stacy, Judy, and Seth*

# ACKNOWLEDGMENTS

The author is extremely grateful for the wit, wisdom, knowledge, and support of many people. Some of them are David Howell, Judith Howell, Stacy Howell, Seth Branstetter, Martha Cooper, Candace Craven, Lynn Gardner, Ellie Kay, Diana Killian, Kelly Mays, Bonnie Stone, Tanya Stowe, and Willian F. Wu, Ph.D. Many thanks to Evan Marshall of the Evan Marshall Agency, and to John Scognamiglio and the hardworking team at Kensington Publishing for all their support.

# PURSES
# and
# POISON

# Chapter 1

"I'm in love," I swore.

"You're in heat," Marcie replied.

My best friend, Marcie Hanover, and I were at the South Coast Plaza, one of L.A.'s trendiest shopping centers, and I was within seconds of performing a carnal act on a display case.

"Forget it, Haley," Marcie told me.

"But it's a *Judith Leiber*," I said, caressing the glass case with my palms. Inside was the most gorgeous evening bag I'd ever laid eyes on—and I've seen a lot of bags. Marcie has, too. We readily admit to our handbag addiction.

In fact, over the last couple of months the two of us had moved beyond being compulsive, crazed, white twenty-somethings obsessed with designer purses. We were no longer simply handbag whores. Now we were handbag whore businesswomen.

Or trying to be.

"You can't get that bag," Marcie insisted, gesturing at the display case.

"Austrian crystals," I said—actually, I think I moaned— "elegantly handcrafted."

"No."

"It's got a satin lining."

"Walk away from the case, Haley."

"And comes in a gorgeous box."

"Step back. Now."

"With a keepsake bag!"

"It's two thousand dollars!"

Best friends can really spoil a mood sometimes.

Marcie was right, though. Marcie is almost always right. I couldn't get the bag—right now, anyway—thanks to the new direction my life had taken.

Only a couple of months ago I, Haley Randolph, with my dark hair worthy of a salon-shampoo print-ad in *Vogue,* my long pageant legs, and my beauty-queen genes—even though they're mostly recessive—had figured everything out. And not only did I know what I wanted, but I also knew how to get it. Yeah, yeah, I knew I was twenty-four now. A huge chunk of my life was gone already. But that wasn't the point. The point was that I was going for it.

Marcie and I left the store and moved through the mall with the rest of the late morning crowd. That gorgeous evening bag had taken possession of my brain; I'd probably lie awake all night figuring a way to get it.

"Are we still going to that new club tomorrow night?" Marcie asked.

Hearing about an opportunity to party snapped me out of my Judith Leiber stupor.

"Yeah, sure," I said.

"No homework this weekend?" Marcie asked.

Damn. Homework. I'd forgotten about it. Again.

In a startling moment of clarity worthy of a Lifetime Channel movie, I'd made the decision to forgo my career, such as it was, in accounting, and blow off a move to San Francisco to pursue a higher education. I'd wanted a real career, a profession. Something of substance, importance, where I could have a positive impact on the lives of others—plus, make a lot of money and buy great handbags, of course.

I still didn't know exactly what sort of position that would be, and didn't really care, as long as I could be the person in charge and everybody else had to do what I said.

Businesses wouldn't let you make the big decisions, take over, and run things unless you had credentials—go figure—so I was now pursuing my bachelor's degree. The college counselor, who was obviously overdue for a stint in rehab, thought that because I had every weekday free, I should take a full load. That's six classes, or something.

But I didn't want to overwhelm myself by taking on too much, so I cut my schedule down a little. The classes I picked were tough, though. Both of them.

So far, college seemed a lot like high school, so I didn't understand what the fuss was all about. Plus, the instructors were taking themselves way too seriously. They expected us to complete every single assignment and actually pay attention in class. I was just there to complete the course; they seemed to think I wanted to *learn* something.

I wasn't worried about my grades. English was easy—all I'd done so far was copy stuff off the Internet—and I'd be able to keep up the good grades in Health, as long as that girl who sat in front of me didn't start covering her paper.

Marcie and I left the mall and said good-bye in the parking lot, and I took the freeway to Santa Clarita, a really great upscale area about thirty minutes north of Los Angeles. I had an apartment there, which was terrific, and a job there that wasn't. But that's okay, because I was on my path toward a highly successful future . . . somewhere, doing something.

Holt's Department Store was seven minutes from my place—six, if I ran the light at the corner. It was a midrange store that sold clothing and shoes for the whole family, jewelry, accessories, and housewares, mostly.

The corporate buyer in charge of the clothing ought to

be taken out behind one of the stores and beaten—or worse, be forced to wear Holt's clothing. Believe me, no one lies awake at night plotting a way to purchase anything on our racks.

I had started working there last fall just before Thanksgiving as a salesclerk. It was supposed to be through the holidays, but then all sorts of crap happened. I ended up with a hundred thousand dollars in the bank and a gorgeous boyfriend.

Somehow, things hadn't turned out exactly as I'd imagined. Having a hundred grand wasn't as much fun as I thought it would be, and Ty Cameron, the man I thought I'd fallen in love with, well, I wasn't sure where things stood with him.

Which was totally *his* fault, of course.

That's why I desperately needed that Judith Leiber evening bag. If a beautifully boxed clutch with Austrian crystals, a satin lining, and a keepsake bag couldn't cheer you up, was there any hope for mankind?

I pulled into the parking lot in front of the Holt's store. It was almost empty. The store was closed until 6:00 p.m. today to get ready for "our biggest sale of the season." That's what the sign in the front window said. But, really, the inventory team was working inside and didn't want to be bothered with customers.

I know exactly how they feel.

I swung around back and parked. The area outside the loading dock had been completely transformed. A big white tent-top had been erected. Latticework screens circled the tent and blocked out the view of the Dumpsters. Tables were decorated with pastels, and a runway led from a curtained platform. Another table held a couple dozen wrapped gifts. Potted green plants and blooming flowers were everywhere. One of the loading dock doors was open and I saw the caterer's staff working inside the stockroom.

Holt's had decided to treat us employees to a luncheon and

a fashion show of the new line of spring clothing we were going to carry. They were also raffling off prizes.

I had to admit, the place looked great and the idea was a good one. I didn't really *want* to admit it, though, since the whole concept was Sarah Covington's, Holt's vice president of marketing.

I hate Sarah Covington.

Which is all *her* fault, of course.

An RV was parked near the stage, and I could hear teenage girls inside, giggling and chattering. I guessed they were the models, excited about strutting the spring fashions on the makeshift catwalk.

Two of my friends were already seated at a table. Bella was tall, black, and working at Holt's to save for beauty school. Girlfriend knew hair. I was thinking she was into an international landmark phase. Today, her hair looked like the Eiffel Tower. Next to her was Sandy. White, young, pretty, and, judging by the idiot she dated, had the word *doormat* tattooed across her back.

They'd saved me a seat, which was way cool, so I gave them a wave as I headed for the steps leading up to the loading dock. Then Rita planted herself in front of me and folded her arms.

"The store is off-limits," she said. "You can't go in there."

Rita was the cashiers' supervisor, though from the way she dressed—stretch pants and tops with farm animals on the front—you'd think she was the corporate clothing buyer.

Rita hated me. I hated her first. Then she took it to the next level when she jacked the purse party business idea Marcie and I came up with and stole all our customers. Now I double-hated her.

"The inventory team is working in the store," Rita said. "Absolutely nobody is allowed inside."

"If I throw a stick, will you leave?" I said to her.

"*Nobody.*" Rita sneered and leaned closer. "And that includes you, princess, no matter *who* you're sleeping with."

Rita gave me one last nasty look and stomped away.

I was pretty sure she was referring to my sort-of boyfriend, Ty Cameron. He was the fifth generation of his family to own and run the Holt's stores.

You'd think that would entitle me to a few perks around here—I don't think there's anything wrong with preferential treatment as long as it benefits *me*—but no. I was still pulling down seven bucks an hour; plus, I had to actually wait on customers.

Contrary to what Rita and most everyone else thought, Ty and I weren't having sex. Yet. Which was totally his fault. Okay, well, maybe some of my fault, too.

I bounded up the steps to the loading dock. The servers were bustling around getting ready to take out the first course. I recognized the caterer, Marilyn something-or-other. Everything looked and smelled great.

In the corner sat dozens of bouquets of chocolate-dipped fruit, cut into the shapes of flowers, and arranged in little terra-cotta pots. They were from Edible Elegance, my mom's latest experiment with living in the real world.

My mom was a former beauty queen. Really. Before she married my dad and had my brother, sister, and me, Mom was prancing the runways, performing—I'm not sure what Mom's "talent" was; she told me, but I wasn't paying attention—and wishing for world peace.

Mom never really hung up her crown. Once a beauty queen, always a beauty queen, apparently—sort of like the marines, except the marines aren't quite as ruthless. She was still involved with the pageant world and a coven, as I liked to think of them, of other ex-queens, though I wasn't sure how, exactly; I wasn't paying attention to that either.

Just where Mom got the idea of the Edible Elegance fruit bouquets I don't know—I doubt Mom knew, either—but they'd been making a splash at L.A. events for a few months now. I helped out with the business, sometimes.

So you'd think that my mom was a hardworking, inventive, highly motivated businesswoman. Right?

No. My mom's idea of running a business was to hire a manager, turn the whole thing over to her, and see what happened. This, of course, drove the old geezer who oversaw the trust fund Mom's grandmother left her—along with a fabulous house in LaCanada Flintridge—absolutely crazy.

That's my mom.

I checked out the fruit bouquets. Everything looked great. The crew Mom's manager hired had done a terrific job. They'd added a chocolate name tag to some of the bouquets, which I hadn't seen before, and I thought the personalization was a nice touch. I guess Mom was still coming up with some ideas after all.

Outside I heard Jeanette Avery, the store manager, on the mic welcoming everyone to the luncheon. Jeanette was in her fifties, looking to retire in a few years. She was dedicated to Holt's. This inexplicably manifested itself in her attire. She always dressed in Holt's clothing. Today, she had on a purple-and-yellow-striped dress. The remaining nine dresses that had been shipped to the store were on the clearance rack.

I was about to head outside and take my seat with Bella and Sandy when I noticed someone in the domestics department section of the stockroom. At first I thought it was a member of the inventory team, sent to the store for the day, then saw the gold vest, white shirt, and bow tie, and realized it was one of the servers. A girl, twenty years old, maybe, leaning heavily against the big shelving unit.

She didn't look so good.

I walked over, and the closer I got, the worse she looked. Sweaty, yet flushed, palm on her stomach like she might throw up.

"Need some help?" I asked.

She jumped as if I startled her, and pushed herself up straight.

"No, I'm fine," she insisted. "I'm great. Just great."

"No offense, but you look like crap," I said.

She gulped hard, as if she was trying to keep something down. "I'll be okay. I—I will."

I could tell she didn't believe it—and I certainly didn't believe it—so I nodded toward the food station where the salads were being plated.

"I'll go tell them you're sick and you need to go home."

"No!" she said, suddenly springing toward me. "Don't do that. You'll get me in all sorts of trouble. I need this job. If I don't finish out the day, I don't get paid. And I'll never get hired again."

"Yeah, but if you're sick—"

"Look, I need the money. I've got school and rent and *everything.*"

I started feeling a little queasy myself. Money problems, job problems. It all seemed eerily familiar.

But I couldn't let this girl get sick and ruin the day. The store employees had been through a lot these past few months. They deserved a nice luncheon, a sneak peek at the spring line, and a prize raffle in a vomit-free environment.

Plus, Holt's had gone to a lot of trouble and expense to set this up. That witch Sarah Covington—Ty thought the world revolved around her, he let her intrude on everything, and I do mean *everything*—had put a great deal of effort into it.

And Ty was my boyfriend. Sort of. This was his store, his luncheon, his reputation. I couldn't just stand there and do nothing.

"I'll serve for you," I said.

Her eyes widened—they looked really watery. "You can't do that—"

"I've done it before," I told her, which wasn't true, but what was the big deal? All you had to do was set plates on the table.

Besides, I knew the caterer, sort of. Marilyn whatever-her-last-name-was had catered several events I'd attended; plus, I'd seen her at my mom's house—Mom certainly wasn't going to cook at her own dinner party.

I was sure Marilyn didn't know who I was, but if I mentioned Mom—something I rarely do—I knew she'd be okay with me filling in, rather than be shorthanded or have the server barf all over everything.

"It will be fine," I told her. "Just give me your vest and tie, and take off. Nobody ever looks at the wait staff, anyway. I doubt anybody will even notice."

I knew my friends outside would notice. But so what? I'd just tell them I'd spit in their dessert if they gave me a hard time.

"Look," I said, "if you throw up in the food, they'll send you home, and you won't get paid, anyway. Plus, they won't hire you again."

She stewed on that for about a minute, then gave me her vest and tie, and slipped away.

I dashed up the big concrete stairs to the second floor of the stockroom, feeling pretty good about myself that I'd done something to help out that girl. And I'd probably saved the entire promotional event. Ty would surely be impressed. Sarah Covington wouldn't have done what I was doing.

I'll have to work that into the conversation with Ty, somehow.

In the juniors section of the stockroom I pulled a white blouse off a hanger—just why on earth Holt's carried white blouses, I didn't know. No one was in the stockroom—it was off-limits to employees today and the inventory team was still working in the store—so I changed into the blouse, put on the vest, which was a little big but oh well, and the bow tie, and got back downstairs in time to grab a tray of salads and head outside.

Wow, look at me go. Making the big decisions, putting them into action—and I didn't even have my bachelor's degree yet.

Then I froze at the top of the loading dock stairs.

Oh my God. *Oh my God.*

There stood Claudia Gray.

Claudia Gray. Gorgeous—and I mean *gorgeous*—poised, confident, beauty queen, and high fashion model Claudia Gray.

Not only did she know my mother, not only did she know all of my mother's friends, but she was Ty's ex-girlfriend.

Oh my God. Now I thought *I* might throw up.

What was she doing here? Then I saw her talking to some of the models and realized she must be their pageant coach.

I ducked back into the loading dock, nearly causing a pileup among the servers behind me.

I couldn't go out there. I couldn't. Claudia looked fabulous, and I had on a caterer's uniform.

What if Claudia recognized me? What if she told my mother—and my mother's megabitchy pack of backstabbing friends—that she saw me here? At *Holt's*?

I never quite got around to telling Mom that I worked here. I never quite got around to telling Mom a lot of things. She didn't know about all that crap I had gone through last fall: how I lost that fabulous job; how I ratted out her tennis club's gorgeous pro; how only I and five of Drew Barrymore's closest friends ended up with a so-hot-it-smokes red leather Notorious handbag. Mom didn't even know I was sort-of dating Ty.

"Keep it moving, will you?" the server behind me said as he skirted past me and down the steps.

Oh my God. I had to do something.

I put down the tray and ran to the stockroom. I pulled a blond wig off a naked mannequin, twisted my hair into a knot, and yanked it on. Then I grabbed a pair of sunglasses from the accessories department section, slid them on, reclaimed my tray of salads, and started serving.

Nobody noticed me. I served the entree, the fruit bouquets, Jeanette made endless remarks, Claudia emceed the fashion show, I refilled coffee, tea, and lemonade, and nobody recognized me.

Whew! What a relief. Seemed like the day was coming off pretty well, thanks to yours truly.

The prize raffle was winding down, the caterers were packing up, and I'd had enough. My feet hurt and the mannequin's wig was making my head itch.

Marilyn hadn't said a word to me, and I hadn't heard any of the servers ask about the other girl. Nobody missed her, which miffed me a bit, since I'd single-handedly saved the entire day, but oh well. Marilyn would just mail her paycheck, and nobody would be the wiser.

I'd still have to find a way to work it into a conversation with Ty, though.

I went upstairs to the juniors section of the stockroom and changed back into my sweater. The white blouse was rumpled and didn't smell quite so fresh, so I shoved it behind the hair dryers; I'd just enter it as a return in the inventory computer when I clocked in and put the wig back later.

I went downstairs hoping Claudia would be gone when I looked outside. Maybe I could hang out with Bella and Sandy for a while, see who'd won a prize at the raffle.

But before I reached the loading dock, I heard screams from inside the store. I ran through the swinging door that opened near the customer service booth and saw a crowd of people outside the women's restroom. The door stood open and I saw more people inside. Men and women. Everybody looked stunned. Two women were crying and somebody was still screaming.

I pushed my way inside the restroom. The crowd had broken back in a semicircle near the diaper changing station. On the floor of the handicapped stall lay Claudia Gray. Dead.

# Chapter 2

For once in her life, Claudia didn't look so good. She lay facedown on the floor, her head near the toilet. There was a big gash over her left eye. Blood had soaked her hair and puddled under her cheek, along with some other really gross-looking stuff.

I stepped into the stall just far enough to bend down and get a closer look at her. Her pupils were fixed and dilated. I touched her neck—which creeped me out big time—but didn't feel a pulse.

Claudia was dead.

I launched into take-charge mode.

"Everybody move back," I said, waving my arms toward the door. "Don't touch anything."

Slowly, everyone left the restroom, some sniffling, some white faced, others craning their necks for another look. I didn't recognize anybody. They must have all been on the inventory team.

"You." I pointed to a tall guy. "Keep everybody together. And make sure nobody leaves the store."

See how I'm meant to be in charge?

I pointed to a heavyset woman wearing jeans and a man's T-shirt. I picked her because she looked like a lesbian, and you can always count on a lesbian in a crisis.

"Stand at the door," I told her. "Don't let anyone go inside."

She took up her position without a word.

I grabbed the telephone at the customer service booth and called 9-1-1, then headed into the stockroom. The police would want to question everyone who was present, so I had to keep the catering crew and the employees from leaving. I had to tell Jeanette what had happened.

My steps slowed as I approached the loading dock.

Then I'd have to call Ty and tell him his ex-girlfriend was dead.

Oh, crap.

Claudia would have loved all the attention—if she hadn't been dead, of course.

Two police cars, a fire truck, and an ambulance were parked behind Holt's, their lights flashing. Yellow crime scene tape was everywhere. Men and women in uniforms and plainclothes roamed in and out of the loading dock, talking into radios, on cell phones. Equipment was being hauled around.

The caterer's staff, the inventory team, the Holt's store employees, and the teenage models were corralled inside the white latticework fence under the tent-top. Some of the teen girls were crying. I stood next to Jeanette near the curtained stage, away from the loading dock but close enough to see what was happening. We both sort of stood there, not talking to each other.

I'd called Ty but he hadn't picked up, so I left a message on his voice mail to call me right away. I hadn't heard back from him.

Jeanette gasped—I thought for a moment she'd caught the reflection of her dress in a car windshield somewhere—but realized she'd seen the homicide detectives pull up.

Then I gasped, too. Oh my God. The same two detectives who'd been here the last time someone was murdered at Holt's.

Detective Madison grasped the door frame and, after a couple of tries, heaved himself out of the passenger seat. He'd lost more hair since the last time I saw him—I'd like to think I was responsible for that, in some small way—and leaned back slightly to offset his basketball belly.

Beside him stood Detective Shuman. Young, kind of good looking, wearing a shirt and tie that didn't quite go together.

Shuman and I had history.

Detective Madison spotted me. Fifty people in the crowd and it was me he homed in on. Great.

"I knew I'd find you in the middle of this," he said, looking delighted that he might have a second chance to pin a murder on me.

"I thought you retired," I said.

He gave me a smug look, then walked toward the loading dock. Shuman held back.

"We've got to stop meeting like this," I said to him.

He pressed his lips together—I know he wanted to smile—and said, "I'll catch up with you later."

About a minute later, a Porsche 911 Turbo pulled up and Ty jumped out. Oh my God, he was so handsome. Tall, athletic build, light brown hair, gorgeous blue eyes. He dressed in the most incredible suits, and—and when did he get a Porsche?

Never mind. No time for that now. I was going to have to tell him about Claudia. This would be a major moment in our relationship. How should I say it?

Why can't they cover something like this in that stupid health class I'm taking?

Or maybe they did.

Anyway, I had to handle this just right.

I'd take him aside. Yes, of course, that would be perfect. Just the two of us, out of the glare of the public eye, so I could break the upsetting news in private. I'd take his hands, look deep into his eyes, and say that Claudia had passed— I'd leave out the big gash on her forehead, the blood, and the other gross-looking stuff on her face, and the part about her lying in the handicapped stall. He'd be stunned, of course. He'd grab me. Hold me. Cling tight to my warm, living body, thankful that I was here with him, sharing this difficult time, and—

Wait. He walked right past me.

"Ty?" I hurried to catch up as he strode toward the loading dock.

He glanced at me, but kept going.

"Ty, something happened. I need to tell you about—"

"Sarah told me."

He kept going. I stopped and watched him disappear inside.

Sarah told him? *Sarah?*

I'd seen Jeanette on her cell phone earlier, so she probably notified somebody at the Holt's corporate office. Sarah must have a network of spies in the building, feeding her information so she could be the first to tell Ty everything.

See why I hate her?

By the time the cops started interviewing the teenage models, their parents had shown up, brought to the store by frantic cell phone calls from the girls. There was a lot of hugging and crying.

From what I overhead of their statements to the cops, none of the models had seen anything unusual, which didn't surprise me. Teenage girls—particularly teenage models— don't usually look at anything but a mirror.

They all went home with their parents, since the RV Claudia had driven them to the store in couldn't be moved, while the cops took statements from everyone else.

Ty came down the loading dock steps looking grim. I

didn't know if the detectives let him see Claudia's body, but I hoped not.

I didn't know how deeply involved he had been with Claudia. They'd dated, but I didn't know for how long—swapping stories with your new boyfriend about former lovers wasn't usually a good idea.

Ty headed toward Jeanette and me. I walked forward and intercepted him.

"I'm so sorry about Claudia," I said.

He looked at me and nodded.

"Has somebody notified her family?" I asked.

"They spoke with her mother."

I flashed on my mom answering the door at her house, seeing two policemen waiting, *knowing*. I didn't like that mental picture. I shook it off.

I didn't know how things had been left between Ty and Claudia's family after their breakup, but I couldn't imagine that would be an issue at a time like this.

"Do you think we should go see her mom?" I asked. "We could stop by the house and—"

"I already phoned her."

Okay, that surprised me.

"Well, then maybe we should—"

I didn't get to finish the sentence. Ty walked away. Again. He headed across the parking lot to where a Beemer had just pulled up. Sarah Covington got out.

She looked fabulous, of course, in a Donna Karan business suit.

I have on black pants and a white sweater.

"Give me your keys."

Bella appeared next to me, holding out her hand. Beside her stood Sandy with a blender tucked under her arm.

I glanced back at Sarah. She was talking and Ty had leaned down a little to hear her better.

"You won something in the prize raffle," Bella said. "I'll put it in your car."

My spirits lifted a little. Wow, I'd won a prize? Something good had happened today?

I pulled my keys from my pants pocket. "Is it cool?" I asked.

"Did you forget where you're working, all of a sudden?" Bella asked. "This is *Holt's*."

I gasped. "Oh my God, it's not clothes, is it?"

Bella's lips curled distastefully. "Let's just say that skank ho Rita was jealous that she didn't win it herself."

Could today get any worse?

Bella took my keys and left.

"So, where were you?" Sandy asked. "We saved you a seat."

I looked at Sarah again. She was still talking. Ty was still listening.

"I got sort of . . . tied up," I said. No point going into the whole sick-server story.

"I won a blender," she said, holding up the box.

Now she had my attention. "Bring it to my place. I could use a margarita."

"My boyfriend already said I have to give it to him," Sandy said. "He's on this special diet that will increase his creativity and enhance his artistic talents."

"He does tattoos."

"It's art, Haley," she said.

I stole another look at Sarah. Jeez, doesn't that bitch ever shut up?

"Couldn't we break it in with at least one batch of margaritas?" I asked, sounding a little desperate.

"I have to take it to him tonight. Right after I pick up his roommate's mother from the airport," Sandy said, then gazed behind me. "Wow, who are all of those people?"

I turned and saw that two Mercedeses had pulled up alongside Sarah's BMW and Ty's Porsche. Two men in Armani suits got out.

I didn't know them, but I knew their type.

"Lawyers," I said to Sandy. I didn't add that they were from the Pike Warner law firm because I didn't want to have to explain how I knew that choice bit of info.

The lawyers, Sarah, and Ty formed up in a tight huddle, which kind of irked me. I wanted to be in the huddle, too. Why did I have to wait for a college degree to get in the huddle?

But I already knew what they were talking about. Liability and damage control.

You'd think they would have a plan already in place, after what had happened here last fall.

"Hi, Haley," somebody said.

Troy walked up. He was just out of high school, worked part-time in the men's department, and seemed to be doofing his way through life.

"Wow . . ." he said, sounding awestruck. "You're the coolest."

Apparently, word had gotten around how I'd taken charge of everything in the women's restroom. And it was pretty cool.

Troy's eyes were wide and his mouth hung open a little. "I never figured you'd do . . . *that*."

Ty, Sarah, and the two lawyers were on the move now, heading toward Jeanette. I saw my chance, so I hurried over.

I wedged myself into the new huddle, anxious to take my rightful place at my sort-of boyfriend's side, but Sarah and Jeanette beat me to it. Then I realized that Troy was standing next to me. What was he doing here?

Introductions were made, including Troy—he didn't say anything, just stared at me, which was sort of embarrassing—and I found out the attorneys from the Pike Warner law firm were Peter McKenzie and Gabe Richards. They were mid-thirties, probably, on their way up the corporate ladder. I didn't know either of them and, hopefully, they didn't recognize me.

"Don't I know you?" McKenzie asked.

Crap. The last thing I wanted to do was go into everything that had happened at Pike Warner last fall.

"We've never met," I said, which was true, but it was possible he'd seen my name on documents that had circulated through the firm.

"Here's what we're up against," Ty said, glancing at his wristwatch. "The store is scheduled to open in less than two hours. If that doesn't happen—"

"It will be a media disaster," Sarah declared.

Peter McKenzie glanced down at me and frowned. I knew he was trying to remember where he knew me from. Why wasn't he paying attention to the huddle?

"We'll have helicopters circling, camera crews crawling all over the place," Sarah said. "We *do not* want to headline the eleven p.m. news. We *have* to open, as scheduled."

Troy gulped hard right next to my ear. Why wouldn't he go away?

"What about the inventory team?" Jeanette asked. "Their work is only half finished. They're supposed to be out of here by six, and at the San Diego store tomorrow. If that doesn't happen, I'll have to reschedule them. That means closing the store another entire day, changing all of our advertising—and you know what that will do to profits, especially this time of year."

*Think, think.* I had to think of something. This was a disaster, all right, a marketing and financial catastrophe. Reputation and money were on the line.

I was just as capable as anyone in the huddle—except maybe Troy, who kept breathing on me—of thinking up a solution, but I had to come up with it before Sarah.

Ty nodded toward the store. "I talked to the detectives. They can wrap up everything in a half hour."

Everybody breathed a sigh of relief. Ty had the solution all along.

He's so hot.

"That gives the inventory team ninety minutes to finish their work," Ty said.

"Can they do that?" Jeanette asked.

"They'll have to," Ty said.

He's so forceful, sometimes. It's way hot.

"So, as long as the police finish up their work in the next few minutes—" Jeanette began.

"We'll be fine," Ty said.

Crisis averted. Reputation saved. Financial problem resolved.

I love being in the huddle.

Detective Madison waddled down the loading dock stairs, Shuman behind him.

"We're shutting you down for the night," Madison announced.

"What?" Sarah exclaimed.

Tension in the huddle spun up again, higher this time. Ty stepped out in front, confronting the two detectives. Troy circled around to my other side, fixated on my left cheek.

"We've got another possible murder victim," Madison said.

Jeanette gasped. Gabe Richards and Sarah Covington put their heads together and started whispering.

"What the hell is a *possible* murder victim?" Ty demanded.

"We've got to take this place apart, piece by piece," Madison said.

Sarah whipped out her cell phone and frantically pushed buttons. Richards went for his BlackBerry. McKenzie pointed at me with a big goofy grin on his face and said, "Mount Rushmore." Troy snorted.

What a couple of idiots. They should be voted out of the huddle.

Never mind about that now. I had to do something to help Ty. His family had shepherded the Holt's Department Store through many a crisis, dating back to the 1800s. He had five generations riding on his shoulders. I knew I could do something to help.

"We've got a missing person," Detective Madison said. "Possibly a second murder victim, somewhere in the store."

Shuman looked at his notepad. "The caterer can't account for one of the servers."

What?

"None of the other servers recalls seeing her since shortly after they arrived," Shuman said. "But they report there was a server on duty that nobody recognized. And we found a disguise hidden upstairs in the stockroom."

A disguise? Upstairs in the stockroom?

"Looks like whoever this mystery person is might have murdered the server, put on her uniform and a disguise, then murdered Claudia Gray," Madison said.

Oh my God. *Oh my God.*

That's *me.* I'm the one who—

Oh, crap.

# Chapter 3

I had met Evelyn Croft last fall when I started working at Holt's. She was a department manager. We were nothing alike. Evelyn was fortyish, neat, trim, and could have worked as a docent giving tours in one of those old southern mansions. And I'm, well, I'm *me*.

But we were connected in some weird—and not so weird—ways.

Like today. I needed retail therapy—the only way I could possibly get over what had happened yesterday—and only Evelyn could help me with that.

That's because Evelyn had eighty grand of my money tucked away in her savings account.

I pulled up to the curb in front of her house. You wouldn't be surprised to see Evelyn outside in a big hat and gardening gloves, cutting flowers from her garden—if she weren't so afraid to leave her house these days.

She never talked about Holt's. Not after the murder and all that other crap that had happened last fall. If she mentioned it at all, she simply referred to it as "the incident" caused by "that certain someone." Which was great with me, especially today, because Holt's was the very last thing I wanted to be reminded of.

As I walked toward the front door, I saw the blinds on the living room window move slightly. I rang the bell.

"It's me," I called. I knew the drill.

The security system beeped. Chains rattled. Locks turned. A lot of precautions for this quiet neighborhood of family homes.

It had taken a long time for Evelyn to recover from last fall's physical injuries, but emotionally she wasn't all that strong. She never had been, really, and "the incident" had only made it worse.

The door opened a little and Evelyn's face appeared. Her gaze darted back and forth.

"It's just me," I said, trying to keep things light. "Just like I said on the phone."

I'd called ahead. Everyone had to call ahead.

She gave me a hesitant smile, then opened the door. I stepped inside.

Evelyn had on a mauve sweatshirt with a ruffle collar, denim jeans that she'd ironed, and white ankle socks. Her hair was perfect.

She slammed the door behind me and made quick work of the chains, locks, and security system.

"Well, Haley." Evelyn drew in a big breath and twisted her fingers together. "It's good to see you."

If it had been anyone else, I would have offered a big hug. But not with Evelyn.

I handed her the white plastic bag of groceries I'd picked up on my way over.

"Can I put these away for you?" I asked.

"Oh no, I can manage. Go have a seat. I'll be right there," Evelyn said, and disappeared into the kitchen.

I took my usual seat on the sofa in the living room. The place looked as if a florist had exploded in here. Floral slipcovers in pink, mint green, and white; floral arrangements; floral artwork; floral throw pillows she'd embroidered herself. Somehow, it worked in Evelyn's home.

A moment later she came into the living room carrying a tray with a tea service and a plate of cookies, and set it

on the coffee table. She passed me an envelope—reimburse-
ment for the groceries I'd bought—and poured.

When I first started coming over, bringing her things she
couldn't have delivered, I told her that the cost was no big
deal. But Evelyn had insisted, and since I didn't want to
upset her further, I rolled with it.

I knew Evelyn didn't need financial help. I happened to
be sitting across the dinner table from Ty—one of our supposed dates—when he told his attorney at Pike Warner not
to negotiate, just pay all of her medical expenses and give
her a half million bucks.

He's generous and decisive like that.

Why aren't I having sex with him?

"How are your classes?" Evelyn asked. She handed me
a teacup and took the chair next to the window.

"We're studying the nervous system in health," I said.

We were really studying STDs, but since I wasn't sure
Evelyn had ever had sex I didn't think it was a topic of
conversation she could run with.

I ate one of the cookies. Evelyn always served the same
kind. Dry, brittle, tasteless. Just once I wished she'd bust out
a package of Oreos. I could do without the tea, too, but I
didn't see her cracking open a Corona, even with chilled
mugs.

"I heard what happened yesterday at Holt's," Evelyn
said softly.

I jumped, nearly spilling my tea. What? Evelyn was talking about Holt's? I didn't want to be reminded of what had
happened yesterday. That's why I came here today.

"That poor girl dying in the store like that." Evelyn shook
her head sadly. "It was all over the news last night—every
channel."

"Well, you know, I think the newspeople really made
too much of it," I said. "Evelyn, there was something I
wanted to talk to you about while I'm—"

"And the Internet. My goodness, bloggers are going crazy.

Another beauty queen, gone. And, of course, that brought up the story of that darling little girl in Colorado."

I had to distract her. I lifted my cup. "This is great tea."

"And what about that girl they're calling the Missing Server?" Evelyn asked.

"Are there any more cookies?" I asked.

"They still haven't found her. After searching the entire store for hours."

"Did I mention that I got an A on my last English paper?"

"And now the store is closed again today," Evelyn went on. "It must be an absolute mess in there. I hate to think of how hard all the employees are going to have to work to get it presentable."

"It was a really hard paper, too."

"Jeanette must be beside herself, thinking of the lost income," Evelyn said. "This is a huge financial blow to the entire Holt's chain."

"I have to go now." I popped off the couch and headed for the door.

I simply could not stay here and listen to another word about what had happened yesterday. The whole thing had turned into a nightmare—a complete nightmare. Even though anyone in my position would have done the same thing.

"You're leaving?" Evelyn asked, sounding disappointed.

"I have to get to the store. Help with the cleanup," I said.

"But when you phoned, you said there was something you wanted to talk to me about," Evelyn said, putting her teacup aside.

Oh yeah. *That.*

I'd rehearsed my speech on the drive over, planned how I would present my case. And now, after being reminded of yesterday's fiasco, I needed a massive dose of retail therapy more than ever.

I put on a bright smile. "I'm going to this big charity

function. It's at the Biltmore Hotel. My whole family goes every year. Dinner and dancing. Very formal."

"Oh, it's a ball?" Evelyn asked, with a Cinderella twinkle in her eye.

"Yeah," I said. "A formal ball. With evening gowns and tuxedos."

"I'll bet you and your mom are going shopping together for dresses," Evelyn said, looking all dreamy.

Not if I could get out of it.

But I worked up an equally dreamy smile and said, "Mom always buys my dress for the occasion, but what I really need is a new evening bag. I found one that's perfect."

Evelyn morphed into the evil stepmother at light-speed. She shook her head and said, "I don't think so."

I'd expected some resistance, so I said, "It's a *Judith Lieber*."

"A what?"

Oh my God. How could someone *not* know what a Judith Lieber bag was? Only the world's most glamorous, gorgeous evening bags *ever*. They transcended fashion. They were art. Sort of.

"It has Austrian crystals," I said—actually, I think I moaned. "Elegantly handcrafted."

"Sounds expensive."

"And a satin lining," I said.

Evelyn shook her head. "No, no."

"It comes with a gorgeous box." I was whining now.

"Out of the question."

"And a keepsake bag!"

"No!" Evelyn said.

She picks now, of all times, to be assertive?

"I'm just following your instructions, Haley."

I hate it when other people are right.

When I'd gotten that big chunk of money last fall, I'd paid for my college classes and books, zeroed out my credit cards, and paid my rent and car payment ahead a few months. I bought some essentials, too, like a gorgeous Louis Vuitton tote, and the fabulous Coach handbag, wallet, and cosmetic bag combo set I'd had my eye on.

And there were so many more things I could have bought.

I knew me. I knew that all that money could disappear if I didn't do something drastic. Putting it in a savings account, or an IRA, or a mutual fund, or something boring like that was a possibility. But I knew I would suffer the financial penalty and take it out. So that left putting it in the safekeeping of a friend or family member. Money is the best way to ruin a friendship, so I didn't entrust it to Marcie; I liked her too much for that. And there was no way I would turn it over to my mom or dad. They would have asked how I'd gotten the money and I wasn't about to go into all of that with them.

So that left one person I could turn to. Evelyn. She was trustworthy and honest; plus, I knew that with her Holt's settlement, she didn't need any money so she wouldn't take mine. I made her promise not to give me any funds unless it was for something like medical bills, rent, or school. It had all made perfect sense.

Until I spotted that Judith Leiber bag.

"Okay, okay," I said, shaking off my disappointment. "Two thousand dollars for an evening—"

"Two thousand dollars?" Evelyn exclaimed.

"It's a very reasonable price," I explained. "Anyway, I'll figure out something else."

"You're not upset with me, are you?" Evelyn asked, twisting her fingers together.

I really wasn't, so I smiled. "No. Of course not. But I really do have to go."

"Oh well, of course. I was just hoping . . . well, that is . . . I wondered if you'd mind . . ." She moved to the blinds and pulled them open a quarter inch. "My neighbor. I think something's wrong."

I went to the window and she stepped aside so I could look out.

"Across the street, on the corner," Evelyn said.

The place looked like every other house on the block. Well-tended lawn, painted trim, clipped shrubbery.

"You want me to go over there and check on them?" I asked.

"No! Oh no!" Evelyn shook her head. "No, don't do that. Please. It's just that, well, I've known Cecil for about twenty years, ever since I've lived here. His wife died a few years ago. A traffic accident. Very sad. And now Cecil has a new girlfriend."

"What's the problem?"

Evelyn twisted her fingers together. "I think the new girlfriend killed him."

Great. I had to find out what was up with Evelyn's neighbor. Plus, I didn't get my own money to buy that Judith Leiber evening bag.

And my day wasn't over. Now I had to go to work. At Holt's.

I waved good-bye to Evelyn, jumped in my car, and headed for the freeway.

I wasn't scheduled to work until the evening, usually, but today was an exception. Everyone was coming in to get the store back in shape after the cops tore everything apart looking for the missing server.

Yeah, yeah, I know it was all my fault. But anybody in my place would have done the same thing. I mean, what choice did I have? I couldn't announce that I was the missing server the cops were trying to find.

Everybody was standing there. Sarah couldn't wait for me to look like an idiot—especially in front of Ty. And Ty would have been embarrassed by me. Plus, I didn't want him to know that I'd done the whole save-the-event thing to try and impress him. I'd have looked totally desperate.

And I certainly couldn't say that I was afraid Claudia would recognize me and blab to the ex-queen's cult that I was working as a caterer. How pathetic would that make me look?

And those attorneys from Pike Warner. They would have gone back to the firm and told the whole story to everybody. I didn't want anything added to all the other stuff they were saying about me there.

Detective Madison couldn't wait for me to screw up again. He would have found some way to twist the whole thing into making me a murder suspect. Again.

Once word got out, who knows who else would have found out? I would have looked like a complete idiot to absolutely everyone.

I exited the freeway, heading toward Holt's.

It didn't matter now, anyway. Everything had turned out okay, pretty much.

Holt's store employees got a whole day off yesterday, and I'd heard Ty say he was paying everyone extra for the hard job of getting the entire store back into shape today. The inventory team would have to come back, but oh well, they traveled from store to store all the time. Jeanette's quarterly bonus would suffer, but it's not like she used her money for anything worthwhile, like decent clothes or designer handbags.

True, Holt's had been all over the news, but there was no such thing as bad publicity; that's what everybody says, anyway. The department store had been in business for over a hundred years and had survived worse scandals.

Anyway, it didn't matter now that I'd stood there silently and let all that stuff happen. The whole thing was over with. The media had shone their spotlight on Holt's for a while, but it had already moved on to the next big story. That's just the way it was with newspeople. By the 6:00 p.m. news broadcast tonight, it would all be forgotten.

I parked in front of the Holt's store thinking this would be an easy day here. No customers. Every day at Holt's would be easier if it weren't for the customers.

Big signs were up in the windows announcing that we would reopen tomorrow for our "biggest sale of the season." Even so, I noticed a crowd of about two dozen people gathered at the corner of the building. I guess some people just couldn't wait for a great sale.

It felt kind of good to be at the store, back to normal, back to the regular routine of life. Nobody knew what I'd done yesterday—and nobody ever would—so I was clear on that. And, aside from Claudia being murdered, everything was okay again.

Colleen—to be generous, I'll call her "slow"—stood inside the big plate-glass doors, on guard duty. When I walked up, she pointed to the sign that said the store was closed.

"I work here," I said to her through the glass.

She gave me an apologetic shrug and pointed to the sign again.

Colleen knew I worked here. She saw me just about every day. Plus, I had my Holt's name tag in its lanyard hanging around my neck.

I might have to downgrade her from "slow."

"I . . . work . . . here," I said, pronouncing each word carefully.

Colleen shook her head again, and I screamed, "Open the damn door!"

She turned the key in the lock and jerked the door open.

"There are no customers trying to rush the store. They're all waiting at the corner of the building," I told her, and managed not to add "dumbass."

"Those aren't customers," Colleen said, relocking the door. "That's the volunteer search party."

"The—the *what*?"

"For that girl that's missing. The one that worked for the caterer."

I gasped and hurried away.

How could this be happening? All of this was supposed to be forgotten. There *couldn't* be a volunteer search party outside our store. Jeez, I hoped those people were just a tour group, or something.

I headed toward the back of the store.

Every department was a mess, thanks to the efforts of the police. All the mannequins had been stripped and were covered in that black fingerprint powder they show on all the TV crime dramas. Dozens of employees were busy cleaning, scrubbing, refolding, straightening, and restocking merchandise.

I spotted Bella at the shelves of T-shirts. She rolled her eyes when I walked over.

"You believe this mess?" she asked, waving her arms. "Those cops, they ought to get their butts back in here and clean this up."

"Did you see the store on TV this morning?" Sandy asked, popping up from behind a rack of blouses. "We made the network news shows. From New York."

The *network* broadcast? This *morning*? No, no, that couldn't be. People were supposed to *forget*.

"Which show was it?" Bella asked. "The one with that crazy-ass bitch who looks like she needs to easy up on her Zoloft? Or the one with that slut who looks like a talking blowup doll?"

"They're calling her the Missing Server," Sandy said. "There's a nationwide search for her."

Oh my God. This can't be happening.

"I've got to go punch in," I said, and headed toward the break room.

Where was a sensational celebrity scandal when you needed one? Or a mass suicide? Something *huge* needed to happen. And soon, to distract the media.

I took a deep breath, trying to calm myself. Another salacious tragedy had to strike almost immediately for this whole Missing Server thing to be forgotten. And it would. It always does. Everything would be fine—*it had to be.*

Then something great happened. I spotted Ty coming out of Jeanette's office. He looked terrific in his Armani suit. My heart did that little flip-flop and my belly felt kind of gooey, just like they did every time I saw him. I didn't know he'd be here today, so this was a great surprise.

Ty spotted me and walked over. He looked intense, but Ty almost always looked that way. His expression would melt any second now, as soon as he got closer.

I pictured it in my head.

We'll have a private moment. He'll lean down and whisper in my ear—just like he did with Sarah, only not as far because I'm enviably taller—something about how great it is to see me, how he misses me, how he wants the two of us to try and recapture that really hot moment in his apartment last fall before—

"The detectives are here," Ty said.

Hmm. Not exactly what I'd expected to hear, but that's okay. This was a public place, after all, and we were both at work. Having an intimate conversation wouldn't be appropriate.

I was surprised that Detectives Madison and Shuman were here again. I thought they'd completed their investigation at the store yesterday.

Ty leaned down a little and lowered his voice. "They want to talk to you. Privately."

What?

"They think you know something about yesterday that you're not telling them," Ty said.

My throat constricted.

His brows drew together. "You don't know anything that you haven't told them, do you, Haley?"

I gulped hard, trying desperately for my innocent look.

"I know you're nervous, but don't worry." Ty grasped my arm. "I'll go with in you, and I'll stay right beside you the entire time."

Oh, crap.

# Chapter 4

Ty looked down at me, exuding comfort and concern. I'd never gotten that look from him before, and it was nice—or it would have been if there was any way possible I could have been comforted at this particular moment.

Still holding my arm, Ty turned and we headed toward Jeanette's office, only to stop again. Troy and four other guys blocked the aisle. They were young, like Troy, and worked in the men's department with him.

Troy's mouth hung open a bit, and all of them stared and seemed to be breathing kind of hard.

"Hey, Haley," Troy said, then snorted.

The other guys clustered around him leaned forward a bit, eyes wide, jaws slack. They all yucked a goofy laugh, and kept gawking at me.

What was wrong with those guys?

Ty and I moved around them, down the aisle toward Jeanette's office.

I stopped dead in my tracks.

I couldn't go in there. I couldn't. What was I going to tell the detectives? How would I explain what happened? Especially with Ty standing right next to me?

I sure could use a Snickers bar right now.

"What's wrong?" he asked.

"I need to ask you something," I said, hoping he wouldn't see that I was stalling.

Should I just bolt? Jump in my car and disappear, never to be heard from again?

That might make me look guilty.

Ty was still watching me. I was still getting the concerned look. I had to say something.

"Yesterday when I called you about Claudia's death, why didn't you call me back?" I asked.

Ty shrugged. "I'd already heard the news from Sarah."

"Yeah, but I left a message saying it was an emergency. Weren't you concerned that something had happened to me?"

"I knew nothing had happened to you. You called me."

Oh. Yeah, right, I did. And it made sense, just like everything that involved Ty. But what if I'd called from the emergency room? What if I was down to my last breath?

I would have asked Ty both those questions, but he'd already walked away. He opened the door to Jeanette's office, swinging it wide so I had no choice but to go inside.

I felt like I was walking into the principal's office.

Detective Madison sat behind Jeanette's desk. Shuman stood behind him, off to the right.

I liked Shuman. We had a little thing going. Nothing romantic—but maybe there could be. He had a girlfriend who worked at the D.A.'s office that he was crazy about. I liked that about him. I helped their relationship along last fall, and he helped me with those murder charges. An even exchange, I think.

"So, Miss Randolph," Detective Madison said, giving me a snarky grin. "You again."

I took the chair in front of the desk and Ty sat beside me. Why was he in here? Why did he pick now, of all times, to be the concerned boyfriend?

"Just like old times, huh?" Detective Madison reared back in the chair. "You, me, a murder victim."

"Claudia was murdered?" I asked. I figured she probably was, but this delayed his questioning a little.

"Poisoned," Madison declared.

I turned to Ty and touched his hand.

"This will be hard for you to hear," I said, managing to sound compassionate. "You should wait outside."

"I'm fine," he told me.

"No, really, I insist," I said.

Ty ignored me and asked the detective, "What sort of poison?"

Shuman checked his notes. "The lab is still working on the tox screen."

"So you're investigating the caterer?" I asked.

I hated to throw Marilyn what's-her-name in front of the bus, but the police probably already had her at the top of their list.

"Right now," Detective Madison said, looking smug and pointing a stubby finger at me, "we're investigating *you*."

"Me?" I exclaimed. I tried for innocent outrage, but didn't quite pull it off.

"What can you tell us about yesterday?" Shuman asked.

"Nothing." Okay, that sounded kind of guilty.

"Nothing?" Madison snorted a laugh. "Well, let me tell you something about yesterday. You were seen entering the loading dock."

That fat cow Rita must have ratted me out.

"Even though you knew the stockroom and store were off-limits," Madison added. "And you were seen at the caterer's food station, messing around with those fruit bouquets."

Oh my God. *Oh my God.* The fruit bouquets—*Mom's* fruit bouquets. I didn't want to tell Madison they were from my mom's business. He'd be all over that. I couldn't let him drag her into a murder investigation.

"I was just checking them out," I explained. "I thought I recognized the caterer. Marilyn something-or-other."

I'm dying for a Snickers bar now.

"So the caterer can vouch for you?" Shuman asked, his pen poised over his notebook.

This wasn't good. This definitely was not good. The caterer couldn't vouch for me because she hadn't even known I was there.

So what could I say but, "Sure?"

"Nobody saw you during the luncheon," Madison told me. "You want to explain where you were?"

I couldn't explain. Not now. Not in front of Ty. I couldn't admit to all the problems I'd caused—which hadn't seemed like such a big deal at the time—and have everybody know what I'd done. The reasons—which were perfectly logical yesterday—seemed pretty lame right now.

"You were seen on the video surveillance tape going into the loading dock," Madison said. "But you weren't seen again until after Claudia Gray was murdered. Surveillance tape doesn't lie."

Damn that videotape. I always forgot about it.

"Well, Miss Randolph?" Madison sneered, like he knew I didn't have a good explanation.

Shuman looked at me weird now. So did Ty.

Where was Sarah Covington? She was always interrupting Ty. Why couldn't she show up the one time I needed her?

I had to tell them *something*. What sort of explanation could I give? Alien encounter? Out-of-body experience? Cramps?

"Okay, well, when I was in the loading dock, I heard a noise—a strange noise—in the stockroom," I said. It didn't come off as a total lie, which I was thankful for.

Detective Shuman leaned forward a bit, as if I were about to reveal something significant. Madison looked disappointed that I might.

"What sort of noise?" Madison demanded.

"Don't get all excited," I told him. "I'm not going to solve *this* case for you, too."

Shuman stifled a laugh and Madison narrowed his already beady eyes at me. I could only imagine the flak Madison had taken, after what had happened last fall.

"It was kittens," I announced. "I heard kittens in the stockroom, so I went to investigate."

Okay, it was possible. I'd seen birds flying around in one of those home improvement stores, and once I'd seen a stray dog that had gotten into the food court at the Grove shopping center.

"Kittens," Madison repeated, not bothering to hide his doubt.

Shuman looked at me really weird now. So did Ty.

"A big party going on outside, food, a fashion show, a prize raffle, and you're in the stockroom the whole time, looking for kittens," Madison said.

"I'm an animal lover," I told him. "I've been in parades and everything."

"So, where are these kittens now?" Madison wanted to know.

I rolled my eyes as if the answer should be obvious—I was getting really good at this police questioning thing—and said, "I couldn't find them. That's why I was in the stockroom the entire time."

"Until you heard screams coming from the store?" Shuman asked.

"Exactly."

I could feel Ty glaring at me. I didn't dare look at him.

"Well, then," Madison declared, "maybe we need to get Animal Control out here and find those kittens."

I could seriously kill someone for a Snickers bar right now.

"Maybe we need to keep the store shut down until we find them," Madison said.

No, no, no!

"Not so fast," Ty said. "Look, Detective, I've cooperated with you throughout this entire investigation, but I will not allow this store to be closed another day. Not for a litter of kittens."

"They're probably gone now, anyway," Shuman said. "After all the chaos yesterday, the mom moved them."

Madison looked as if he wanted to murder him for speaking up. I could have kissed him.

I popped out of my chair while I had the chance.

"I have to get to work," I said.

Ty got up when I did. I guess he was antsy about sitting there any longer. He hadn't been on his cell phone for a good ten minutes.

He opened the door and there stood Sarah Covington. She looked right through me. The two of them drew together as if they were magnetized and moved down the hallway a few feet, Sarah talking low and urgently, Ty listening carefully.

You'd think since she was a vice president she could make a decision or two on her own, without dragging Ty into every little thing that came along. I was thinking she just made up problems to take to him.

"I know about Claudia Gray and your boyfriend," Detective Madison called.

How had he found out so quickly that Ty and Claudia used to date?

I turned and saw Madison still seated at Jeanette's desk, still watching me, still looking smug. I guess he expected me to go back into the office, after hearing that comment. But no way was I getting close to him again.

Madison smirked. "Claudia was quite the looker. On the covers of all the big magazines. Appearing at those fashion shows. Everybody probably wondered what Cameron saw in *you*."

My stomach jerked into a knot and my cheeks heated up.

Madison hoisted himself out of the desk chair and walked over to me.

"You must have wondered the same thing yourself," he added, looking me up and down.

I knew he was comparing me to Claudia, and I wished I could say it didn't matter. But it did. I knew how gorgeous she was. I didn't need Madison to tell me I didn't measure up.

"So, maybe you decided to do something about it," he suggested, leaning closer. "Maybe you decided to get rid of the old girlfriend before Cameron came to his senses and realized what a mistake he'd made."

Breath went out of me. My cheeks flamed.

"Maybe you heard the same thing that I heard," Madison said, moving even closer. "That the two of them were getting back together."

I gulped, stunned. I knew the shock showed on my face because the detective grinned sadistically.

"Sounds like a motive for murder to me," he said, looking altogether pleased with himself.

Madison chuckled and walked out of the office. Shuman followed, but I couldn't even look at him. I grasped the door casing trying to hold myself up.

People thought I wasn't good enough for Ty. That didn't surprise me. All anyone had to do was look at Claudia and me. She was stunning and, as my ex-beauty-queen mom had often said, I was merely pretty.

I couldn't compete with Claudia in the looks department. But that's not why Ty was attracted to me. He said his grandmother thought I had spirit, and he liked the way I'd told him the truth about how awful Holt's clothing was, and that I—I . . .

I got a yucky feeling in the pit of my stomach. Why *did* Ty want to date me?

I thought back and realized he'd never really said. I mean, I could think of a million reasons he'd want to date me, but what had Ty actually said?

Then my stomach started feeling really yucky. Was Detective Madison telling me the truth? Had Ty been getting back together with Claudia?

A zillion thoughts flew through my mind. Ty canceling our dates, being late for our dates, talking on the phone through our dates. Always distracted, supposedly consumed with business. Plus, we hadn't slept together yet.

I looked down the hallway. Ty and Sarah had split up, both of them on their cell phones. I'm not big on suspense, so I headed toward Ty, ready to ask him exactly what was going on.

But as I passed Sarah, two words she said caught my attention: "Ty" and "Europe."

I froze behind her, blatantly listening to her conversation. She slapped her phone closed a few seconds later and opened her Louis Vuitton organizer.

"Ty . . . Ty's going to Europe?" I managed to ask.

"For several weeks," Sarah said, frantically flipping pages.

My heart sank.

Ty was going to Europe for several weeks. And he'd never even told me.

# Chapter 5

It was a Fendi day. Definitely a Fendi day.

The January weather was fabulous, as always in the Golden State, as I walked along Wilshire Boulevard. Shirtsleeve weather, as my father's relatives from back East like to say, on the rare occasions when they can tolerate my mother long enough to visit. They're always impressed by it while I, a native, take it for granted. I freely admit to being a California-weather wimp. Extreme heat, cold, or humidity and I freak out.

I'd selected the Fendi bag this morning because it so perfectly complemented the Chanel suit I had on—the kind I used to wear every day before last fall—and I needed to present just the right image. Facing down a vice president at the prestigious, old-money Golden State Bank & Trust would take some finesse—something I'm a little short on, but hey, that's what the Fendi and Chanel were for.

A reverent hush hung over the lobby of the GSB&T as I walked through the big glass door. It was exquisitely appointed in rich dark wood, sumptuous leather furniture, and fine artwork. Their branch offices that spread out across the West offered a more contemporary look, catering to the masses. But here at their main office, old money, good taste, and quiet sophistication reigned supreme. It was sort of like being in someone's rich grandmother's house.

The bank's greeter, a young woman wearing a gray skirt, a navy blue blazer, and a necktie, for some reason, approached.

"Good morning, ma'am," she said quietly, giving me the GSB&T smile called for in their customer care handbook, no doubt. "How may I assist you?"

I hoisted my Louis Vuitton organizer—a surprise gift from Ty, which proved he was crazy about me, didn't it?—so she could see it and be jealous.

"I'm here to see Bradley," I told her, managing to sound as if calling unannounced on a vice president at the B & T were the most routine of events.

"Is Mr. Olsen expecting you?" the greeter asked.

"No," I told her, giving her an eyebrow bob that indicated making an appointment was oh so far beneath me.

I may not have gotten my mom's looks, but I can summon her I'm-better-than-you gene when I need it.

And I needed it today. I didn't know if Bradley Olsen's secretary would schedule an appointment for me if I called—I'm pretty sure my picture, with a red circle and a line drawn through it, was plastered next to her telephone—but I figured if I showed up, he wouldn't refuse to see me.

The Golden State Bank & Trust had gotten caught up in that whole mess last fall, and while you'd think Bradley Olsen would be grateful that their involvement was settled quietly—meaning no lawsuit or unseemly publicity—I just didn't know how he'd feel about being reminded of the whole thing. When I'd brought Evelyn in here before Christmas to open that account with my settlement money, Mr. Olsen didn't seem all that glad to see me.

"Tell him Haley Randolph is here," I told the greeter. "And Ty Cameron will be joining us momentarily."

Ty wasn't coming—he didn't even know I was here—but what was the point of having a sort-of boyfriend if you couldn't use him, occasionally?

The customer greeter must have recognized the Cameron

name as one of their biggest and oldest depositors—I think their account number is "one"—because she invited me to be seated, offered to bring me coffee, then took off. As I'd discovered last fall, the B & T was anxious to make the Camerons happy.

A moment later, the customer greeter returned and escorted me though the silent corridors, the heels of my Jimmy Choos clicking on the marble floor, and into Bradley Olsen's well-appointed office.

He stood next to a desk big enough to land a squadron of F-22s on, and was as impeccable as his surroundings. Already over the hump and into his fifties, I guessed. Tall, trim, a touch of gray at his temples, an expensive suit and conservative necktie.

He didn't look surprised to see me—or glad, either.

"Good morning, Miss Randolph," he said, and gestured to a chair. "Please, have a seat. Can I offer you coffee? Tea, perhaps?"

"No, thank you," I said, and sat down, placing my Fendi bag and Louis Vuitton organizer on the edge of his desk where he would be sure to see them and know that I deserved to be here.

He sat and an awkward moment passed until he finally said, "So, how is Ms. Croft?"

"Evelyn?" I was surprised he remembered her. The new account we opened with a mere eighty grand was hardly cause for excitement at the Golden State B & T.

"Fully recovered," I reported. Physically, that was true. I didn't think Evelyn would want me telling the bank VP that she was too afraid to walk out her own front door these days.

"I'm so glad to hear that." Mr. Olsen looked relieved. "Really, I'm so glad. Please give her my warmest regards."

Another uncomfortable moment passed as he glanced from me to his office doorway.

"Should we wait for Mr. Cameron?" Mr. Olsen asked.

I made a show of looking at my watch, then shook my head.

"He must have been delayed. There's a situation with advertisers," I said, which could have been true. I'd heard him on the phone handling all sorts of problems every time we'd been out together.

"For Wallace Incorporated?" Olsen asked.

Wallace Inc. was the new store Ty was opening, his own venture separate from Holt's. The deal had been in the works for months. Golden State Bank & Trust was handling the financing, or something. Ty had explained it but I'd drifted off.

Olsen frowned. "Nothing serious, I hope."

Oh God, now he thought there was a problem with Ty opening the store on time.

"Nothing Ty can't handle," I said, and waved my hand to demonstrate that it was no big deal.

Olsen's frown deepened. "So there *is* a problem."

"No. There's no problem," I insisted, and forced a smile. "It's a situation. That's all. Just a simple, routine, everyday situation."

He frowned for another moment, then scratched a note on a slip of paper, and turned to me again. "So, Miss Randolph, what can I do for you this morning?"

"I'd like some information," I said.

Mr. Olsen's smile returned, as if he could see this would be easy and he could hand me off to an assistant and get on to dealing with people more important than me.

I took a piece of paper from my Louis Vuitton organizer and handed it to him. On it, Evelyn had written everything she knew about her neighbor Cecil Hartley, whom she believed had been murdered by his new girlfriend.

"I'd like you to give me information on this man," I said.

Mr. Olsen slipped on his reading glasses and stared down at the paper for a moment.

"I don't understand," he said, looking at me over the top of his glasses.

"It's all right there," I said. To Evelyn's information, I'd added a list of info I needed. "His credit cards, when he last used them, where they were used. That sort of thing."

Mr. Olsen frowned a completely new kind of frown.

"This is highly irregular," he told me.

I knew that. I also knew that Cecil Hartley was probably alive and well. Evelyn had told me he'd bought a new motor home a few months ago, so I figured he and the new girlfriend were on some cross-country adventure—or whatever it was old people did in those things—and would return home sooner or later.

But Evelyn had been adamant—too many crime dramas on the Lifetime Channel, I suspect—and convinced beyond all doubt that Barb, the new girlfriend, had somehow done Cecil in. So I figured if I could show her that he was using his credit cards somewhere, it would prove he was alive and kicking. I also figured that the easiest way to get that information was from Bradley Olsen.

Only Bradley Olsen didn't seem all that anxious to help out.

He stared at me, completely stunned, as if I'd just asked him to take off his clothes—yuck—and dance on the desk.

"This is also illegal," he said, his voice getting a little higher. "I can't simply check into someone's credit history on a whim. There are policies and procedures, federal laws and government regulations. You *do* know that, don't you?"

"Of course I know that," I said—really I didn't, but no need to tell him that.

At this point, I could have reminded him of the incident last fall when he and the Golden State Bank & Trust had come way close to a huge scandal, but had been saved from public humiliation by yours truly—okay, it was really Ty, but he wouldn't have done it if it hadn't been for me. Anyway, I could have said that. I didn't want to, though. Nobody likes being reminded of their screwups.

I know this from personal experience.

But I didn't see any reason to actually tell him the truth, either. That complicating things sometimes.

So I said, "It's for Evelyn. She's thinking of investing with this guy and I think he's up to no good. Preying on her because she's lonely."

Olsen's expression morphed back into concerned-banker mode. Or so I thought until he said, "Ms. Croft is lonely? Why, I assumed she had a husband, children. Surely a woman like her would have a very full life."

Okay, that was weird. But he seemed to be on my side now, so I went with it.

"I'm afraid this Cecil Hartley is some sort of gigolo," I said. "I don't want to see her get hurt."

"Neither do I. So, yes, of course. Of course, I'll check into it. I can't have a lovely lady like Ms. Croft—" He stopped suddenly and said, "That is, I owe it to her as a Golden State Bank and Trust customer to thoroughly investigate any business opportunity."

I figured I should get out of there while things were still going my way, but I couldn't resist adding, "I'll be sure to let Ty know how helpful you've been."

Of course, there was no way I'd ever mention this to Ty.

Olsen pushed to his feet and stood tall. "I'll get on it immediately," he declared.

Bradley Olsen, man on a mission.

It seemed a shame to ruin a perfectly wonderful day by going to work, but that's what my life was these days.

I swung into a parking space at my apartment complex and sat there for a moment contemplating things. I had just enough time to get inside, change clothes, then call my best friend, Marcie, at work before I headed to Holt's. I needed to talk to her about this whole Ty-going-to-Europe thing. And, of course, tell her about the school supplies I'd just bought.

After leaving Bradley Olsen's office this morning I'd stopped by the mall to check on that Judith Leiber evening bag I was dying to have. It was still in the case, still gorgeous. I stayed until the security guard started to stare. But I could hardly tear myself away. I felt sort of like a soldier saying good-bye to a lover in one of those old war movies.

I'm pretty sure it called my name when I left.

So, to ease my heartache, I'd taken a quick turn through the mall just to see what was new in the stores. It's important to stay on top of all the latest fashion trends. And wouldn't you know it, Nordstrom had awesome new Kate Spade bags that had just arrived.

That left me in a bit of a dilemma, since I'd promised myself that I wouldn't spend money on anything except essentials and things I needed for school. Then it occurred to me that the purse would look great with the new pair of jeans I'd bought last week for school, so technically, that made the bag a school expense. So what could I do but buy it? Along with a matching wallet, of course.

You know, if it weren't for the homework, this school thing wouldn't be so bad.

I got out of my car and popped my trunk to get out my packages, and noticed a car door opening at a nearby space. Detective Shuman got out.

I froze. What was Shuman doing here? At my apartment? In the middle of the afternoon?

Then I gulped. Oh my God. *Oh my God*. Was he here to arrest me?

My gaze darted from car to car. Was Detective Madison here, too? He wouldn't want to miss this.

Should I jump behind the wheel? Tear out of the parking lot? I envisioned videotape shot from a news chopper above the L.A. freeways as I led a caravan of police cars on a high-speed chase to the Mexican border. But how would I live down there? What would become of me?

I'm definitely taking Spanish next semester.

Detective Shuman walked over and I saw that he was alone.

"I don't see Madison, so I guess I'm not under arrest," I said.

"Not today," he said.

Shuman looked kind of good, with the afternoon sunlight shining on his brown hair. It gave him golden highlights that I hadn't noticed before. Since that crab-ass Madison wasn't with him, I figured this visit wasn't about police business. Probably something to do with his girlfriend.

I pulled my shopping bags out of the trunk.

"I won a latte machine at the Holt's prize raffle," I said, nodding to the box Bella had put in my trunk. "Bring it upstairs and we'll try it out."

"I don't think that's a latte machine," Shuman said, after a quick peek into the trunk. "I need to talk to you about Claudia Gray's murder."

"You found the murderer already?" I asked, hoping that somehow a miracle had happened and this nightmare was over.

Shuman shook his head. "No. I want to find out why you lied about what you were doing in the stockroom that day."

# Chapter 6

"Husqvarna Viking," I said, gesturing to the box that Shuman had just placed on the coffee table in front of my sofa. "It's that French company that makes latte machines."

Shuman spun the box around and pointed to the words and picture on the other side.

"It's a sewing machine," he said.

"*What?*"

I dropped my shopping bags on the sofa. A sewing machine? I'd won a sewing machine at the Holt's raffle? What was I supposed to do—what would *anybody* do—with a sewing machine?

Leave it to Holt's to give such a lame prize.

"Look, Haley," Shuman said, "I know you and Detective Madison don't get along. But lying to the police—especially in a homicide investigation—isn't going to help matters."

Maybe inviting a homicide detective into my home wasn't such a good idea.

"If Madison would stop fixating on me, he probably could have solved this case already," I said, and gestured to the kitchen. "Want something to drink?"

"What were you really doing in the stockroom?"

"I sure could go for a Snickers bar right about now," I told him, and headed for the kitchen cabinet where I kept my stash.

Shuman followed. "We're going to find out what really happened that day," he told me.

It came across as a warning, rather than a threat, but my heart jumped, just the same.

Oh my God. What if they found my DNA in that blouse I wore, or on the sunglasses? What if they found one of my hairs in the wig?

I was pretty sure my DNA hadn't been registered anywhere. But what if the detectives sneaked around Holt's and found a stray hair someplace, like they do on those TV shows, and compared it to the ones inside the wig? I couldn't let that happen. I'd have to be careful not to let any of it get loose.

But which is worse? Going to prison or wearing a hair net?

"Oh, look. Oreos." I ripped open the package and shoved one in my mouth—whole, not even twisting off the top, which showed how stressed I was.

"So, who's this missing server, anyway?" I managed to ask, hoping to distract him.

Shuman didn't answer me, just got a weird look on his face.

So weird that I put down the Oreos.

"The lab found out how Claudia was poisoned," he said. "It was the fruit bouquet from Edible Elegance."

I gasped. Oh my God. My *mom's* fruit bouquets?

"No—no, that doesn't make sense," I told him, relieved that I'd come up with a plausible objection. "If the fruit bouquets were poisoned, why didn't anybody else die—or at least get sick?"

"Every bouquet prepared for the VIPs at the head table had a name tag on it," Shuman said.

I remembered seeing the chocolate name tags, and think-ing how cool they were.

"Somebody intended to murder Claudia," Shuman said.

My stomach twisted into a knot. I knew what he was going to say next.

"Edible Elegance is your mom's company. Right?"

"Well, yeah, but . . ."

"It looks like your mom found out Ty was going to break up with you because he wanted to resume his relationship with Claudia. So your mom poisoned Claudia's fruit bou-quet. She murdered her."

I shook my head frantically. "No. That's not possible."

"So Ty wasn't planning to get back together with Clau-dia?" Shuman asked.

"Well . . ."

"Things are okay between you two?"

"Well . . ."

I should have been able to tell Shuman that things were perfect between Ty and me, but I couldn't. I didn't know how things were between the two of us—which was all Ty's fault. And, as a result, my mom was a mur-der suspect.

"Look, no matter what's going on with Ty and me, it has nothing to do with my mom. She absolutely would not murder anyone," I insisted.

Shuman shrugged. "It's her company. She has unrestricted access to the ingredients, the finished product, everything."

"She doesn't even know where they're made," I exclaimed.

A woman who lists "walking comfortably in five-inch stilettos" under "major accomplishments" on her résumé isn't exactly a hands-on business owner. But how could I convince Shuman of that?

"Does Detective Madison know about this?" I asked.

Shuman shook his head. "I just found out."

And he'd come here first, to tell me, to warn me. I appreciated that, but it didn't alleviate my worry.

"When Madison finds out, he'll go nuts. He'll stop investigating," I said. "Is there any way you can hold off on telling him?"

"This is a homicide investigation," Shuman said, looking and sounding just like a detective. "A high-profile murder has been committed. A lot of important people in L.A. are pressuring the department. The media has us under a microscope. Didn't you see the prayer vigil last night for the missing server?"

A prayer vigil? Oh my God.

"I don't want Madison anywhere near my mom," I said.

"Then if you know anything else about what happened in the stockroom the day Claudia was murdered, now's the time to tell me."

Shuman gave me a hard-ass cop stare that he must have gotten an A-plus on in the academy. It gave me a chill. It made me want to confess to *something*.

But would telling Shuman about substituting for the sick server help? Or would it make things worse? Would the facts end up being twisted to fit their theory, and make things harder for my mom?

Confessing that I'd donned a disguise for the sole purpose of hiding from Claudia might lead the detectives to believe Mom and I had been in on the murder together. And how would that help anything?

"If I knew anything that would help, I'd tell you," I said to Shuman, which was true—sort of.

I don't think Shuman bought it but he gave up, which was just as good. I followed him to the door.

"Please don't tell Detective Madison that my mom owns Edible Elegance," I said, sounding desperate.

He paused in the doorway. "I can't keep this kind of information from him."

We just looked at each other for a few seconds; then Shuman left.

I changed into khaki pants and a sweater while I was on the phone with Juanita, my mom's housekeeper that I'd known for most of my life. Mom was distraught, Juanita reported—which could have been because of anything from Claudia's death to Vera Wang's new spring line—and resting. Okay by me, because I didn't really want to talk to her, anyway. Juanita gave me the info I needed and I took off.

Marilyn—whose last name was Carmichael, I'd learned from Juanita—owned Pacific Coast Catering Company in Sherman Oaks. If I hurried I could get there, talk to Marilyn, and still get to Holt's on time, or close to it, anyway.

I cruised down the 5 freeway, cutting off slower cars, as necessary, thinking this would probably be my only chance to talk to Marilyn about what had happened at the Holt's luncheon. Once the police announced that Claudia had been poisoned, Pacific Coast Catering would be besieged by reporters. And if Shuman couldn't—or wouldn't—keep a lid on the news that Edible Elegance was the true culprit, Marilyn certainly wouldn't speak with me then.

The catering company was located in a strip mall off Sepulveda Boulevard. I whipped into a parking space and went inside.

The showroom boasted the latest trend in decorating, lots of deep green, brown, and bronze, a place where Marilyn's upscale clientele would feel right at home. Several wrought-iron tables were placed around the room where customers could sit and flip through books of menus and photos of food. The scent of cookies wafted in from the back room where the food was prepared.

Marilyn came out through the curtained doorway looking a bit leery about who she might find in her store; undoubtedly, the detectives had already been here, perhaps even the press.

I'm guessing Marilyn was pushing sixty. Short, wide. Sensible suit, sensible shoes. White hair that she must have styled by breathing in helium that caused it to inflate like a balloon, then shellacked it into place with enough spray to withstand a Category 5 hurricane.

I introduced myself and reminded her of who my mom was, something I don't usually do—unless it benefits me, of course.

Marilyn's well-practiced smile stayed frozen on her face. "Your mother . . . your mother . . . she's, ah, she's the lady who . . ."

"You've catered dinner parties for her. You remember, the one that celebrated National Liposuction Appreciation Day," I said.

"Oh, sure. Sure, sure," Marilyn said, bobbing her head. Her hair didn't move.

"Mom does the fruit bouquets," I added.

Marilyn's expression froze again. "Fruit bouquets?"

"Edible Elegance," I said.

Her eyes darted back and forth. "Hmm . . ."

I was thinking Marilyn was off her meds, which might explain why she didn't notice that, at the Holt's luncheon, one of her servers had disappeared and a stranger had taken her place, wearing a cheesy disguise, no less.

"Strawberry, pineapple, and pear slices cut into the shape of flowers, dipped in chocolate," I explained.

"Oh, sure. Sure, sure," Marilyn said, looking relieved. "Of course I remember."

"Mom wanted me to stop by and make sure you were doing okay," I lied, "after what happened at the Holt's event."

"Your mother, she's such a dear. So thoughtful and caring."

Now I'm positive Marilyn is off her meds.

"So, how are things?" I asked, trying to get her back on track.

"Fine, fine. Just fine."

"The police haven't been here?" I asked.

"Oh yes! Of course." Marilyn tapped her forehead with her fingertips. "Yes, the police came and asked questions about . . . about—oh, now let me think. What's her name?"

God only knows what Marilyn was trying to remember.

"The missing server?" I asked.

"Sure, sure. That's it."

Marilyn struck out across the office to the desk in the corner. I followed. She rifled through the drawers and finally came up with a big binder.

"I have all that here . . . somewhere," Marilyn said, flipping through the pages. She stopped and squinted down at something.

"Now, where did I put my glasses," she muttered, patting her suit, even though it had no pockets.

"Would you like me to look?" I asked, taking the binder from her before she could answer.

I scanned the page and saw that it was a personnel roster. Apparently, Marilyn wasn't comfortable using a computer for things like this. I'm guessing she was still using a VCR and hoped to one day figure out how to program it.

"Is that it?" Marilyn asked, craning her neck to see the page. "Is Jamie's name on there?"

Information on Jamie Kirkwood—the missing server—was all there.

"I just don't understand what the fuss is all about,"

Marilyn said, looking completely baffled. "I mean, it's a tragedy, of course, that Claudia died. But all this media coverage about the mysterious Missing Server?"

Marilyn made little quotations in the air, then went on. "There's no mystery. The police know exactly who she is. I gave them Jamie's name, her address, everything."

"I guess they haven't been able to find her," I said.

"Well, I don't know why not," Marilyn declared.

Marilyn had a point, and I wondered the same.

"The police have been here twice. And reporters keep calling, asking all sorts of questions. Like I know something about poor Claudia dying at the luncheon."

I'm guessing that Marilyn didn't know yet that Claudia was poisoned. I certainly wasn't going to tell her.

The telephone on the desk rang. Marilyn eyed it as if, for a second or two, she wasn't sure what to do, then answered. She listened for a moment, then said, "No comment," and hung up.

"My lawyer advised me not to respond to any questions," Marilyn explained.

She'd spoken to her lawyer already. Not surprising. This was, after all, Los Angeles.

"Is Jamie one of your regular servers?" I asked.

"She just showed up one day, asking for work," Marilyn explained. "That happens all the time. Word gets around. Especially among the college crowd."

"Mrs. Carmichael?" a woman called from the curtain doorway. She had on a white uniform and a hair net—not a great look. "Everything's ready."

"I've got to run," Marilyn said.

"Who hired you for the luncheon at Holt's?" I asked.

She paused and squeezed her eyes shut for a second. "I got a call from someone at their corporate office. A woman. Her name was . . . hmm, let me think. Sally? Sandra? No, no. Oh, now who was—oh yes. It was Sarah."

"Sarah Covington?"

"Yes. Sure, sure," Marilyn declared. "Got to run. Give my best to your mom."

My heart pounded and I felt a little dizzy, as I jotted Jamie's info on a slip of paper.

Wouldn't it be cool if I could pin this whole murder on Sarah?

# Chapter 7

Although Marilyn Carmichael had probably forgotten her own question a millisecond after it left her lips, the thought fused to my brain like cellulite on thighs, and it was all I could think of as I drove to Holt's.

Why hadn't the police been able to find Jamie Kirkwood, the everybody-is-making-too-big-of-a-deal-about-her Missing Server?

I guess it wasn't unusual that the cops hadn't released her identity to the media yet. They probably didn't want her put in the spotlight and questioned by the press until they'd had a chance to do that themselves. And the world is full of whack jobs, so maybe, in a way, they were trying to protect her.

But that didn't explain why Jamie hadn't simply come forward. I mean, even though the media coverage was way overhyped, how could she *not* know the police wanted to talk with her?

I whipped into the Holt's parking lot. It was packed. Seemed the news of Claudia's murder had actually drawn shoppers to the store, which was kind of sick, but there it was. I imagined Jeanette and the rest of the corporate team—except for Ty, of course—salivating over the potential profits.

Maybe Sarah would come up with an "After Murder Sale" ad campaign.

Then I spotted a television news van parked at the curb in front of the store. Oh my God. What were they doing here? Had someone else been murdered?

I didn't see police cars, an ambulance, or circling helicopters, so I figured this was some sort of follow-up story. Jeez, why couldn't they just let this go?

I whipped into a parking space far from the news van and the looky-loos surrounding it, and sat there for a moment stewing on Jamie Kirkwood.

I wondered why, in media-crazed L.A., a friend or family member hadn't ratted her out. Surely there was a book deal in this for someone, or at least a mention on The View.

I could think of only two reasons why Jamie hadn't come forward voluntarily.

One: she didn't want to be in the center of the publicity storm that had built until she'd found a good lawyer.

Or two: she'd killed Claudia.

I got a sick little feeling in the pit of my stomach. If Jamie had killed Claudia, that meant I'd aided in her crime and her escape.

Oh, crap.

I bolted from my car, ignored the crowd of gawkers surrounding the news van, and dashed into the store. Customers choked the aisles, their arms laden with merchandise, and for once, I was glad to see them. I wanted to be busy tonight, too busy to think about Claudia, Jamie, Mom's fruit bouquets, or how big my butt would look in a prison-orange jumpsuit.

I hurried into the employee break room where the time clock was located and found Rita standing at the whiteboard, arms crossed, and glaring. No one else was in there. That meant only one thing.

I was late. And Rita was loving it.

Someone up the Holt's corporate chain—someone who had surely never met Rita and likely never set foot in an actual Holt's store—had promoted her to the position of cashiers' supervisor. That meant she was the time clock monitor—or time clock Nazi, as *someone* had started calling her.

At each shift change, Rita positioned herself by the time clock, and if anyone was late clocking in, she wrote their name on the whiteboard. Four lates in a month and you got fired.

"You're late," Rita declared.

"I guess that Hooked on Phonics.is really working for you, huh?" I said as I pulled my time card from its slot.

"Everybody else gets here on time," Rita said. "I got here on time, and I was busy *all day*."

I waved my time card—I still hadn't punched in—at the top she was wearing. Purple, with a milk cow on the front.

"It must take a while to achieve that signature look of yours," I told her. "I'm surprised you made it here at all."

I don't think Rita picked up on my sarcasm. She was in high bitch mode.

"We were busy," Rita went on. "Tiffany and I. We gave a purse party for one of the ladies on the morning replenishment team. Her sister works for a big company. We sold two hundred handbags."

My temper shot up. Rita had stolen the purse party idea from Marcie and me. We thought of it first and everything. Now Rita and her friend Tiffany were taking all the good customers—and making a fortune.

I hate her.

Rita glared at me and the time card in my hand, waiting for me to punch in. I wouldn't give her the satisfaction.

"You're supposed to work in domestics tonight," Rita said, nodding to the schedule posted beside the time clock. "But I want you in infants and children's wear instead."

Crap. I hated that department. Screaming babies, whining kids, stroller gridlock. The moms spoke a whole different language there, asking for things like sleepers, onesies, and some chick named Dora.

Rita knew I hated that department. She made that change in the schedule just to irk me.

"Still making the big decisions, huh?" I rolled my eyes. "I'm surprised you haven't made store manager yet."

I huffed to the back of the break room before Rita could answer, wrote the time down on my card, then stored my handbag in my locker. When I came back, Rita was gone. I saw that she'd written my name on the whiteboard and that she'd misspelled it, which, I'm certain, she'd done on purpose.

I erased my name and left the break room.

Lots of screwups happened with time cards. Almost a daily occurrence. So, with mine in hand, I headed for Jeanette's office intending to have her sign off on my card, after I gave her some bogus reason why I'd forgotten to punch in. But farther down the hallway I saw that the door to the training room was open and that employees were seated there, talking among themselves.

Hmm . . . was this a meeting I was supposed to attend? I hadn't seen a notice posted in the employee break room— all I'd seen was that fat cow Rita in her fat cow shirt. I wasn't big on meetings, but attending was a great way to avoid infants and children's wear.

I found a seat on the back row near the door behind that heavyset guy from menswear—a good place for dozing, making it a favorite spot of mine—and noticed that Ty was at the front of the room on his cell phone.

Ty seldom came to the store. He was always at the corporate office, or in a meeting, or something. I knew he was only here because of Claudia's murder.

Seeing him, I felt my heart doing its usual little flip-flop. Only this time something else was going on in there. An ache.

Had Ty really been trying to get back together with Claudia before she was murdered?

I still wondered if Detective Madison had told me the truth. And if so, how had he known? Who had told him? One of Claudia's friends? Someone in her family?

That little ache in my heart got worse. Sarah knew about Ty's trip to Europe—the one he hadn't mentioned to me—along with just about everything else that went on in his life. Maybe she knew he intended to get back together with Claudia. Maybe she'd mentioned it to Detective Madison.

I got out of my chair and approached Ty just as he closed his cell phone. My heart did a bigger flip-flop when he saw me, and a tiny smile cracked the corner of his mouth.

"How's it going?" I asked.

"The usual," he said.

I presented him with my time card. "Would you initial this? I didn't punch in when I got here."

Ty pulled a pen from the breast pocket of his suit jacket, looked at the start time I'd noted on my card, and raised an eyebrow. "You were ten minutes early?"

"Twelve, really, but I just rounded off to ten," I said.

He scrawled his initials on my card and handed it back to me. I stood there for a moment, thinking that he might want to know how I was doing, or ask me out, or something. But he didn't—which didn't prove anything. He could still be nuts about me. He just didn't want to make me the target of store gossip by getting personal right now. And *that* proved how much he cared about me. Right?

I resumed my seat on the back row behind that big guy from menswear as Ty addressed the employees. Jeanette sat off to the side, nodding wisely as he talked about the untimely death of Claudia Gray, the condolences expressed by everyone at the Holt's "family," the hardship it had caused the employees, blah, blah, blah. He said all the right things, and sounded sincere.

I guessed that guy sitting in front of me was getting antsy—

or maybe, like me, he was sick of hearing about Claudia—because he glanced back toward the door. He must have caught a glimpse of me from the corner of his eye, because he spun around so quickly I thought he might flip his chair over.

Since he was staring straight at me, I gave him a little head nod. He kept watching me.

Ty told all employees not to speak with the news media camped out in our parking lot. No one in the store was authorized to speak on behalf of Holt's. If questioned, simply reply "no comment." The corporate lawyers had probably told Ty this would avoid a huge lawsuit somehow, but Ty didn't say so.

The longer I sat there, the weirder I felt—and not because that guy from menswear kept staring at me. Some sort of volcano was building inside me. My feelings roiled like hot lava, ready to spew out.

I couldn't get the thought of Ty and Claudia together again out of my head. Or the question of why Ty had never told me the reason he liked me. Or why he was going to Europe and hadn't told me.

Then it came to me. I'd confront him. Right after the meeting. Yeah, that's what I'd do. And I didn't care if anyone in the store overheard us, or if they knew the two of us were—

"Haley."

The sound of my name snapped me out of my mental tirade. I glanced around. Jeanette stood in front of the room pointing at me. Everyone stared, except Ty, who was in the corner talking quietly on his cell phone.

I'm pretty sure I just missed something important.

Jeanette smiled. "It seems Haley has no objections, so everyone, please see her."

See me? About what?

Oh my God. What just happened?

"Okay, that's it," Jeanette declared. "Thanks for your hard work."

Everybody rose from their chairs and headed out of the training room. I needed to ask someone what was going on, but I didn't want to look like an idiot with Jeanette and Ty standing there.

"Count me in, Haley," someone called.

"Yeah, me, too," another person said.

All around me, heads nodded and I got a couple of thumbs-ups.

Well, apparently I had a lot of support for whatever had happened. Maybe everyone else would handle it for me and I wouldn't have to bother.

Anyway, I didn't have time to worry about that now. This thing with Ty and Claudia was getting to me big time. I had to find out what had been going on between them before her death. Jeanette and several of the department managers had crowded around Ty—trying to kiss ass, I'm sure—so I couldn't approach him with my questions now. I'd have to find out another way.

I didn't know any of Ty's friends to ask—just because he never introduced me to any of his friends did *not* prove he wasn't wild about me—so I'd have to look elsewhere for info.

The obvious source was Mom. Her family and Ty's family were both from old money, dating back to the founding of California, or something, so they had lots of the same friends. If I alerted Mom to the situation, she'd root out crucial info at warp speed.

But no way could I talk to her about this. One hint, one tiny hint, that Ty was interested in me and she'd have me looking at bridal gowns until I went cross-eyed.

Luckily, I had sources myself. People who knew people. What did I care if they wouldn't want to talk to me?

# Chapter 8

"He said *what*?" Marcie exclaimed.

We sat at opposite ends of my sofa drinking Corona and munching pretzels. I'd called her after I'd finished my shift at Holt's and she'd rushed over.

You can't ask for a better friend than that.

"Yeah," I said, nodding and waving my beer bottle in indignation. "That dumb-ass Detective Madison said that Ty was trying to get back together with Claudia."

"I don't believe it," Marcie declared, as a true friend would. "Ty's crazy about you."

"Yeah?" My spirits lifted. "How do you know?"

Marcie thought for a second, then said, "He just *is*, that's all. I mean, you can tell by the way he looks at you."

Not exactly the definitive proof I was hoping for.

"That detective probably made the whole thing up," Marcie decided.

I'd wondered about that myself. Maybe Madison had concocted the whole story to judge my reaction, to scare me, to shake a confession out of me. I wouldn't put it past him.

"So where did Madison *claim* he got this info?" Marcie wanted to know.

I took another sip of beer. "He didn't say."

"You need to find out," Marcie advised.

"Yeah, I know," I said.

"You think it might be true, don't you?" Marcie said, looking both wise and compassionate, as only a best friend can look at an all-time low point in your life.

"Ty's never actually said why he likes me," I said.

"Most men are like that," Marcie said with a dismissive wave of her beer bottle.

"I found out he's going to Europe for several weeks, and he never even told me," I said.

Marcie shrugged. "It's probably just a business trip."

I drew in a breath and said, "And, well, you know, things have been sort of *weird* with Ty and me."

Marcie translated my words instantly and her eyes widened. "You two still haven't had sex?"

"I don't understand it, either," I told her. "He's always busy, or working, or in a meeting, or *something*."

"Yeah, but why wouldn't he want to have sex?" Marcie asked, apparently as confused as I was.

"Everybody wants to have sex," I said.

Or was that just me?

"Could be a lot of reasons," Marcie said.

"Like what?"

She thought for a moment, and I could see that she was anxious to come up with something that would make me feel better. I hoped she could.

"Maybe he's one of those weird men who're not all that interested in sex," Marcie suggested.

"Disappointing, but a possibility," I said.

"He could have taken a vow of celibacy."

"Yeah, maybe . . . I guess."

Marcie thought for another minute. "Maybe he's a D-I-Y kind of guy."

"Do-it-yourself? *Gross*," I said.

"That only leaves a couple of possibilities," Marcie said, as kindly as anyone could say it. "Either he's really too busy with work—"

"Or he has another girlfriend," I said, my spirits plummeting. "Claudia."

Marcie drained her beer. "So how did he act when he heard Claudia was dead? Was he completely devastated?"

A little spark of hope flared inside me and I sat up straighter on the sofa as I remembered seeing him the day Claudia died.

"No, not really," I said. "Upset. Troubled. But not devastated."

"And since then?"

"No more distracted and preoccupied than usual," I reported.

Marcie nodded wisely. "Okay, so there you are."

"You think this means nothing was going on between them?"

"Makes sense," Marcie concluded.

She was almost always right about things. I hoped she was right about this.

"I've got us another purse party lined up," Marcie reported. "I'll e-mail you the details."

"That awful Rita and her friend are still at it," I told her. "They sold two hundred bags at their last party."

Marcie shrugged. "Whatever."

I'm not a *whatever* kind of gal. I had to do better than Rita and Tiffany. In fact, I wouldn't be happy until we put them out of business.

"Are you saving your share of the profits for that Judith Leiber evening bag?" Marcie asked.

At once, every thought flew out of my head and my one active brain cell presented me with the image of that gorgeous bag I wanted to take to the charity gala at the Biltmore Hotel. I definitely had to get that bag. It was the only thing that could boost my spirits right now.

Marcie rose from the sofa and picked up her handbag—a Fossill Tote in chocolate brown—and spotted the box that I'd dropped next to the end table.

"Hey, cool," she said.

"It's a sewing machine," I told her.

"I know," she said, looking excited. "You should make some tops for yourself."

Yeah, right.

"Want it?" I asked.

Marcie gave me an odd look. "I already have one."

Wow, the things you learn about the people you think you know.

"I can sell it on eBay, if you really don't want it," Marcie offered.

"That'd be great," I told her.

She jotted down info from the side of the box, then headed for the front door. I followed.

"I know things are tough right now," Marcie said, then forced a smile. "But at least we're still alive."

That knocked the Judith Leiber handbag, that stupid sewing machine, and almost everything else out of my head. See how Marcie was right about most things? Yeah, I was having my share of problems—more than my share, really—but I was alive.

That's more than could be said for Claudia.

Several cars jammed the circular drive of the Gray home, so I nosed my Honda against the curb and got out. I'd selected a black Prada handbag for the occasion, and it went nicely with the conservative skirt and sweater I wore. Perfect attire for my covert, fact-finding operation.

Talking with Marcie last night made me even more determined to learn the truth about Ty and Claudia. Everything Marcie said made perfect sense, and I had little real info to support my paranoia. I had to find out more.

Since I'm not big on suspense and my confrontation skills are superior, I figured the best way to handle the situation was just ask Ty straight out.

But I couldn't do it.

I didn't want to see the look on Ty's face if my suspicions were true, and I sure as heck didn't want to look like a desperate, clingy girlfriend if they weren't true.

I'd stayed up late last night doing homework for my English class, and e-mailed the assignment a full forty-five seconds before the midnight deadline, along with an explanation that I wouldn't be in class because of a death. I sent the same e-mail to my health class instructor. I usually went with the touch-of-the-stomach-flu excuse, a personal favorite of mine, but figured that Claudia's demise might as well serve some purpose in my life, other than make me question my entire relationship with my sort-of boyfriend.

This morning I'd stopped off at the florist's and bought what the guy behind the counter assured me was a "subdued flower arrangement." So now, under the guise of paying my respects, I headed up the walkway toward Claudia's parents' house in Brentwood.

I'd known Claudia and her family for years. Mom had that whole model, beauty pageant connection with Claudia and her mother; plus, while not exactly old money, the Gray family was well off enough to travel in the same social circles as my mom's.

Claudia and I had never been friends. She was a few years older than me. We knew each other well enough to speak if we happened to run into each other, but that was about it. It suited both of us.

As I approached the front door, it was opened by the housekeeper. She wore a black uniform. Her face was drawn and her eyes downcast.

I stepped into the foyer and was slammed from all sides by a wave of grief and despair.

Sorrow radiated from every room of the house. It washed over me, seeped into me, and knocked me for a mental loop.

Oh my God. *Oh my God.* What had I been thinking? Coming here, at a time like this, to ask questions about

*Claudia and Ty?* What was the matter with me? How could I have been so selfish?

See how this thing with Ty was making me crazy?

"Everyone is in the family room," the housekeeper said in a low voice as she gestured down the hallway.

No way was I going to hang around and see the family. I couldn't face any of them—I wasn't sure I could even face myself.

I shoved the floral arrangement—which looked anything but "subdued" at the moment—at the housekeeper and turned to go. Someone called my name.

I looked back and saw Rebecca, Claudia's younger sister.

Now, more than ever, I wanted to run out the door. But I couldn't.

Rebecca came forward. She had an Audrey Hepburn kind of thing going with black skinny jeans, a sweater, and flats. Her dark hair was pulled back in a simple ponytail.

She was a few years younger than me—twenty, I think, or maybe twenty-one now. Rebecca was the "smart one" in the family, excelling in her premed classes. She'd already done a stint with Habitat for Humanity in New Orleans, helped build a water treatment plant in Africa, and collected thousands of dollars to save the rain forest through a Web site she'd built.

I knew this because, over time, I'd dragged it out of Mom as she'd raved about Claudia and the magazine covers she'd appeared on and the fashion shows she'd done.

Despite all of Rebecca's accomplishments, I'd always felt connected to her. Her older sister was beautiful, while Rebecca, like me, was merely pretty.

But Rebecca didn't look so good right now. Puffy, red eyes. Dark circles. Pink nose. Stooped shoulders, as if she couldn't stand upright under the weight of her sister's death.

Not even a Snickers bar would make me feel better right now.

"Haley, you're so sweet to stop by," Rebecca said, walking forward with some effort. She grasped my arm. "Come in."

I heard voices from deep in the house. I absolutely could not face anyone—especially the parents—with my conscience screaming at me over the stupid reason I'd come here.

Which, now that I thought about it, is all Ty's fault.

"I don't want to intrude," I said, which was true, but for selfish reasons.

Rebecca nodded. "Let's go back here."

Still latched on to my arm, she led me down the hallway to a den that I doubted got much use. Decorated in deep blues, it had mahogany bookcases filled with leather-bound volumes, and oil paintings of ships on the walls.

"I'm so sorry," I said. "About . . . everything."

Rebecca nodded and wiped her nose with the tissue crumpled in her hand.

"How're your mom and dad?" I asked.

"Awful."

Tears spilled down her cheeks, and she looked up at me, bewildered.

"I don't know how this could have happened," Rebecca said. "It—it wasn't supposed to be like this."

She started full-on crying and I just stood there, not sure what to do.

But I'm female, right? I'm *supposed* to know how to handle things like this. It's in my DNA, isn't it?

Rebecca kept crying and I kept standing there, waiting for my XY—or maybe they were XX—chromosomes to kick in. I think we covered that in health class—or maybe we didn't.

Anyway, nothing kicked in.

I tried desperately to recall a similar situation and glean knowledge from how it had been handled.

Nothing came to me.

Then I tried to imagine what my mom would do in my

place. I flashed on the mental picture of Mom demanding Juanita bring her a glass of wine, then telling Rebecca to fix her makeup.

I could do better.

"Sit down," I told Rebecca, firmly but gently.

We sat on the rock-hard sofa. I perched on the edge, my knees nearly touching Rebecca's. She cried for a few more minutes, then wiped her cheeks with the tissue.

"I—I just don't understand," Rebecca said.

I wasn't sure if the police had told the family yet that Claudia had been poisoned. But I'm sure word hadn't spread that my mom's fruit bouquets were the culprit. I wouldn't have been invited in, otherwise.

"Have the detectives been here?" I asked, as gently as I could.

Rebecca nodded. "They—they said it wasn't an . . . an accident. Somebody killed Claudia on purpose."

Another wave of sobs overtook her, and suddenly I saw myself in her place, overcome with grief if my own sister were to die. My sister and I weren't exactly the best of friends—she was a lot like mom, with all that modeling and beauty pageant stuff—but I still loved her. What would I do if she'd been murdered?

"But it *wasn't* on purpose," Rebecca insisted, worrying the tissue in her fingers. "It *wasn't*. How could anybody think that?"

Honestly, Claudia was so gorgeous, so accomplished, it's a wonder she had any friends at all and that somebody hadn't done her in years ago.

Then I felt guilty for thinking that, so I said, "Claudia meant a lot to so many people."

Rebecca dabbed at her eyes. "People have come by and phoned, almost nonstop. Friends, the pageant girls she coached. Even her coworkers, and she'd only worked there a couple of months."

"Claudia had a job?" I asked. "A real job?"

"L.A. Affairs."

Judging from the name, you might think L.A. Affairs was an escort service, but no, it was an event planning company. Their clientele was mostly celebrities and wealthy Hollywood insiders.

"Mom—" Rebecca gulped and a fresh wave of tears poured down her cheeks. "Mom didn't get to see her that . . . last day. She made me go instead. Now Mom's angry with herself for not going to the runway show, for not—"

"You came to the runway show? At Holt's?" I asked. "I didn't see you."

Rebecca gulped and her tears stopped. "You . . . you were there?"

I realized I had to come up with a good reason for being there—I still wasn't about to tell anybody that I worked at Holt's.

"I was checking out the chocolate fruit bouquets. My mom's new business. I help out, sometimes," I said.

Rebecca's breath stopped for a few seconds, and I got a really yucky feeling in the pit of my stomach.

Maybe the detectives *had* told the family that the fruit bouquets had poisoned Claudia.

"Those were *your mom's*? I—I didn't know. I thought the caterer had done them." Rebecca shook her head. "I was only at the store for a few minutes. Mom made me drop off Claudia's passport. Then I left."

"Did you see anything unusual that day?" I asked.

Rebecca looked away. I guess maybe I shouldn't have asked her to remember details about the day her sister died, especially since she'd been at the scene.

Maybe I'm more like Mom than I like to believe.

Not a great feeling.

"I know Claudia had problems with the mother of one of the girls she coached," Rebecca said. "The mom wanted her to do more, but Claudia insisted she wasn't ready."

I opened my mouth, but Rebecca anticipated my question. After all, she'd been through this drill with the homicide detectives when they'd come to question the family.

"I don't know who it was. Claudia never said." Rebecca drew a ragged breath. "She had a stalker."

"Claudia had a stalker?" I repeated, stunned. "Who was it?"

Rebecca fiddled with the tissue for a moment. "She didn't know."

The idea of a stalker creeped me out big time, so I couldn't let it go.

"She must have had some idea," I said. "Somebody she'd worked with? A photographer, maybe? Or somebody—"

"She had no idea," Rebecca told me.

"That's why she was needed her passport, wasn't it?" I said, thinking of how desperate Claudia must have been, and feeling even more guilty for every unkind thought I'd ever had about her. "She was leaving the country to get away from him."

"No, no, that's not the reason," Rebecca said. She sank back onto the sofa and said, "I just wish all of this would go away."

I felt like an insensitive idiot for coming here, for being consumed with my own sort-of boyfriend problems when Rebecca's family had suffered this devastating loss. And as much as I'd like to blame Ty for bringing me to this point, the truth was that this was all on me.

I had to make up for this. I had to do something.

Then it came to me: I had to find Claudia's murderer.

Nothing would make up for my callous disregard for their loss, but at least it would help them to know the killer had been found and would pay for his crime. It was the best I could do. I hoped it would be good enough.

"I'll make it go away," I told Rebecca. "I'll find Claudia's murderer."

Her gaze whipped toward me. "What?"

"I've done it before," I told her. "Last fall. I solved a

murder. The police were stumped, but I figured it out. All by myself. And there were other crimes, too. I figured out who was behind all of them."

"But . . ."

I took Rebecca's hand and gave it a reassuring squeeze. "I swear to you, I'll find Claudia's killer. And I won't let anything—anything—stop me."

Rebecca just stared, too overcome to speak. I couldn't blame her. The conviction I heard in my own voice startled even me.

"This stalker. He sounds like a good place to start," I said. "If you think of anything else that might help, let me know, will you?"

"Yeah, yeah, sure," Rebecca said, wiping her nose.

Her voice sounded a little stronger now, so I figured my vow to find Claudia's killer had started the healing process. I felt stronger, too, ready to take on this investigation, make things right.

My mind skipped ahead, making a mental list of people to talk to, things to check out. I knew I had to start with Claudia herself.

"So, where was she going for vacation?" I asked. My stomach tingled, like this might be just the clue I needed to solve her murder.

"Claudia wasn't going on vacation. It was work. She's— she was—leaving next week. Some big modeling assignment in Europe."

The tingle in my stomach turned into a hard brick.

Claudia had been going to Europe?

So was Ty.

# Chapter 9

It was a Fendi day. Definitely a Fendi day.

A Fendi handbag would look perfect with the really sharp, brown Armani business suit I had on, but I'd carried Fendi the last time I'd visited the Golden State Bank & Trust, so this morning I had to do something different.

That made it a Louis Vuitton day.

According to my mom, too much Louis makes it look like you're trying too hard; just one of her pearls of fashion wisdom that have served so many so well. So I'd left my LV organizer in the car—the one Ty surprised me with, which proved his devotion to me, didn't it?—and just carried my purse.

I'd gotten a call from Bradley Olsen's secretary yesterday saying Mr. Olsen would like to meet with me this morning. I'd also gotten a call from my mom wanting us to go shopping today for gowns to wear to the charity gala at the Biltmore Hotel.

No way was I doing that.

I told her I had class. That's the one good thing about going to college. It's the perfect reason to get out of absolutely everything. Over the past few weeks, I've used that excuse with Mom so many times that, to anyone else, it would seem that I was in class twenty-four-seven.

Mom hadn't noticed.

In her call yesterday, she'd also asked who I was taking to the charity gala. I'd expected that Ty and I would attend together, but now . . . well, it was just one more reason not to call Mom back.

When I'd heard from Mr. Olsen's secretary I figured he'd gotten the info I'd requested on Evelyn's neighbor, the one she's convinced was offed by his new girlfriend, and that Olsen would tell me that Cecil Hartley was alive and kicking, and living the high life in an RV park somewhere in Arizona.

That left me feeling really good that I could mark this chore off my list—and ease Evelyn's mind, of course.

As I approached the B & T, the big glass door swung open and out walked Ty. My heart did its usual little flutter whenever I saw him.

Oh my God. He was so handsome. And he was wearing Armani. Just like me!

See? This proved we thought alike. We were on the same mental and emotional plane. We were *meant* to be together.

Ty wasn't exhibiting my joy of life right now, though. He was frowning—more than usual.

But that was okay. Actually, perfect. He'll spot me any second now. He'll stop dead in his tracks. His eyes will light up and a huge smile will break out over his face. He'll rush to me. Take me in his arms, right here on busy Wilshire Boulevard, not caring who might be watching. He'll tell me he's desperate for me. He'll ignore all his meetings today and whisk me away to a plush hotel suite overlooking the ocean where we'll—

Wait. He walked past me.

"Ty?"

He didn't stop. But that was to be expected. After all, he just left the B & T, probably some big meeting with Bradley Olsen.

"Ty!"

He still didn't stop. It was probably a *really big* meeting.

I hurried after him. "Ty!"

He glanced back, spotted me, then stopped.

His eyes lit up—a tiny flare, but I saw it—and the left corner of his mouth turned up ever so slightly—not everyone could spot it, just people like me who knew him well. Really.

"Sorry," Ty said. "I didn't see you standing there."

"Problems?" I asked.

"Olsen." Ty looked annoyed and nodded toward the B & T. "Somehow he got the idea there were problems with Wallace Incorporated opening on time."

Oh, crap.

I think maybe I gave Bradley Olsen that idea—he totally misinterpreted an innocent remark—the last time I was here.

But no use telling Ty. He already had enough on him. And I was sure he'd already cleared up the situation.

Besides, there was no need to dwell on the negative. This was the perfect opportunity for Ty to ask me out. We weren't at work, he wasn't in a meeting, and most important, Sarah Covington wasn't hanging around distracting him.

"So everything is set for the opening?" I asked.

Wallace Inc. was Ty's personal, pet project, totally separate from the family owned Holt's chain of stores. It was the reason he was doing double work these days.

In a way, Wallace Inc. was my pet project, too. Ty had consulted with me on the location. We'd discussed it over a romantic dinner.

At least, that's the way I'm choosing to remember it at the moment.

I hoped Ty remembered it that way too because it was a good lead in to him inviting me out again.

"Everything's on schedule. I just hired a store manager," Ty said, then nodded toward the B & T again. "Are you here to see Olsen?"

How did we get back on the subject of business? I wanted to talk about personal things like dinner, and why he liked me, and why we weren't having sex yet.

"Just some investment questions for Evelyn," I said.

"How's she doing?" Ty asked, looking concerned now.

I was not getting into the whole won't-come-out-of-her-house thing with him, or the murdered-neighbor thing.

"Evelyn's great," I said.

Okay, it didn't appear that I would get a dinner invitation out of him at the moment. I'd have to settle for lunch. But lunch was good. Nothing wrong with having lunch together.

I waved my hand toward the B & T and said, "I'm just here for a quick appointment. A few minutes, at most. Then I'm free for the afternoon."

"Give Evelyn my best," Ty said.

What's wrong with him?

"What sort of investment is Evelyn making?" Ty asked.

How could somebody this dense actually run a major corporation?

"A restaurant. Just down the street. Great place for lunch," I said.

See how he makes me lie? What's the matter with him?

Ty frowned. "Restaurants can be problematic. I should talk to Evelyn."

"Maybe you should try the restaurant first," I suggested, nodding in what I hoped was a wise, rather than desperate, fashion.

Ty hesitated, then glanced at his watch.

Why doesn't he *get it*?

The answer came to me: he was too busy right now. *And* he was too polite to say so.

Sure, that was it. He was on his way to a meeting crucial to the carefully orchestrated opening of Wallace Inc. and didn't have time for lunch with me. Lots of people—dozens, probably—were standing by, waiting for him to show up to give them instructions so the project could continue. Jobs and tens of thousands of dollars were on the line.

Okay, this was good—really good. If we had lunch right now, Ty would want to sit down across the table from me, gaze longingly into my eyes, savor every moment, hang on to my every word, learn every little thing that had been on my mind lately.

But I couldn't let him do that. I couldn't let him sacrifice his dream of opening Wallace Inc. on time just for lunch with me.

See what a great girlfriend I am?

"I've got to go," I said.

Ty looked surprised. "Sure. Okay. I guess I'll . . . see you around."

I headed down the sidewalk, and at the door to Golden State Bank & Trust, I looked back. Ty was already gone.

Wow, that was fast. Guess that meeting he was headed to was really important.

I told myself I'd done the right thing, but really, I hated it when I had to do the right thing.

In the B & T the same customer greeter was on duty wearing the same idiotic outfit. She remembered my name and glanced longingly at my Louis Vuitton bag, which cheered me up a little, and escorted me back to Bradley's Olsen's office.

He stood at attention beside his desk when I walked in.

"Good morning, Miss Randolph," he declared with a big—for a conservative banker, of course—smile. I guess he was over whatever he and Ty had talked about.

I sat down in the chair in front of his desk. Had Ty been sitting here? It felt warm, really warm. My heart ached again.

Why couldn't he have delayed that meeting for a half hour to have a quick lunch with me?

Why hadn't he just told me straight out that he'd wanted to get back together with Claudia?

Why hadn't he mentioned his trip to Europe?

Why didn't he want to have sex with me?

Mr. Olsen remained standing, watching the door. "Is Miss Croft joining us?" he asked.

I hadn't told Evelyn I was coming here today. Better to contact her when I had the situation resolved. She worried about everything, especially since last fall.

"No," I said, placing my Louis Vuitton handbag strategically on his desk top, where it could be seen and appreciated. "Evelyn couldn't make it today."

"Oh." Mr. Olsen just stood there for a minute, then frowned. "She isn't ill, I hope."

"Evelyn's fine," I assured him.

"Vacationing, perhaps?" he asked, smiling.

"No, no, just busy today," I said.

"Something fun with friends?"

Jeez, what was with him? He'd met Evelyn only once and he was asking a million questions. And Ty wouldn't even ask me out to lunch—after I practically put the smackdown on him for an invitation.

"What did you find out about Cecil Hartley?" I asked, anxious to move the conversation along so I could leave— not that I had any lunch plans, of course.

I was going to have to visit that Judith Leiber evening bag. It was the only way to salvage the afternoon.

Mr. Olsen got down to business. He lowered himself into his chair, slipped on reading glasses, and picked up a file.

"I'm pleased to report that everything seems in order," he announced. "This Mr. Cecil Hartley has substantial assets. A sizeable bank account, mutual funds, a solid retirement plan, and a home with considerable equity."

"So that's good?" I asked.

My mind really wasn't on Cecil Hartley or even Evelyn right now because all I could think of was Ty.

He wouldn't even ask me to lunch. I mean, it was just lunch. Nothing long-term. Nothing serious.

Mr. Olsen glanced at the file again. "Perhaps a little too much credit card debt, but nothing to be alarmed about, given his assets."

I *had* to find out what was going on with Ty. This whole thing was making me crazy.

I sat up straighter in the chair, realizing that Mr. Olsen had been blabbing on and on and I'd not been listening. I just wanted a straight answer from him. I didn't want to have to figure anything out right now.

"So that's good?" I asked again.

"Yes," Mr. Olsen said, putting down the file. "I'd say that Mr. Hartley's financial condition is good. Very good."

I needed to get out of there. I needed to phone Marcie and have her brainstorm the problems with my relationship over a few beers—no, wait, I think this called for tequila. And chocolate.

But I wanted to be done with this Cecil Hartley thing, too, so I pulled myself together enough to ask a question.

"He's used his ATM card and his credit cards?" I asked. "Recently?"

Mr. Olsen consulted the file, flipped a couple of papers, then nodded.

"Just last night. A place in Nevada called Department 56—not sure what that is—and a gas station." He frowned. "A considerable purchase."

"It's an RV," I said, recalling how Evelyn told me she'd seen Cecil and the girlfriend in his new motor home.

"Well, then, that explains it."

"His checking account is being used? Checks, I mean, not just the debit card?" I asked.

Mr. Olsen consulted another page in the file. "Checks written regularly for utilities, insurance, taxes. That sort of thing. I could go over this in more detail with Miss Croft, if you'd like."

I wasn't going to take up any more of his time with Evelyn's wild-goose chase. She just had too much time on her hands and spent it spying on her neighbors. Maybe I'd get her an Xbox, or something.

"That's not necessary," I told him, and got to my feet

"Please tell Miss Croft that, at this point, I see no reason for her not to consider Mr. Hartley's investment suggestions," Mr. Olsen said, pulling off his reading glasses. "I'll keep an eye on things, though, and I'll let her know immediately if something untoward comes up."

"Thanks," I said, and left the office.

I stood outside on the sidewalk for a while. The weather was great. Expensive cars drove past. Good-looking people in fantastic clothing went about their business. Ty wasn't there, of course, but in my mind I could still see him.

Then a hard body brushed against me. A hand landed lightly on my shoulder. Warm breath puffed against my ear and whispered, "How about lunch?"

I whirled around.

It wasn't Ty.

# Chapter 10

I had met Jack Bishop a few months ago. He worked for a private security firm and did freelance investigations. We'd been friends before all that stuff happened last fall, so he'd wound up in the middle of it. I'd helped him out with a few investigations in return.

He sat across the table from me in a trendy restaurant just a few blocks from the Golden State Bank & Trust. He was way hot. Dark hair, great body. The kind of guy you could count on for sweaty sex—not that I knew from personal experience, though. He looked particularly good right now in a gray turtleneck and black sport coat.

I guess I must have looked pretty good, too, in my Armani suit because Jack had been looking me up and down since I saw him in front of the B & T a few minutes ago

"How's everything going?" he asked.

"Doing the college thing," I said, "and working."

"You're still at Holt's?" Jack looked surprised.

Anyone who knew me well was aware that I'm not exactly cut out for working with the public. But I needed spending money and the job at Holt's provided it. Plus, the hours suited me, and I had friends there. Also, I'd learned the best places to hide from customers and which supervisors would let me get away with most anything. That made Holt's very close to my dream job.

"I figured that, with the settlement you got last fall," Jack said, "you wouldn't need to work."

"I just need a little cash for extras," I said.

The waitress served our lunch. Jack had ordered a big, meaty sandwich that looked delicious. I'd ordered a salad. I didn't want a salad, but neither did I want to eat like a truck driver in front of him.

The guy at the table next to us glanced at me. He looked me up and down, sort of like Jack had been doing.

Wow, this suit really attracted lot of attention. Maybe I should wear it more often.

"So what happened with the money from your settlement?" Jack said.

"I still have it," I said, stabbing at my salad. "Most of it."

The guy at the table next to us leaned forward and said something to the man he was having lunch with. That guy looked at me, too.

They probably thought I was a lawyer, or a corporate executive, or something. Was that what life would be like when I get my bachelor's degree? Cool.

"Everything's okay with you? Financially?" he asked.

I didn't expect Jack to ask about money. But he was full of surprises, like showing up in front of the GSB & T just now.

"Everything's great," I told him.

"Heard anything from your old friend Kirk Keegan?" Jack asked.

I rolled my eyes at the mention of Kirk's name. He'd been involved in that stuff last fall, but not in a good way, and he blamed me for all the things that went wrong.

"Kirk's way off my radar," I told Jack.

"Nobody's seen or heard from him," he said. "You should watch out."

I shrugged and said, "What's up with you? Working any cool cases?"

"Everything I do is cool," Jack said, and gave me a swarthy

grin that sent a heat wave through me. "Heard anything about Cameron's old girlfriend being murdered?"

Jack was one of the few people who knew that Ty and I were dating, but he didn't know about the sort-of part.

"Detective Madison seems to think I'm involved—again," I told him.

"Because Cameron and Claudia were getting back to-gether?" Jack asked.

Oh my God. How did Jack know that? Did absolutely everybody know that Ty wanted to get back with Claudia—except me?

"Where did you hear that?" I demanded.

Jack shrugged but didn't say anything. I knew I wouldn't get anything out of him that he wasn't ready to give up.

"I had nothing to do with Claudia's death," I told him. "One of those psycho pageant moms was mad at her. Plus, she had a stalker."

Jack frowned. "Why haven't you told police about this?"

"Claudia's sister already told them," I said.

He studied his sandwich a minute, then started eating again. I pushed my salad around my plate for a few min-utes, and then we got up to leave.

"If you need help with anything, let me know," Jack said.

For a moment I considered asking him to find Jamie Kirkwood, the missing server everybody was making such a fuss about. But I didn't want to burn a favor with Jack, not yet, anyway.

I smiled. "If you come across a really cool case and need help, call me."

Jack gave me a hot smile. "I haven't collected on the last time I helped you."

A shiver went through me. I knew he wouldn't name a price, just give me his standard answer, and he didn't dis-appoint.

"I'll let you know what I want," Jack said, "when I want it."

*    *    *

Seeing Jack made me realize that I had to get down to the business of solving Claudia's murder. I had a lot at stake, and a lot to check out. I didn't have much time, either.

Detective Shuman, if he already hadn't, would tell Madison that my mom's fruit bouquets had poisoned Claudia, and it would hit the fan then. Nobody would talk to me after that.

Traffic was light on the 5 freeway as I headed north, so I had plenty of room to weave in and out without thinking much about it, giving me the perfect opportunity to consider my suspects.

At the top of my list was Jamie Kirkwood, the Missing Server that I'd subbed for at the luncheon. She'd had the perfect opportunity to poison Claudia's fruit bouquet, and pretending to be sick so she could leave was a great cover. Not coming forward to talk to the police made her look guilty, but that was about all I knew that might implicate her. Motive? Who knew? Did she have access to the poison itself? I didn't even know what, exactly, had killed Claudia.

Rebecca had given me two more suspects: a whacked-out pageant mom and a stalker. That made three suspects—and I hadn't even started digging yet.

I swerved left, cutting off an SUV creeping along at the speed limit in the fast lane, and an awful thought hit me.

Would my mom turn out to be one of those suspects?

Part of me—most of me, really—knew Mom would never murder someone, under normal circumstances. But everyone else's "normal" wasn't the same as my mom's—that's the beauty of living in your own world.

Had Mom somehow found out about Ty and me sort-of dating? I'd never told her. Had someone else? Wouldn't she have mentioned it to me if she'd known?

Mom got distracted pretty easily—especially if the new issue of *Vogue* just arrived—but she'd have remembered that I was dating the hottest bachelor known to all her friends.

My cell phone rang. I fished it out of my purse and looked at the caller ID. Mom. I tossed the phone onto the seat. I didn't need to talk to her to know what she wanted. I could read her mind as clearly as a clearance sale tag at Nordstrom.

The charity gala at the Biltmore was drawing closer and Mom wanted to know who I was going with. She wanted us to go dress shopping together, too. I wasn't ready to commit to either.

Floating around in the depths of my memory was the recollection that Mom and Claudia's mother had been pageant rivals, back in the day. Had that morphed into some sort of my-daughter-is-better-than-your-daughter competition that I didn't know about? A Texas-cheerleader-mom kind of thing?

Starting at age three, I'd been put through the rigors of dance, singing, and music lessons by Mom in her search to discover in me some—any, really—natural talent. By the time I was nine we were down to baton lessons, and after I set the curtains on fire in the den, she'd given up on me.

I'd never made the pageant rounds, so there'd been nothing for my mom and Claudia's mom to compete over. But had their old rivalry resurfaced when it came to which daughter Ty—hot bachelor that he was—would choose?

Then another really awful thought hit me: if *I* could think these things about Mom, what must Detective Madison be thinking?

The Edible Elegance base of operations stood out like a red Gucci bag at a funeral sandwiched between a car stereo installation place and a painting contractor in an industrial park in Altadena.

Today, just like every other day I'd been here, a group of

men stood around in paint-splattered clothes. I'd never heard any of them speak English, so I figured it was just a matter of time before the INS raided the complex, shutting down Mom's business along with the others, and miring our family in a lengthy and expensive lawsuit.

Mom would have known that if she'd visited the site before signing the lease.

Debbie, the manager whom Mom had hired for no particular reason that I was aware of, waved through the window of the Edible Elegance office attached to the workroom. She recognized me immediately; I doubt she'd know Mom if she were standing next to me.

My Armani suit attracted a lot of attention from the men clustered outside the painting contractor business when I got out of the car. Wow, just like at the restaurant. One of the guys did a double take, punched another in the arm, pointed, and said something in Spanish. Within two seconds all of them were staring.

Then it hit me. Maybe I'd spilled something on the front of my jacket and hadn't realized it. Was that why everyone was staring? Jeez, how embarrassing.

I put my nose in the air pretending absolutely nothing could possibly be wrong, just as I'd seen Mom do a zillion times, and walked into the office of Edible Elegance. I stole a quick glance at myself as I crossed the threshold. No trail of salad dressing dribbled down my jacket. Whew. I guess it was just like Mom said: when you wear great clothes, people notice. Even painting day-laborers, it seemed.

"Haley, what a nice surprise," Debbie said, coming to her feet and rounding the desk to greet me.

Debbie had probably passed fifty several years ago but was fighting it. I had to hand it to her for that. Slim, trim, and just a little bottom heavy, she no doubt spent hours in the gym every day. The '80s were her favorite decade, apparently, because she still dressed in velveteen warm-up suits and styled her coal-black hair around a visor.

And no, I have no idea why Mom hired her.

"Has my mom been by lately?" I asked.

"No, no, I haven't seen her in a while." Debbie gave me a big smile and declared, "Orders are pouring in! L.A. loves us!"

She waved her hand toward the fax machine and telephone, both of which were silent, but still, I admired her enthusiasm. I decided to let her enjoy it while she could. Any moment now, Detective Madison would gleefully announce that Edible Elegance had poisoned Claudia, Mom's attorney would shut down the business, and Debbie would be out of a job.

Still, I needed info, and I had to get it without alarming her.

"Have the police been here?" I asked.

Debbie's eyes widened. Okay, maybe I needed to work on my interview skills.

"The police?" Debbie's gaze darted to the door, like she expected a SWAT team to repel from a hovering helicopter at any second. Then she gave me a nervous laugh. "Well, whatever for?"

"Someone died at the Holt's luncheon," I said.

"Oh, *that*." Debbie laughed again, but sobered quickly. "That pageant coach. I heard about her on the news. So sad. But no, the police haven't been here. Why would they?"

"Routine stuff, since Edible Elegance was part of the event," I explained.

"I don't know what I could tell them," Debbie said, shaking her head. "I mean, I drove the van to the store, unloaded the bouquets, and had Marilyn sign for them. That's it."

"Did you see anything . . . unusual?" I asked.

Debbie's lips turned down. "I was only there for a few minutes, and I wasn't really looking around."

"So the fruit bouquets are selling well?" I asked, changing the subject like I'd seen the detectives on *Law & Order* do.

Debbie perked up. "Terrific!"

"What's with the chocolate name tags?" I asked.

Adding the name tags had made it possible for the killer to target Claudia. Whoever ordered the fruit bouquets for the event would know that, and according to Marilyn at Pacific Coast Catering, that person was Sarah Covington. So if Sarah had requested the name tags along with the bouquets, I'd be one step closer to pinning this whole murder on her.

I couldn't wait to see Ty's face when they carted her off to jail.

The scene played out in my mind like a movie trailer.

I'll be with him, of course. He'll be stunned that his judgment had been so bad. I'll take his hand, look into his eyes, and assure him that he's not to blame, it was all Sarah. Then he'll tighten his grip on my hand, touch my cheek, realize that I'm the only woman in the world for him.

Sarah's trial could take years. I was going to have to find a way to speed this up.

Debbie laughed, bringing me back into the moment.

"Weren't those name tags just the most darling things?" she said. "A nice touch, I thought. They were your mom's idea."

My heart started to beat a little faster. Mom had done that? Mom? She'd thought up the name tags?

My whole line of thinking reversed, and I was desperate to hear that Edible Elegance had been using the name tags for weeks and I'd not known it.

"When did you begin using them?" I asked.

"Just started," Debbie said, nodding so hard the visor bounced up and down. "We used them for the first time at the Holt's event. Everybody loved them—absolutely everybody!"

Except Claudia.

My stomach looped into a knot the size of a Prada satchel. I had to go. I mumbled something about keeping up the good work, and raced to my car. Outside, guys from the car stereo installation place had joined the painters and all of them stared.

What was wrong with everybody today? This was the last time I'd wear this suit.

I jumped into my car and was ready to pull away when Debbie dashed out of the office, waving frantically. I buzzed down my window.

"I just thought of something," she told me, leaning down. "I *did* see something kind of unusual at Holt's that day. Well, no, actually, I *heard* something. Two women arguing."

My spirits lifted a little. "Who were they?"

Debbie shook her head. "They were on the other side of the delivery van. I couldn't see who it was. Sorry."

"What were they fighting about?" I asked.

"I couldn't make it out." Debbie's lips turned down again. "Sorry."

This whole thing was weird, I thought as I pulled out of the complex. I couldn't figure why my mom would get so involved with an event—especially one at Holt's, of all places—that she'd come up with the idea for chocolate name tags.

Except that, of course, she'd added the name tags so Claudia could more easily be murdered.

But if Mom had done that, she'd first have to have a reason to kill Claudia, decide to do it, come up with the means and method, get the poison, go to Edible Elegance's location, actually go into the workroom, and put the poison on the fruit bouquet. I couldn't see Mom doing any of those things.

But Detective Madison would.

This meant only one thing: I was going to have to go see Mom.

Crap.

# Chapter 11

"**I**'m overwhelmed. Completely overwhelmed," Mom declared as I walked through the front door of the house.

My mom was tall, like me, with dark brown hair. She always looked like she expected to answer the door and a photographer from *Vogue* would snap her picture. Today she had on Kenneth Cole pumps, pants, a cowl-neck sweater by Michael Kors, three tennis bracelets, a necklace, and diamond stud earrings. My mom's idea of lounge wear.

"What's wrong?" I asked.

Note: she didn't say hello or ask how I was doing.

"How could I not be overwhelmed?" Mom demanded, gesturing to the ceiling with the wineglass she carried. "Things are *frantic* around here."

I followed her to the family room off the kitchen. The house was perfectly still. No one else was in sight except Juanita, the housekeeper, who stood in the kitchen wiping down the countertops.

Mom's idea of frantic.

She sighed heavily. "So *much* is happening."

It didn't matter how many times I asked—or whether I asked at all—Mom would get to the point sooner or later. But I didn't have that kind of time. I had to get to Holt's for my shift.

"Listen, Mom, I need to ask you about Edible Elegance," I said. "At the—"

"What?"

"Edible Elegance," I said again. "The chocolate-covered fruit bouquets? The business you started?"

Mom waved away my words with a flick of her hand. "I can't concern myself with that at a time like this."

Then I felt bad. After all, one of her oldest—though certainly not dearest—friends had just lost her daughter. Mom shared the pain Claudia's family suffered, the horror of her murder, their future without Claudia in it.

"I know," I said softly. "It's really bad about Claudia."

"Who?"

What had I been thinking?

"Claudia Gray," I said. "She died the other day."

"Oh yes. Of course." Mom sipped her wine. "I've spoken with Cynthia. She's devastated. The entire family is devastated. Such a tragedy. I have no idea what I'll wear to the funeral."

"So look, Mom, about Edible Elegance," I said.

"There's an investigator involved, you know," Mom said.

Patience . . . patience . . . patience. Wait for it . . . wait for it . . .

"He specializes in—" Mom glimpsed herself in the mirror above the fireplace.

At this rate, I'd be lucky to make tomorrow's shift at Holt's.

"Who hired an investigator?" I asked.

Mom turned her head left, then right, studying her reflection. "The family."

"Claudia's family?" I asked.

She touched the back of her hair. "He specializes in this sort of thing. Much more efficient than the police."

Not efficient enough to find out that Edible Elegance had poisoned Claudia, I hoped.

"The fruit bouquets have chocolate name tags on them now," I said. "Where did the idea come from?"

Mom turned to me. "How would I possible know?"

"Well, Mom, it's your company," I said.

"That's what staff is for."

Mom walked to the edge of the kitchen and placed her wineglass on the counter. Juanita stopped working and poured her another glass.

"Your father is involved in some big project," Mom said. "He's never home on time anymore."

My dad was an aerospace engineer. He was always involved in a big project.

"I told him to bring those young men on his team home with him," Mom said. "I'm sure they could use a home-cooked meal."

Not that my mom would do the cooking, of course.

"Who's your date for the charity gala?" Mom asked.

Damn. She'd hit me with it out of the blue. Caught me totally off guard. At times, Mom could be very crafty.

But I wasn't about to give her any info. And I knew how to throw her off the scent.

"Whose dresses look good to you?" I asked.

Mom launched into an explanation of the subtle and almost undetectable differences in the designer lines, and I drifted off.

I still didn't see my mom murdering Claudia, but if she was determined to accomplish something, she could do it. She'd been hardened by her beauty pageant experiences—you didn't get to be third runner-up in the Miss America contest without trashing a tiara or two, or breaking an occasional nail.

If Mom had, in fact, ordered the chocolate name tags on the fruit bouquets, she would have needed a list of people seated at the head table, and she'd have gotten it from Holt's. That thought cheered me up a bit because the list would have come from Sarah Covington, which meant I could pin her with, at least, accessory to murder.

So how did Mom get the list? How did she send it to Debbie at Edible Elegance? Even though Mom wasn't exactly a computer whiz, she could handle e-mail.

"Mom?" I butted into her rambling explanation of the YSL strapless gowns. "Is that a spot on your sweater?"

She looked down, horrified, even though there was no spot, and hurried away.

I dashed into the den and pulled up Mom's e-mail on the family computer. I'd figured out her password a long time ago—her own name—and checked her mailbox. Nothing received from Holt's. Nothing sent to Edible Elegance or Debbie personally, which was good, since I'd really like to clear my mom of murder.

By the time I got back into the family room, Mom was there. She'd changed her sweater. Afraid she'd ask about my date again, or try to get me to meet her for a shopping trip to pick out gowns for the charity gala, I headed her off with another subject.

"I'm really worried about the way Debbie is running the business," I said.

Mom gazed at me. "Who's Debbie?"

Okay, I'm out of here.

"Got to go to class," I said, and headed for the door.

Mom called after me, but I pretended not to hear as I dashed out of the house.

Just as I got to my car, a white four-door Volvo pulled up and four guys got out. They were engineers, the guys on my dad's team whom Mom had invited for dinner. I figured them for early thirties; it takes a long time to endure all that schooling and get what they considered a good job somewhere.

Engineers, as a group, are brilliant. They've sent men to the moon, put computers in our pockets, and made the most remote spot on the planet a mere cell phone call away. But aside from that, they're kind of weird.

I knew these guys were engineers because, thanks to my dad's job, I'd been looking at them all of my life. You can always tell an engineer, and these were no exception.

All four of them crowded at the hood of the car. Judging by the pants the driver wore, he believed it was still Hammer time. Another guy had on plaid shorts and mandals—man sandals. The third one wore powder-blue sweatpants and black dress shoes. The other guy had on a jacket he must have been wearing since junior high.

Clothing manufacturers really need to put expiration labels in their clothes so men will know when to stop wearing them.

They all stopped when they saw me and clustered together, rising on their toes and craning their necks to see me. And it wasn't my Armani suit this time. Among them, these guys probably had more degrees than dates.

"Hey, guys," I called, and gave them a finger wave.

They all mumbled something and the guy in the mandals sort of waved. I think he was going for the Vulcan live-long-and-prosper hand gesture—which really translates to I'm-a-dork-and-a-loser—then caught himself.

The guy in the eighth grade jacket stepped away from the pack and approached me with his hand out.

"Doug Eisner," he said.

I took his hand and warmth zinged up my arm, which kind of surprised me.

I'd figured him for the president of the Klingon Dictionary Club, but now that he was closer I could see that he was kind of handsome, in a dorky engineer sort of way. Tall, brown hair that was about seven years out of style, and not a bad build considering all the time he spent hunched over a computer.

"I'm Haley," I said.

The guys behind him stared openmouthed, as if I were a trophy Doug had just brought down at a big game hunt.

Doug nodded toward the street. "Your dad is right behind us. We're having dinner here tonight."

Engineers, as a group, are social misfits. But that's okay because they knew it. It had taken a lot for Doug to step forward and actually speak aloud, and the fact that he'd put together two complete sentences was impressive. So I didn't want to just blow him off and leave even though, with each second I stood here, the chances of him launching into a mind-numbing explanation of their current project grew. No way could I listen to that.

"Enjoy," I said, and gave them all another wave.

"You're not staying?" Doug asked.

"No, I've got to—"

I wasn't about to tell him I was leaving for my shift at Holt's tonight. He might mention it to Mom in a desperate attempt to make dinner conversation. And I didn't want to use my I've-got-class excuse, either. Not that I was embarrassed about the two classes I was taking—Doug had probably forgotten more than I was ever going to learn in school—but it just wasn't something I wanted to get into with him.

"I'm seeing a friend," I said. "She's sick."

I reached for my door handle, but Doug stepped over and opened it for me.

"Maybe some other time?" he asked.

"Yeah, sure," I said, and got into my car and drove away.

I glanced at the house in the rearview mirror—my favorite way of seeing it—glad that I'd accomplished something here.

I knew Mom hadn't been in contact with Holt's or Debbie to pass on the list of names for the chocolate tags. If the police checked her computer, they'd see that.

Mom could have faxed the list, of course. I didn't think she knew how to operate a fax machine, and I couldn't picture her running into Staples to use one available to the general public, so that didn't seem likely.

Detective Madison popped into my mind and I imagined him asking, "But what better way to cover it up?"

Oh, crap.

I ran by my apartment and changed out of my Armani suit and into khaki pants and a brown sweater. I freshened my hair and makeup—as Mom says: if you're pretty, people will like you—and got to the store a full ninety seconds before my shift started. In the employees' break room about a dozen people stood by the time clock. Rita had posted herself beside the whiteboard, red marker in her hand, anxious to take names and ruin lives.

"I want all of this stuff out of here by closing," Rita said to me, and nodded across the room.

Heaped on the table beside the refrigerator were cases and bags of—oh my God, was that cat food?

"What are you telling *me* for?" I demanded.

"*You're* the one who said there were cats in the stockroom," Rita told me. "*You're* the one who volunteered to feed them."

Volunteered? Me? No way.

I'd adopted a strict policy of never volunteering for anything back in fourth grade when I offered to bring cookies to the class Valentine party, and Mom put Chips Ahoy cookies in a plastic container and tried to pass them off as home baked. How embarrassing.

"You've been sniffing your marking pen too long," I told Rita. "I never said I'd—"

"You told Jeanette you'd do it at the meeting," she said.

Okay, this sort of rang a bell. I'd drifted off and then Jeanette had called my name and . . .

Maybe I should start paying attention in the meetings.

I felt the employees at the time clock staring at me now. They'd all spent part of their pittance of a salary to help feed the nonexistent cats in our stockroom. So what could I do?

"This is great," I said, gesturing to the mountain of cat food on the table. "Those little kitties will be well fed."

Everybody smiled, shoved their time cards into the time clock, feeling like they'd done something good. And I guess it was good for me, too—feeding the supposed cats would be the perfect excuse for leaving the sales floor.

I took up my usual spot in line—dead last—and checked the work schedule clamped to a clipboard on the wall. I was assigned to domestics—that's retail speak for bedroom stuff—then found Bella's name on the list and saw where she was working tonight.

The store seemed kind of quiet as I headed for the housewares department, or maybe I'd just gotten good at tuning out the canned music, screaming children, and complaining customers. I kept my lanyard with my name tag on it inside my pocket so nobody would ask me to help them, and found Bella loading dishes onto one of the U-boats we used to move merchandise around the store.

"Damn, I wish this place would make up its mind," Bella grumbled.

Her international landmark phase continued. Tonight her hair looked like the Chrysler Building.

She heaved another stack of plates onto the cart. "I just put all this mess out here two weeks ago, and now I'm moving it someplace else. Got to make room for the new department."

I perked up. "Designer clothes?"

"At Holt's?" Bella rolled her eyes. "They're putting the new sewing department here."

Maybe Jeanette had covered that in the meeting.

"We got some old lady gonna give lessons," Bella said. She stopped and looked up at me. "Hey, what did you do with that sewing machine you won in the raffle?"

"I'm trying to get rid of it," I told her. "Want it?"

Bella went back to moving dishes. "You ought to learn to sew. Make some of those knockoff purses you're selling."

"Guatemalan housewives make them for about five cents an hour," I told her. "I can't beat that price."

She paused and pursed her lips. "Maybe I'll buy that machine from you. I'll make my own signature brand of headbands and scarves when I get out of beauty school. Sell them to those stupid movie stars for a hundred bucks each."

"My friend Marcie listed it on eBay for me. If nobody bids on it, it's yours," I said. "Listen, I wanted to ask you about the luncheon the other day. Did you see anybody fighting?"

Debbie had told me that she'd overheard an argument between two women. I figured it was the pageant mom trying to steamroll Claudia into letting her daughter do more. Bella would've had a front-row seat for whatever went down.

"You mean an Ike-and-Tina kind of thing?" Bella asked, moving dishes again.

"More a Rosie-and-just-about-everybody kind of thing," I said. "An older woman? The mom of one of the models arguing with the pageant coach that died?"

"Didn't see anything like that," Bella told me. "But I did catch one of the girls bitching her out."

Teenage models complained, whined, and pouted about nearly everything, and their coach usually took the brunt of it, so what Bella had seen didn't really surprise me—except that she'd seen only one of the models doing it.

"Did you hear they found who that Missing Server was?" Bella asked. "It was all over the TV today. Had her name and picture splashed across the Internet. Still can't find her, though. Everybody's still looking for her."

I got that queasy feeling in my stomach, like when you ask for a Fendi purse for your birthday, but you're afraid to open the package because you're not sure if you really got it.

Detective Shuman had already told me that Jamie Kirkwood had been ID'd as the missing server. I hadn't actually looked forward to him finding her since Jamie might tell them about my involvement that day, and that I'd kept it from the police—which anyone in my position would have done.

"I bet she'll get a book deal," Bella said. "Or one of those crazy-ass TV producers will want to do her life story."

But Jamie didn't seem like the kind of girl who'd be anxious to spill her guts about everything that went down that day. She wouldn't want to get into trouble with Marilyn because she needed that catering job, and I was guessing Jamie wouldn't want to deepen her involvement with the police.

"Or, at least, the cover of *People*," Bella said.

Or Jamie might want to lay the whole thing on me, just to get free of the cops.

Crap.

# Chapter 12

"We're resolving this issue with Ty right now," Marcie declared as she stepped through my front door. She pulled a stack papers from her tote—a fantastic Tory Burch—and announced, "A relationship quiz."

Oh my God. Of course. A relationship quiz. The perfect way to figure out what was going on with Ty and me. Why hadn't I thought of that before?

"I'll get beer," I said, and headed for my kitchen.

"And lots of chocolate," Marcie called.

Chocolate was a given. No personal dilemma could possibly get resolved without it.

We sat at opposite ends of my couch, beer in hand, two full bags of Snickers bars at the ready. When Marcie had called after I'd left Holt's tonight and said she needed to drop by, I'd figured it was something to do with our next purse party. This was tons better.

Marcie waved an ink pen in my directions and consulted the papers she'd brought. "This quiz is titled 'Is He Mr. Now Or Mr. Never?' "

I already knew the answer, of course. Ty was my Mr. Now. But things had been weird between us, so reaffirming that we were perfect for each other through the scientific process of a relationship quiz would ease my mind.

"Okay, first question in the Major Issues section," Marcie said. "Does he share the same political views as you?"

"We never really talked about politics," I said. "But that doesn't mean we wouldn't agree."

"Of course not," Marcie said, and made a note on the paper. "Okay, next question. Do the two of you agree on a religion?"

"Well, we never actually discussed religion," I admitted.

Marcie looked up from the quiz. "What religion is Ty?"

"I don't know—but I'm sure I'll love it when I find out."

"And he'll love yours," Marcie said, making another mark on the paper. "How about other issues like global warming, abortion, and stem cell research?"

I got a yucky feeling in my stomach. "I don't think 'major issues' is a big factor in our relationship. Maybe we should move on."

"Good idea," Marcie said. She flipped the page. "Do the two of you like the same sports teams?"

"I'm not sure which sports team Ty likes," I said.

"Okay, how about his favorite food?"

"I don't know what it is."

"Favorite vacation spot?"

"I don't think that ever came up."

"His favorite color?"

"He looks great in blue," I said.

"Close enough," Marcie declared, and marked the page. "Now, name three romantic things he's done for you in the past week."

Okay, I could do this. I *had* to do this. Our relationship was hanging in the balance. I squeezed my eyes shut, waiting for a romantic memory to pop up.

It didn't.

"Uh, I can't really think of anything romantic," I said, then added, "Right now, that is."

"How about something thoughtful?" Marcie asked.

I shook my head. "Nothing's coming to mind."

"Something helpful?" she asked.

"Ty's really busy," I said.

"Oh, okay. Sure," Marcie said, then turned the page. "Now, name five things the two of you have in common."

"Five?" I gulped down a swallow of beer. "Wow. Five, huh? That's a lot."

"Okay, then name four."

"Actually, we haven't really known each other all that long and—"

"Three?"

"Well . . ."

"One?" Marcie asked, her pen poised over the quiz. "Come on, Haley, you can think of *one*, can't you?"

"Of course I can," I declared. "But, well . . ."

"We'll come back to that one," Marcie said, and jotted a note on the paper. "Now, what's the most important characteristic you're looking for in a man?"

"That's easy," I said, relieved. "He should be fun at a party."

Marcie looked up at me. "That's not one of the options on the quiz."

"It's not?" I asked. Okay, that was weird. "Then how about that he likes to dance?"

Marcie shook her head.

"He's strong enough to pick me up if I pass out at a club?" I tried.

Marcie looked at the quiz and frowned. "That's not on here, either."

"Jeez, what kind of quiz is this?" I demanded. "Where did you find it?"

"On the Internet."

"Not from *Cosmo*?" I heaved a sign of relief. "No wonder I'm not getting any of the answers right. What kind of credibility can a relationship quiz have if it wasn't published in *Cosmo*?"

"Yeah, I guess this was a bad idea," Marcie agreed, and slipped the papers back into her tote.

I studied the bag for a minute, then asked, "So what's the result?"

"Are you sure you want to know?" Marcie asked.

Okay, I knew things didn't look so good for Ty and me right now, but sometimes those quizzes have a way of pointing out the positives, rather than the negatives in a relationship. And it looked as if Ty and I needed all the positives we could get.

Marcie pulled out the papers again and did a quick calculation. She frowned again.

"Ty's not your Mr. Never," she said.

My spirits lifted. "See? I knew we were meant to be together."

Her frown deepened. "He's not your Mr. Now, either. According to your quiz score, you might make out with him at a bar, but you wouldn't date him."

I shoved a Snickers bar in my mouth.

"I'd better go," Marcie said, and got up from the couch. She gestured to the sewing machine still sitting in my living room. "I checked on eBay before I came over. No bids yet."

"Bella said she might want it," I said. "She's got some wild notion about designing a line of headbands and scarves."

"Sounds like a good idea," Marcie said.

Maybe it was. I was kind of bummed right now. Nothing sounded good to me.

"You should make your own line of bags," Marcie said, then smiled and nodded. "You could be the next Judith Leiber."

That kind of cheered me up. It would be great to be a

Judith Leiber type of designer. Everyone would be jealous of me. I probably wouldn't even need a college degree for it.

Then my spirits plummeted again.

"Crap," I said. "I have homework tonight."

"Another English paper?" Marcie asked.

"Health," I told her. "We're studying circulation or corneas—I don't know, something that starts with a *c*."

I hated that class. As soon as it was over I was going to go get drunk so I could burn out some brain cells and hopefully forget everything I'd learned.

Marcie opened the door but lingered for a minute, the way a best friend would.

"I know things are tough for you and Ty right now," she said, "but they'll get better. I have a good feeling about the two of you."

That boosted my spirits a bit. Marcie was almost always right about these things.

She left and I slumped onto my sofa cradling the last of my beer in one hand, a bag of Snickers bars in the other.

Okay, so things didn't look so good for Ty and me, according to Marcie's relationship quiz. But no quiz could take into account how hard Ty worked, how many hours he put in every day, all the responsibility he carried on his shoulders, all the people who depended on him. He'd been spread thin for months, running Holt's and trying to get Wallace Inc. open. He really had very little time to spend with anyone—which proved that it wasn't *me*.

I needed retail therapy in a major way. Nothing less than that Judith Leiber evening bag would pull me through right now. Somehow I had to get my hands on it.

I pulled up in front of Evelyn's house the next morning and killed the engine. The neighborhood was quiet. A few newspapers still lay in driveways, and one health-conscious old guy jogged in a sweat-stained T-shirt.

A few days ago I'd phoned Evelyn with the info Bradley Olsen at the GSB & T had given me about her supposedly missing, maybe-murdered neighbor Cecil, and assured her everything was fine. She'd seemed okay with it.

Then, this morning—way too early—Evelyn had called all twisted up about Cecil again. She'd begged me to come over. It didn't really suit me, but I'd dragged myself out of bed, pulled on sweats, put my hair in a ponytail, and driven over. I pretty much looked like crap.

But I couldn't refuse Evelyn, especially since she was probably lonely, and more than likely this was just an excuse to get me over here. Besides, I could hit her up again for the money to buy my Judith Leiber evening bag.

A Honda Pilot was parked in the driveway, which was a surprise. Evelyn seldom had company since "the incident" last fall. Two people at her house at once? Maybe Evelyn was ready to party.

I saw the blinds at the living room window move a fraction of an inch as I headed up the walk. Still, I rang the bell, and called out to identify myself. Locks turned, the security system peeped, and finally, the door opened.

"Haley, thank you so much for coming," Evelyn said, repeating her ritual of securing the door. "I know it's early and you're very busy, but, well, I just had to do *something* and I didn't know who else—"

"It's fine, Evelyn," I told her. I just couldn't stop trying to make things better for Evelyn.

She looked neat and tidy, dressed in jeans that she'd ironed, a pink T-shirt, and a white cardigan sweater.

"Please, come in. I want you to meet someone," Evelyn said, and led the way into the living room.

Christine, whose last name I missed, was the someone Evelyn wanted me to meet. I figured her for about thirty, blond hair styled in a crooked ponytail, no makeup. She looked worse than I did but had a better excuse—the infant baby cradled in her arms.

"This is Annie," Christine whispered, pulling back the pink blanket.

Women are weird when it comes to their babies. They want to show them off, but don't really like people getting too close or actually touching them.

"Oh, wow," I said. "She's a real—"

"Shh," Christine hissed, and drew the baby away as if I'd just exhaled anthrax. "Don't wake her."

"Sorry," I whispered.

"Christine is Cecil's daughter," Evelyn explained in a low voice.

Okay, so now I knew why I was here. Evelyn and Christine intended to tag-team me about Cecil and the new girlfriend.

Evelyn knew me well. On the table in front of the sofa sat a tray of cinnamon buns. They were bad for me, of course, but Evelyn had gone to so much trouble, how could I refuse?

Evelyn headed to the kitchen for coffee—I thought that's what she said, she'd spoken so quietly I wasn't sure—and I sat in the chair near Christine. She was so fascinated with her sleeping baby I wasn't sure she remembered I was in the room, so I headed into the kitchen after Evelyn.

Of all the times I'd been to the house, I'd never been in the kitchen. It looked neat and tidy, just like the rest of the place and Evelyn herself. The cabinets, appliances, floor, and walls were crisp white; she'd spiced things up with touches of pink and mint green.

"How are your classes?" Evelyn asked as she took cups and saucers from the cupboard.

I hated them. They were boring and dull, and I didn't know how I was going to endure years of this abuse. But Evelyn didn't want to hear that.

"Great," I said, then realized this would be a good opportunity to hit her up for money—my own money—for that evening bag.

"You know, I have some pretty big school expenses coming up," I said, which was a total lie, of course, but we were talking about a Judith Leiber evening bag. Desperate measures were justified.

Evelyn paused at the frige, a carton of creamer in her hand.

"You're not just saying that to get money for the evening bag you wanted, are you?"

Damn. When did Evelyn get so sharp?

"It's a fantastic bag, and I desperately need it."

"I'm just doing what you asked," Evelyn reminded me, placing the sugar bowl on a flowered tray.

Yes, I know I made her swear not to give me an extra dime unless it was a real emergency, but how was I to know she'd actually *do* it?

"You have a nice monthly income," Evelyn pointed out. "Can't you cut corners somewhere?"

"I'm cutting corners," I told her, my thoughts scrambling around to come up with a believable example. "I won a sewing machine and I'm thinking of making my own clothes."

"Oh, I love to sew!" Evelyn said, looking all dreamy-eyed. "If you need help, just let me know."

This wasn't the direction I wanted this conversation to go, but Evelyn picked up the tray and headed out of the kitchen before I could say anything else.

I followed her into the living room. Christine was still mesmerized by her baby; I doubted she knew either of us had been out of the room. Evelyn poured coffee and served the cinnamon buns. I took two, just to be polite.

"Christine is very worried about Cecil," Evelyn whispered.

"Did something else happen?" I whispered back.

"It's just everything," Christine said as she sipped coffee with one hand and straightened the baby's blanket with the other. "Look, I admit I don't like Barb."

"Barb seems a bit . . . rough," Evelyn explained in a low voice. "She wears jeans and those leather jackets with some sort of skull on the back. Hardly Cecil's type."

"And I could never find out much about her," Christine said softly. She glanced down at the baby—to make sure she was still there, I guess—then went on. "When I asked Barb about her family or where she worked, she was very evasive."

"I only spoke with her once," Evelyn murmured. "We didn't hit it off."

"After Mom died, Barb showed up out of nowhere. Dad was lonely and I think she took advantage. Within no time at all, she'd moved in with Dad," Christine said, rocking little Annie for no apparent reason. "Then, suddenly, Barb up and moved out. Dad was devastated. When she finally agreed to come back, he started doing everything he could to keep her from leaving again. He bought her a car, let her redecorate the house. Anything she wanted, he went along with it. Dad bought that motor home last fall because Barb asked for it."

It crossed my mind that Christine was more worried about Barb running through all of Cecil's money—her inheritance—than her dad's love life. But I didn't say so. I took a third cinnamon bun—just so I'd look interested, of course.

"Cecil is a completely different man," Evelyn said quietly. "He used to stop by here occasionally, help out with little things, just to be neighborly. After Barb moved in, he wouldn't even wave from his yard."

"Barb's the jealous type?" I asked.

Evelyn's cheeks flushed and her back stiffened. "Cecil

was always a perfect gentleman. We were friends. Neighbors. That's all."

In her own way, Evelyn was an attractive woman. I could see that Barb might be jealous.

"I hardly ever see Dad anymore," Christine said, holding little Annie tighter and rocking at a frantic pace. "Barb won't let him come over unless she's with him. He's hardly seen Annie at all."

"And now no one has seen or heard from him for weeks," Evelyn said.

"Dad called two weeks before Christmas, saying they were taking the motor home to Arizona to visit Barb's family for the holidays," Christine said. "I couldn't believe it. It was Annie's first Christmas and Dad wasn't going to be here?"

"I spotted the motor home parked on the side street by Cecil's house, just after New Year's," Evelyn said. "It was there for a day, then gone again. I saw Barb going into the house, but I never saw Cecil once."

"Dad never called to let me know he was back in town," Christine said.

"If he was only going to be here for a day, maybe he didn't have time?" I suggested.

"Then why come back for only a day?" Christine asked, jiggling the baby up and down. She shook her head. "See? The whole thing just doesn't make sense."

Okay, she had me there. It didn't make sense. But it didn't add up to murder, either. More like Cecil was having a good time with Barb and enjoying life on the road, free from neighborly good deeds and a daughter who didn't like his girlfriend.

"Dad's never been away for this long before. I think I should go to the police," Christine said, then bit her lip. "But if nothing's wrong, Dad would be upset with me. And Barb would throw such a fit I'd never get to see Dad again—and he'd never get to see little Annie."

"That's why we need you, Haley," Evelyn declared in a low voice. "Is there anything more you can find out?"

Yeah, there was more I could find out, but I'd need help. And I knew just where to find it.

Provided I was willing to pay his price, of course.

# Chapter 13

"**D**o you have this in a size seven?" the customer asked.

I looked across the counter of the customer service booth at the woman holding the ugliest shoe—even by Holt's standards—I'd ever seen, and tried to pull off the newly required we-can-do-that smile. The store had moved past its of-course-you-can slogan—with accompanying smile—and instituted yet another idiotic mantra that we minimum-wage grunts were supposed to carry off.

It wasn't working. At least, not for me. That's because I knew the whole lame-ass promotional plan had been the brainchild of Sarah Covington.

Jeez, and she needed a college degree for that?

"I'll have to check," I told the customer, and took the shoe—ugh, gross—from her.

I turned to Grace, who was working at the inventory computer at the back of the customer service booth. Since Christmas I'd been assigned to almost every department in the store, including customer service. I didn't like working here, but I liked Grace. She was nineteen, with spiked hair that she'd just colored dark red. Grace was in college working toward a real future, so she didn't take things here at Holt's too seriously, which was why we hit it off so well.

"I need to check on shoes," I said to Grace.

She glanced at me, rolled her eyes, and said, "Go for it."

Don't ask me why, but customers think that just because we're in the customer service booth we should provide actual service to anyone at any time. I mean, really, it's crazy.

How would I possibly know if a certain shoe was available in a specific size when I was in the customer service booth and the shoe department was all the way across the store? You'd think they would just ask the clerks in the shoe department. Hardly a day goes by that this didn't happen.

But it was a good excuse to get out onto the sales floor and maybe visit with some friends, so I headed toward the shoe department, the customer trailing along behind. Sophia, the department lead, was straightening the boxes when I walked up.

"Checking for a size," I called as I walked through the door to the stockroom.

The shoe department had its own stockroom. It wasn't nearly as cool as the huge one at the back of the store, but it was still a good place to hide from customers. There were huge racks of shoes in there and a desk the department manager used to do paperwork on.

I pulled out the chair and sat down as the door opened and Sophia walked in. She was Hispanic, short, and solidly built. She'd been supporting her five kids on her Holt's salary for years.

"Damn, that's ugly," Sophia said, taking the customer's shoe from my hand. She tossed it on the desk. "Stupid customers."

No argument from me. I reared back in the chair and put my feet up on the desk.

Even though Sophia had worked here for a long time, she wasn't much for store gossip. She had a lot on her at home. Putting in her time here, then leaving, suited her fine.

But I was pretty sure not much got past her, even if she didn't usually talk smack about people. I figured it wouldn't hurt to ask her about the day Claudia was killed.

"What did you think about the luncheon?" I asked, not wanting to rush her into anything.

"Lucky you," Sophia said. "You won that sewing machine in the raffle."

What's with everybody and sewing, lately?

"Want it?" I asked.

"I've got two already," Sophia said, as if everybody did. "My girls all know how to sew their own clothes."

"What did you think of the fashion show?" I asked, trying to steer her back to the luncheon.

She uttered a disgusted grunt. "Those models. What a bunch of little bitches."

"I heard one of the moms got into a fight with the pageant coach," I said.

Okay, I knew this was a leading question, but I had to find out which mom Debbie had overheard arguing with Claudia.

"I didn't see nothing like that," Sophia said, shaking her head. "Did you find those cats in the stockroom yet?"

After so many of the employees donated cat food, what could I do but put it out for the cats—even if they didn't really exist. What choice did I have?

"Not yet," I said.

"Maybe you need to put out more food for them?" Sophia suggested. She opened a desk drawer and pulled out a bag of Hershey's Kisses. "I checked their bowls. They're not eating."

Great. Now I'd have to sneak back there and empty some of the food.

Sophia held out the bag and I took a few—just to be polite, of course.

"My neighbor has some kittens she's trying to get rid of," she said. "I told her you'd take them."

My feet dropped from the edge of the desk. "What?"

Sophia popped a kiss into her mouth. "You're the cat lady now, right?"

"I'm not the cat lady," I insisted.

"I'll bring them so you can take a look," she said, then disappeared out the door.

Jeez, where do these crazy ideas come from?

I sat back and enjoyed the candy, thinking about what Sophia had said. Neither she nor Bella had seen a mom arguing with Claudia, so I wasn't getting anywhere with the suspect Rebecca had told me about. I'd have to figure another way to find out who it was—other than talk to Rebecca again. I didn't want to do that until I had something concrete to tell her.

I ate two more kisses and left the stockroom. Halfway across the shoe department a woman called to me.

"Did you have them?" she asked.

Oh yeah. The woman who wanted those god-awful shoes in a size 7.

"We're out," I told her.

I took the long way around to stretch my legs a little—and to delay my return to customer service booth hell—and Troy popped out from behind a mannequin in the men's department.

"Hey, Haley," he said. He stared at me like he was in a trance, or something.

He'd been annoying me for a while now, so I said, "What's with you, Troy? You're acting like a complete idiot."

He yucked a goofy laugh and kept staring. I kept walking.

I headed for the break room—I saw no reason not to continue to abuse the time I was out of the customer service booth—to get something to eat. Those Hershey's Kisses had only made me hungry. My shift would end in an hour or so and I needed a little boost to get me through.

Seated at the table near the fridge was that girl who was always eating fruit and those frozen diet meals. I could never remember her name, which was just as well since I hated her because she'd lost so much weight. Forty pounds now, somebody told me. Really, how could I not hate her?

"Hi, Haley," Sandy called. She sat at a table nibbling chips and flipping through *People* magazine, and pointed. "Lots more stuff."

Piled up next to the employee lockers was another dozen bags of cat food, along with six cases of canned food. Jeez, what was I going to do with all this cat food? The trunk of my car was still full from yesterday's haul.

I plopped down in the chair beside Sandy, too overwhelmed to hit the vending machine.

"My mom works with a pet rescue," Sandy said. "She told them what you're doing for the cats. They think it's really cool."

"So," I said, changing the subject, "what's up with you?"

Sandy shrugged. "You know."

I translated this immediately: boyfriend problems.

"What did he do?" I asked.

She sighed. "I had to stop by his place this morning. It was kind of early. When I got there I saw his ex-girlfriend leaving."

"*What?*"

She nodded. "Yeah. I guess she spent the night there."

"You dumped him. Right?" I asked.

She shrugged again. "He said he really likes me. No one understands him like I do."

"Please tell me you dumped him."

"He says I'm his muse," Sandy said.

I couldn't talk to her about this anymore. I changed the subject.

"Did you see anybody arguing with that pageant coach who died at the luncheon?" I asked. No sense trying to be subtle with Sandy.

"Yeah, that caterer lady," Sandy said.

I sat up straighter in the chair. "Marilyn?"

Sandy shrugged. "I don't know her name. She had on a really weird outfit and a thing in her hair. You know, one of those visors old women wear at the beach."

"Debbie," I realized.

Okay, that was weird. Debbie hadn't mentioned that she'd actually spoken with Claudia the day of the luncheon. And she sure hadn't told me that the two of them had argued over something. In fact, Debbie had claimed that she'd overheard Claudia in a row with someone else.

"You're sure?" I asked. "You're positive it was the caterer you saw arguing with Claudia? Not one of the pageant moms?"

"Yeah, I'm sure." Sandy shook her head. "I don't think Claudia was having much fun that day. I mean, even one of the models was giving her a hard time about something."

"It comes with the job," I said.

Sandy was quiet for a moment and I figured we were both thinking about Claudia's last day of life.

Then Sandy said, "Maybe I should plan a romantic weekend for my boyfriend and me. So he'll know how much I love him. What do you think?"

"I think you should dump him," I told her, and left the break room.

Two more hours of my life that I'd never get back crawled past and, finally, I punched out and left the store pushing a U-boat loaded down with bags and cases of cat food. Troy and that heavyset guy from the men's department had offered to help, but I'd turned them down; they kept looking at me weird.

I didn't know what I was going to do with all this cat food. I'd left a bag in the stockroom so the employees would see that I was "feeding" the nonexistent cats. I knew everybody meant well, but this whole thing was working on my nerves.

I popped my trunk and crammed the cases and bags in alongside the cases and bags I'd put in there last night.

Around me, the other employees got into their cars and drove away. The security lights in the parking lot dimmed. I pushed the U-boat back to the store entrance and left it there—if someone stole it, oh well—and headed back to my car.

Not in the best of moods, I considered calling Marcie. It would be great to hang out for a while, but I had a ten-page paper to write for English that was due by midnight that I hadn't even started yet; plus, I had to study for a test in Health, two whole chapters on addiction, which made me wish I were addicted to something.

I hate college.

And I hated that I wasn't getting anywhere with Claudia's death, or clearing Mom—or myself—of murder charges, and that Sandy's boyfriend treated her like crap, and that my own sort-of boyfriend was just that: sort-of.

Bright headlights cut through the darkness as a car whipped into the deserted parking lot. I froze. It sped diagonally across the spaces, directly toward—me.

I ran for my car. My keys? Where were my keys?

I yanked open my purse—a fabulous Gucci satchel—and shoved my hand inside, feeling for the keys. The car's engine roared louder.

Was that Detective Madison coming to arrest me?

I found my keys—thank God—and pulled them out. I kept running. Bright headlights flashed on my face as I clicked the lock on my key.

Could it be Claudia's murderer? Had I stumbled onto him—or her- -and not realized it?

The car turned in a tight circle around my Honda and screeched to a stop next to me.

Was it Kirk Keegan? Had he come after me, as he'd threatened?

My heart raced. I jerked open the car door and jumped inside.

"Haley, wait up!"

Ty. Oh my God, it was Ty.

I lurched out of my car as Ty got out of his. My heart pounded in my chest—but not from relief at seeing him.

"What the hell are you doing?" I screamed. "You scared the crap out of me!"

"I did?" he asked, and looked genuinely surprised. "Sorry, I didn't mean to scare you. I just wanted to catch you before you left."

"I got off work ten minutes ago, Ty! *Ten minutes*," I yelled. "You should know that since you *own* the place!"

"Sorry," he said again.

But I wasn't ready to be soothed or placated, and I sure wasn't ready to forgive. I was angry about—well, about everything, and thinking I was going to be arrested or murdered in the dark, empty parking lot of Holt's, of all places, had fried my last nerve.

"Really, I'm sorry," Ty said once more. Then he smiled down at me, that cute smile of his that I couldn't resist—usually.

"You could have called," I told him.

He heaved a sigh and announced, "I finally have everything handled for the opening of Wallace Incorporated. I need to talk to you. Let's go out for dinner."

"Now?" I asked.

"Sure." He nodded toward his car.

Dinner? With Ty? I'd wanted just that for ages. But right now, at this very moment, it didn't sound all that great.

I had on my Holt's work clothes, so I looked like crap, and I had that homework paper due by midnight. It irked me that Ty had blown in here, announced that he wanted to go to dinner—because it suited *his* schedule—and he expected me to hop in his car, no-notice.

"I had something I wanted to talk to you about," Ty said. "Something special."

Now my heart rate really cranked up, but for a whole different reason.

Oh my God. He was going to invite me to the charity gala at the Biltmore. Our first big night together.

The evening flashed before my eyes.

We'll walk in. I'll be wearing a fabulous gown, Ty in a stunning tuxedo. All eyes will turn to us. Mouths will gape open. People will point. A murmur will go through the crowd. We'll be the stars of the evening. Then afterward, Ty will take me to the exquisite suite he's rented for us at the hotel where we'll—finally—have our first night together.

"I'm leaving for Europe," Ty said. "I'll be there a few weeks and I—"

My best-ever daydream burst.

"You're *what*?" I demanded.

"I'm leaving for Europe," Ty repeated. "I'll be—"

"*When?*"

Ty paused, looking troubled. Obviously, this wasn't the way he'd pictured this conversation going.

"Soon," he said. "I'll be there for several weeks and—"

"What about the charity gala at the Biltmore?" I all but screamed.

He froze. I could see the wheels turning in his mind as he wondered just what the hell I was talking about.

He didn't figure it out because he said, with a good measure of caution, "What about it?"

"We're supposed to go! You and me! Our big debut!"

Ty waved his hands—as if that could somehow calm me—and said, "No, Haley, you don't understand. I want you to go to Europe with me."

I stared at him, trying to process his words, too stunned to speak for a second or two.

"What's wrong?" Ty stared hard at me, trying to glean something from my expression. "You don't have a passport?"

"Of course I have a passport," I snapped.

Most parents took their kids to Disneyland. We went to Paris Fashion Week.

"You're telling me this *now*? *Now*?" I said. "You couldn't have given me some notice?"

"I wanted to surprise you."

Oh. Okay, now I felt like an idiot. And that made me mad again.

"Do you think I have absolutely no life at all? That I'm just standing around, waiting for you to surprise me with something?" I demanded. "I have plans, commitments. I have responsibilities. Things I have to do."

He shrugged. "Cancel them."

His words lodged in my brain. I couldn't seem to understand them.

"Haley, this is Europe I'm talking about," Ty went on. "I've got business, but you can have your days to shop, sightsee, whatever. Then in the evenings we can—"

"You expect me to cancel my plans? Just like that?" I shouted. "I've got school, Ty. My education."

"You can turn in your assignments over e-mail," he said.

"I have other plans. Helping with my mom's business. Purse parties scheduled with Marcie. Tons of things," I said. And the more I thought about it, the madder I got. "I can't believe you'd think I'd take off to Europe with you. Our relationship won't even stand up to an *Internet* dating quiz."

Ty stared at me. I don't think he knew what I was talking about.

"We've hardly had a real date," I said. "You're always late, or you're on the phone, or you don't show up at all."

Now Ty looked as if he understood, but didn't know why I thought that was a problem. And then it hit me: I was being an idiot over Ty.

Oh my God. I really was being an idiot over him. Just like all the other girls I knew. The ones who put up with a load of BS when they deserved better. The girls who kept hanging on when the guy was clearly not interested. The girls I always made fun of.

Not a great feeling.

"I'm not going to Europe with you, Ty," I said. "Forget it."

I turned to get back into my car, but Ty caught the door, stopping me.

"Look, Haley, you know I've been busy with Wallace Incorporated, and—"

"Everybody's busy, Ty," I said. "If I mattered to you, Wallace Incorporated would matter a little less."

He looked really confused. "But you do matter, Haley."

"We've never had an uninterrupted date," I said.

"Okay, no problem. Next date, I'll leave my cell phone at home," Ty promised.

"We haven't even had sex yet."

"We can fix that—right now, if you want."

Okay, that was kind of tempting.

Then I came to my senses. I didn't want sex from Ty, not *just* sex, anyway. I wanted a relationship.

"Forget it," I said to Ty, and turned back to my car.

He jumped in front of me and sighed heavily. "I realize that everything that goes wrong between us will be my fault, but could you at least tell me what's really happening here?"

I huffed, letting him know that I didn't want to talk about it anymore. But I guessed I owed him that much.

"You're too busy to spend time with me, and I'm tired of being in second place," I said. "I'd really looked forward to us going to the charity gala, but obviously it means nothing to you since you're going to Europe instead."

"I'll come back," Ty said, as if the solution were obvious. "I'll come back and we'll go to the gala together."

My spirits lifted for a second, then plummeted again. "You can't make it to dinner with me on time when you're right here in town. You're not going to make it back from Europe."

"I will," he promised. "I'll be there. Count on it."

I shook my head. "I don't want to be disappointed again."

"You won't be. I swear," Ty told me.

I wanted to believe him, but I wasn't going to get my hopes up again.

He grinned. "We could still have sex now, if you want."

I grinned, too. I couldn't help it.

"I'm going home," I said, and got into my car. "I have a paper to write."

Ty stood outside my open car door looking down at me. "You're going to see a different side of me from now on."

I liked the sound of it, but wouldn't let myself believe it.

"Yeah, okay. Whatever," I said.

"See you at the Biltmore."

Ty pushed my door closed and I drove away.

A different side of Ty? I wondered what that would be.

# Chapter 14

There's a fine line between stalking and just hanging around to see what's up. I hoped that nobody who saw me sitting on the front steps of the Palms Apartments, watching the apartment building across the street, knew that subtle difference.

I'd rolled out of bed early this morning—way early—and headed to Westwood Village, a really cool area near the UCLA campus. Old movie theaters showed indie and classic films, there were tons of bookstores, art galleries, shops, and great restaurants.

Nearby were lots of apartment buildings. It was a really nice area, so rent was high; students had to share.

The building directly across Hilgard Avenue from where I sat was where Jamie Kirkwood, the missing-now-found server lived, according to the address I'd copied out of Marilyn Carmichael's personnel records.

I'd knocked on Jamie's apartment door on the second floor when I got there, but no one had answered. I figured she'd refused to open up, fearing it was the press or police, or maybe she'd sacked out in a neighbor's apartment until things died down. Either way, I hoped I could catch her on her way to class, or breakfast, or work, or something this morning. Granted, it wasn't much of a plan, but it was all I had going at this early hour.

For my covert op I'd dressed in jeans, Skechers, and a sweatshirt and carried my backpack—standard college student attire. I thought I blended in pretty well. My health book lay open on my lap. I could have read my next assignment, but saw no need to carry this undercover thing too far.

I pulled my lone notebook from my backpack and dug around until I found the one pen I kept with me—no sense in weighing myself down with school supplies—and wrote the word "suspects" at the top of a fresh page. I needed to see where I was on my investigation; plus, I wanted to look like I was studying—without actually studying, of course.

Voices drifted from across the street. I looked up. Three girls came out of the apartment building. Jamie wasn't with them.

I turned back to my notebook, ready to list my suspects, but my mind drifted back to last night in the Holt's parking lot with Ty, and the stunning revelation that had hit me out of the blue: I'd been making excuses for Ty's behavior, all along.

Bad enough that I didn't know where I stood with him, but could he really have been trying to get back together with Claudia before she died? And his trip to Europe. Was it just coincidence that Claudia was traveling there also?

Yeah, I'd been pretending everything was okay when it wasn't. Letting him treat me badly and not speaking up. And for what? I wasn't even getting any good sex out of him.

A black SUV pulled up to the curb in front of the apartment building across the street and honked the horn. A couple of seconds later, two girls came out. I craned my neck for a better look at them, and saw that neither was Jamie. They climbed into the SUV and drove away.

I looked down at my suspect list but still couldn't write

anything. My brain was still stuck on Ty. He'd promised he would return from Europe in time to take me to the charity gala, and he'd sounded sincere, but I didn't see it happening. I'd told him that. I didn't want him thinking I would hang around waiting for his return, so at least I had my dignity.

. But my *dignity* wouldn't whirl me around the dance floor at the Biltmore charity gala.

I glanced at my watch. I'd been here awhile—nearly a half hour already—and my butt had gone numb from sitting on the hard steps; I was hungry, and the fountain in the yard beside me was giving me a headache.

Maybe I wasn't cut out for undercover work.

But I wasn't ready to give up on finding Jamie. I turned back to my notebook.

I had only one suspect I could identify by name: Debbie. Sandy had said she'd seen her arguing with Claudia the day of the luncheon. Motive? I had no clue.

Next I listed the pageant mom who was, according to Rebecca, upset with Claudia. Her motive was pretty clear. She wanted her daughter to do more and Claudia disagreed.

Bella had mentioned that one of the teen models had gotten into it with Claudia, so I wrote that down, too.

My next unnamed suspect was whoever Debbie had overheard arguing at the luncheon when she'd dropped off the fruit bouquets. Maybe it was Claudia, or maybe not. Debbie wasn't sure.

I paused and looked at my list. Not much to go on. So I added the one nameless suspect who gave me the creeps—Claudia's stalker.

To discover his identity, I'd have to delve further into Claudia's life, and I had a pretty good idea of how I'd do that. And it wouldn't—thank God—include sitting in front of an apartment building.

"What are you doing here?" a voice asked.

My head snapped up. Jamie Kirkwood stood in front of me.

When had she come out of her apartment building? Crossed the street? Walked up to me?

I'm really bad at this undercover stuff.

"Hey, Jamie, are you okay? I've been worried about you," I said. Luckily, I'd thought my approach through earlier, so the words popped out even though she'd caught me off guard.

Jamie looked better than when I'd seen her at the luncheon. Not sick, anyway. She had on jeans and a sweatshirt—standard college wear. They looked worn and ill fitting, but not in a cool way.

"How did you find me?" she asked, looking worried.

"I asked around," I said, then hurried on. "Are you feeling better? You looked really sick the other day."

"Yeah, I'm okay now. It was nothing," she said.

"Did the police talk to you?" I asked, then added, "They're talking to everybody."

Jamie didn't answer right away, like maybe she wasn't sure if she trusted me, or wanted to discuss it. But I guess she decided we had a connection, or something.

"Yeah, they came," Jamie said, and nodded toward her apartment building. "Nearly got me tossed out on the street. My roommates let me live there but they don't want any trouble. I don't want any trouble, either. I've got a full ride and I can't mess it up."

"So what did you tell the cops?" I asked.

"I told them I don't know anything about Claudia Gray dying. And I don't."

"Did you tell them that I subbed for you?" I asked.

She looked concerned now, like not mentioning what we'd done at the luncheon might have just blown up in her face.

"All I said was that I hadn't felt well so I left early," she told me.

Jamie spoke the words as if she'd practiced them, which, I guess, she had. I was relieved to hear it, but for selfish reasons.

"What did you tell them?" she asked.

"Nothing. Just that I was there but didn't see anything," I said.

Jamie looked relieved that we had our stories straight.

"So, did you see anything weird going on at the luncheon?" I asked.

"Everything about it was weird," Jamie declared. She glanced away and shook her head. "Those teenage girls, those models, they've got everything—and they don't appreciate it. They just expect more."

"You've seen those girls before?" I asked. It surprised me a bit. Jamie sure didn't look like she traveled the pageant circuit.

"A couple of times when I served for Marilyn," Jamie said, and uttered a bitter laugh. "Luncheons at the Gray family's house in Brentwood. They were all so stuck-up. Like they thought they were so much better than me."

Actually, those girls probably did think they were better than Jamie. She had her hair in a ponytail, but you could see that it hadn't been cut professionally in a while. Today, like at the luncheon, she wore inexpensive makeup, the kind you get off the clearance rack in the drugstore. Jamie looked like what she was—a struggling scholarship student.

"So why didn't you come forward when the cops first started looking for you?" I asked.

"Because I don't know anything about Claudia Gray dying," she said.

"It must have weirded you out big time to see your face all over TV and the Internet," I said. "Probably freaked out your parents, too."

"No family," Jamie said, and looked away.

I had a better picture of Jamie now. Probably a foster kid from some small town in the middle of nowhere, blessed with a good brain that got her a full scholarship but little else, at the moment. Classes, studying, homework, hunting down odd jobs, feeding herself, and keeping a roof over her head occupied her every waking moment. No wonder she didn't want to get mixed up in Claudia's murder investigation.

Jamie hitched her backpack higher on her shoulder. "I've got to get to class."

I shoved my book, notebook, and pen into my backpack and stood.

"Listen, take my cell phone number," I said. "Maybe we can hang out sometime."

Jamie didn't jump at the chance, but she finally pulled out her phone and punched in my name and number. I took her number too. I already had it from Marilyn's personnel roster, but I didn't want her to know that.

"Hang in there," I said as I turned to walk away.

I'd gone a few feet when Jamie called my name.

"Thanks for the other day at the luncheon." A hint of a smile touched her lips, but not without some effort. "You didn't have to do that. So, thanks."

"Sure," I said.

I stood there for a few minutes as she walked away, glad I wasn't her, then guilty that I'd had the thought.

Despite what you see in the movies, it's okay to look like crap when shopping on Rodeo Drive. All sorts of people go there, not just the beautiful ones dripping in jewels and fabulous clothes.

You might see what appears to be a homeless woman tottering out of a store, only to find a chauffeur-driven Bentley waiting for her at the curb. A girl in a ratty T-shirt and UGG boots might be an actress dodging the paparazzi.

The cool part about the Rodeo Drive shops is that their highly trained sales staff can somehow discern your bank balance when you walk through their doors, and treat you accordingly. If you're a regular customer, they remember you and your bank balance. Or, in my case, they know your mom.

I'd put off shopping with Mom for our gowns to wear to the charity gala for so long that she'd finally gone without me. But I wasn't completely off the hook. She'd picked out a few that she knew I'd just love and had Lillianna—I'm pretty sure everybody who worked there made up their own names—her personal shopper at Chez March, put them aside.

So there I was still in my college student attire of jeans and sweatshirt that I'd worn to Jamie's place this morning, walking into one of the most fabulous shops on the most famous street in the world, not worried in the least that Richard Gere wasn't there to ensure that I got great service.

The elegance of Chez March touched everything in the store, from the ankle-deep carpet, to the crystal chandeliers. The whole place was done in muted tones of gold and ivory, with mannequins dressed in chic fashions, and lots of comfy chairs to accommodate pampered customers. The sales staff all wore beautiful clothing—but not so beautiful as to outshine their wealthy patrons—with carefully coiffed hair and full-on makeup.

I spotted Lillianna at the rear of the store. She looked like someone had just hauled her out of an exhibit at Madame Trousseau's and set her up here at Chez March.

She put on her I-have-to-pretend-you're-better-than-me-so-I'll-get-my-commission smile and came forward, greeted me by name, complimented my mother, then went to fetch the gowns Mom had picked out for me. Since Lillianna, like all the other clerks at Chez March, moved at the pace of a bride approaching the altar, I knew I had a few minutes to kill. I headed for the handbags.

Maybe they had a Judith Leiber evening bag here. Oh my God, wouldn't that be fabulous? My heart skipped a beat as I hurried toward the display case.

My cell phone rang. I yanked it out of the side pocket of my backpack and flipped it open. A number I didn't recognize appeared on the ID screen. Since I'm not big on suspense—and was desperate to get to the handbag display—I answered.

"Uh, Haley?" a man's voice asked.

"Yeah," I said as my gaze swept the purses behind the glass. Judith Leiber . . . Judith Leiber . . . surely there would be a Judith Leiber bag here.

"Uh, hello, Haley. This is, uh, this is Doug—Eisner. Doug Eisner."

I froze. My mind whipped into a frenzy trying to place the name.

"Uh, from the other night," he said. "In your driveway. At your parents' home."

"Oh, right," I said. Doug was one of the engineers who worked with my dad that my mom had invited to dinner. "How did you get my number?"

"The Internet," Doug said.

Okay, that was weird. But at least my mom hadn't given it to him. She'd tried to set me up with one of Dad's engineer friends once before. The guy definitely had his own agenda. In the first three minutes of our date he asked about my education background, work history, and where I saw myself in five years. I felt like I was on a job interview.

"I hope that's all right," Doug said.

"No problem," I said, easing around to the next display cases. There just had to be a Judith Leiber bag here somewhere.

Doug exhaled loudly. "So, I was, uh, I was wondering if you'd like to get together for dinner sometime."

I turned to the next case but instead of spotting a gorgeous evening bag, I saw Rebecca Gray.

"Or, uh, lunch, maybe?" Doug asked.

She spotted me at the same moment, and her eyes widened.

"Coffee?" Doug asked.

What was Rebecca doing here?

"Haley?" Doug asked.

"Yeah, that's great," I said into the phone. "Listen, Doug, I've got to run."

"Oh yes, of course. How about tomorrow?"

"Sure. Bye," I said, then flipped my phone closed.

Rebecca and I did the usual oh-my-gosh-it's-you quick hug thing.

"What are you doing here?" I asked.

Rebecca nodded toward the counter at the rear of the store. "Looking for a gown," she said.

"For the charity gala?" I asked. "Your family is still going?"

It came out sounding kind of judgmental—I mean, jeez, her sister had been murdered a week ago—but Rebecca didn't seem to notice. She looked sort of numb, like when I'd last seen her.

She shrugged. "I guess."

"How's your mom?" I asked.

She glanced away. "She's okay."

I doubted that was true, and it made me feel like a dork for standing here trying to talk to her. I didn't know what to say—and everything I'd said so far came out bad—so I moved on to something I knew Rebecca would want to hear.

"I found that Missing Server the cops were looking for," I said.

"I know. She's been all over the news," Rebecca said, glancing at the handbags in the case.

"No, no, *I* found her," I said. "*Me*. I found her myself just this morning."

Rebecca's head whipped around. "You did?"

I nodded quickly. "I told you I would. Remember? I promised you that day at your house that I'd find Claudia's killer."

"Well, yeah, but . . ."

"I talked to her right in front of her apartment near the campus."

Rebecca just stared at me for a minute, like she couldn't believe I'd actually done what I'd promised.

"So, what did she say?" Rebecca finally asked.

I shrugged. "She told me the same thing she told the cops, that she didn't see anything the day of the luncheon."

"She didn't know anything?" Rebecca asked.

Now I regretted that I'd mentioned it, that I'd gotten her hopes up when the info amounted to nothing.

"Sometimes—lots of time, really—witnesses realize later that they saw something important. That could happen with Jamie," I said. "I got her phone number. I'm going to talk to her again, and I'm sure the cops will, too."

"Wow, that's . . . that's great, Haley." She glanced back toward the stockroom. "I guess I'm not really up to this, after all. Would you tell Talia I had to leave?"

She ducked around me and out the door.

Rebecca didn't look so great, but would I look any better if my sister had been killed a week ago? And my mom was dragging me to a formal event?

It flashed in my mind that maybe I'd thought too harshly of Rebecca and her family for attending the charity gala so soon after Claudia's death. Maybe they needed to put it behind them, get back to their real lives. Who was I to judge?

Lillianna appeared and presented a Vera Wang gown with great fanfare, but I couldn't look at it. I wasn't feeling so good myself, at the moment.

Over the past week I'd wondered how I'd feel if my sister died. Now another, scarier thought zoomed through my mind.

What if I died?

# Chapter 15

Ever since I left Chez March this morning after seeing Rebecca, I couldn't stop contemplating my life—and the possibility of losing it. What would happen if I died? What would I leave behind?

I drove into the Holt's parking lot and nosed into a space near the door, killed the engine, and stared out the windshield, hoping to catch a glimpse a life without me in it.

I figured that by the time I got old, decades and decades from now, medical science would have advanced to the point where people routinely lived to be over a hundred. I had a lot of years left—unless something went wrong, like with Claudia. So, if I died in, say, a few years, I'd likely leave no kids behind. What would be left to show that I'd even been on earth?

Money.

The idea popped into my head. I had that eighty grand in the bank. I could do something with it, set up a foundation, a trust, or something.

I got out of my car and crossed the parking lot contemplating just what sort of worthy cause I should give my money to. It would have to be something grand, of course. Something huge. Something that would make everyone else jealous.

Then it came to me: I could set up a program to give designer handbags to underprivileged young women.

Yes! Perfect. Wow, what a cool idea. Jeez, why was I fooling with college classes when I had these terrific—

"That's her!" a voice yelled.

Off to my right, a half dozen people raced across the parking lot toward me.

"Stay right there!" someone shouted.

In a flash I recognized several Holt's employees running behind a woman in a pink suit. A man loped alongside them carrying some sort of equipment.

"Don't you dare move!" the woman commanded.

They surrounded me, closing me into their tight circle.

The woman turned to the man. "Get ready. We go live in fifteen."

Oh my God. *Oh my God!* A television crew.

"Stop," I said. "I'm not—"

"Haley Randolph, right?" the woman asked, pulling out a microphone. She turned to the cameraman. "How am I?"

"Great," the guy said, hoisting a huge camera onto his shoulder.

"Wait," I said. "What's going on? I don't—"

"All you have to do is answer my questions," the woman said, patting her hair and straightening her jacket. "Act naturally."

"But—"

"This is so cool," I heard Troy say. He stood at my left shoulder, his mouth open slightly, leering at me. That heavyset guy from menswear stood next to him. Three other people from Holt's crowded closer, craning their necks to see.

"Look," I protested, "I don't—"

"We're live here at Holt's Department Store," the woman suddenly announced into the microphone, "where just days ago an untimely death took place. Now, in the wake of that tragedy, new life has been discovered in the form of a mother cat and her litter of kittens."

My heart slammed against my ribs. Oh my God! This was *not* happening.

"With me this evening is Haley Randolph, the young woman who, we're told, found these precious creatures near the very stockroom where, only moments before, model Claudia Gray's murdered body was discovered," the reporter said. "Tell us, Haley, how did it feel when you heard those tiny kittens calling out?"

The reporter shoved the microphone in my face. The camera swung toward me. Silence fell and everybody stared.

Oh my God. I had to say *something*.

I gulped hard. "Good. I mean, I was glad the kittens were safe inside the stockroom."

The reported yanked the microphone away. "And you're heading up the store's efforts to take care of these sweet little kittens and their mother, aren't you?"

She thrust the mic at me again.

"It's really all the employees," I said. "Everyone's chipped in with food for them."

"So there you have it," the reported announced, turning toward the camera again. "An entire store, led by one committed young woman, treasuring life in the face of death. For Channel Three's Making Things Matter segment, I'm Avery Phelps reporting. Back to you, Bob, in the newsroom."

The cameraman and the reporter walked away without another word. Everyone else kept staring. Troy eased closer.

"Wow, Haley, that was so cool," he said, then snorted a laugh.

The guy from menswear looked at me like I was a cinnamon roll with extra frosting.

"I've got to get to work," I said, and pushed my way through the crowd.

Just inside the door, Julie, the Holt's credit greeter, stood beside the table where she handed out half-pound boxes of candy to customers who completed a credit card application.

"Was that a news crew?" Julie asked.

She was nineteen, cute and perky. She had the store's new we-can-do-that smile down pat on the very first try.

"Just something about the cats," I told her.

"I heard them the other day," Julie said.

I stopped. "You what?"

She nodded. "I was in the stockroom and I heard the kittens."

I just stared at her for a second, then kept walking.

I headed for the employee break room, knowing what I'd find when I got there. Rita. I was already picturing her with duct tape across her mouth.

Sure enough, Rita stood by the whiteboard, poised and ready to add my name to the list of employees late for their shift. I snatched my time card out of the slot and fed it into the clock, three seconds early.

"I want you in the sewing department tonight," Rita told me.

"I can read," I shot back, pointing to the work schedule that hung beside the time clock.

"And I want all of this out of here by the end of your shift," she said, and jerked her thumb toward the table in the corner.

My shoulders slumped. More cat food. Plus litter, and all kinds of cat toys. What was I going to do with all this stuff?

Rita glared at me for a few seconds and I glared right back. Finally, she tossed her head and trounced out of the break room. I stewed for a moment, then followed.

I didn't know the first thing about sewing, except that I owned a sewing machine that had proved impossible to get rid of, so I hardly knew what to expect working in that department. Bella had said the woman Holt's had hired to run it was old, so maybe I could slip away when she wasn't looking.

The new department looked about half finished. Seven sewing machines were set up. A number of display units were in place, along with several huge cabinets, and some tables and chairs with thick catalogs on them. I had no idea what any of it was for, even though I watched *Project Runway* faithfully.

The one good thing about the department was that there were ropes up to keep the customers out.

Maybe working here wouldn't be so bad, after all.

"Hey, girl," Bella called. She walked over from the housewares department. "You working here tonight?"

"I guess so," I said, and gestured to the empty department. "Who's the manager?"

"Beats me," Bella said. "You hear what happened to Shannon?"

Shannon supervised the greeting card department. She and Rita were friends. I hate her, of course.

"She got attacked," Bella said, leaning in a little. "In the stockroom."

Okay, I didn't hate her enough to wish something bad would happen to her.

"What happened?" I asked.

"That mama cat back there came after her, attacked her," Bella said.

"*What?*"

"She's off on disability."

I don't believe this.

Bella headed back to housewares and I hung around, waiting for somebody to show up. Then, afraid a customer might jump the ropes and ask me to do something, I started rearranging the catalogs on the tables.

A tiny gray-haired woman walked up. She looked frail, brittle, like maybe if you spun her in a circle body parts would snap off. She wore a Holt's lanyard around her neck, so I figured she was the woman hired to run the sewing department.

"Hi, I'm Marlene," she said, giving me a sweet smile. "We've got a lot to do, dearie, so let's get cracking."

"I'll go back to the stockroom and get the merchandise," I offered. I could stretch that out for at least a half hour.

"No need," she said. "I've already got it all."

Marlene pointed across the aisle. Four U-boats were loaded down with boxes. It would take all evening to stock all that merchandise.

Crap.

Marlene talked until closing. Straight through, with barely a pause for a fresh breath, she talked. I think she even talked while I was on break.

Thread, bobbins, patterns, blah, blah, blah. Anything I took out of a box, she explained—just as if I were interested. She droned on about the leisure suits she'd made back in the '70s, and how she hoped shoulder pads would come back. I got an earful about the lessons she planned to give here at Holt's.

Just as I was seriously considering shoving a wad of rickrack into her mouth, the store closed. I rushed to the break room, cut to the front of the line at the time clock, then grabbed my purse and headed out the door.

"Aren't you taking the cat supplies home?" Julie asked.

Everyone in line at the time clock stared at me, so I forced a smile and said, "Sure. I'm just getting a U-boat."

I dashed back into the stockroom, found a U-boat, and loaded it up with the litter, cat food, and toys. Everyone in the break room pitched in.

Outside, I rolled the U-boat up to my car as everyone else headed home. I popped the trunk and stared down at all the supplies already inside. What was I going to do with all this stuff?

A shadow moved across my face and I looked up to see a man standing next to me. The security light shone from behind so I couldn't see who it was. I got a creepy feeling.

"Uh, hello, Haley," he said.

I glanced around. Everyone else had left the parking lot already. The creepy feeling threatened to mushroom into an all-out panic.

The man took a step closer. "It's Doug—Eisner. Doug Eisner. From the other night? We talked today . . . on the phone."

I shifted to the side, changing the angle of the lighting, and got a better look at him. He looked nice, like he'd shaved and showered before coming here and, thankfully, had left his junior high jacket elsewhere.

"Oh yeah, right," I said, relieved that—as far as I knew, anyway—Doug wasn't a homicidal maniac. "What are you doing here?"

"I saw you on the news tonight," he said, and nodded earnestly.

Damn. I'd hoped no one I knew had seen that news segment. I didn't worry that Mom had seen it—she never watched the news—but someone she knew might mention it to her. This was hardly the story I wanted shared over drinks at the charity gala at the Biltmore.

"Your efforts at pet rescue are to be commended," Doug said. "The ramifications of homeless animals in our communities place undue hardship on many facets of our society."

I just looked at him. What was I supposed to say to that?

"Let me give you a hand with that," Doug said, and started loading the cat supplies into my trunk. He moved some things around and got it all in there, with room to spare. He was stronger than I expected, for someone who didn't lift anything heavier than a mouse.

"So, would you like to go have coffee, maybe? Or something?" Doug asked as he pushed my trunk lid closed.

It hit me as kind of weird that he'd seen me on the news, then shown up here at Holt's.

"Or we can go tomorrow night, as planned," Doug offered.

Tomorrow night? I'd made a date with Doug for tomorrow night?

Then it came back to me. He'd phoned while I was in Chez March this morning.

Headlights cut through the darkness as a car sped across the parking lot toward us. My heart jumped. Was it Ty again? An actual homicidal maniac? The cops coming to arrest me?

Then I mentally chastised myself. I had to stop thinking that every time I saw headlights in the darkness it meant something bad was about to happen.

The car cruised to a stop behind my car, blocking it in. The doors opened and Detectives Madison and Shuman got out.

So much for thinking positive.

Madison hitched up his trousers and planted himself in front of me, and with an expression of smug delight said, "Miss Randolph, we're here to talk to you about the disappearance of Debra Humphrey."

"Who?" I asked.

"The woman who manages Edible Elegance," Madison told me. He swaggered closer. "She's missing. And according to witnesses, you were the last person to see her."

Oh, crap.

# Chapter 16

Detective Madison stared at me, waiting for me to respond to his latest accusation. But I wasn't about to say anything—at least, not with Doug Eisner, an open conduit to my dad's ear—standing next to me.

I turned to Doug. He looked concerned and a little scared. Not that I blamed him, of course.

"This really isn't a good time for me," I said quietly.

"Who is this?" Madison demanded, thrusting his chin toward Doug.

"He's nobody," I told him, then felt bad because it came out sort of insulting. "I didn't mean that you're nobody. But, really, you should go."

Doug's chest puffed up a little and he squared his shoulders.

"No, no, I won't leave you alone here, under these circumstances," he declared.

"Really, it's fine," I told him. "This sort of thing happens to me a lot."

Now Doug looked terrified. "It does?"

"Maybe you'd rather go downtown and discuss this," Madison said in a threatening tone.

"There's nothing to discuss," I told him.

"What were you doing at Edible Elegance?" he asked.

Shuman stood behind him, looking a little concerned. I

wondered if maybe he hadn't told Madison that my mom owned the business. If so, and he was trying to cover for me, I sure didn't want to rat him out. It crossed my mind, too, that Madison knew the truth already and was waiting to see if I would admit to it, some sort of test to see if I was being honest with him.

You'd think Madison would know better by now.

"Witnesses ID'd you at the scene," Madison declared. "And right after you left, the Humphrey woman closed the place and took off. Nobody's seen her since."

Doug eased up next to me and said quietly, "Haley, I recommend you speak with an attorney before making a statement."

"Do you think you need an attorney?" Madison asked, his tone suggesting that he hoped I did.

"This is all a misunderstanding," I said to Doug. "Give me a minute."

I walked away, leaving all three men to stare after me. As I knew they would, Madison and Shuman followed.

"Yes, I stopped by Edible Elegance," I told the detectives when we were out of earshot of Doug. "And, yes, I spoke with Debbie. So what?"

"So what?" Madison echoed. He gestured toward Shuman. "We're investigating a murder, a poisoning. We go to question one of the companies that provided food and what do we find? You've already been there, and the woman we want to talk to has disappeared—in a hurry. What are you trying to hide?"

"Nothing," I insisted, but it came out sounding a little guilty.

Madison leaned closer. "You were seen hanging around those fruit bouquets at the luncheon. That makes me think you and this Humphrey woman were in on this murder together. Did you force her to leave town to cover up your crime? Threaten her?"

"Of course not."

"That's tampering with a witness, with evidence." Madison gave me a smug smile. "All of which will go quite nicely with a second murder charge."

I gasped, but he walked away, hopefully not seeing that my hands had started to shake.

Madison thought I'd murdered Claudia *and* Debbie? He didn't even know if Debbie was dead. Jeez, he was out to get me, all right.

Shuman hung back, his expression grim. I didn't know if he was upset with this turn in the investigation, with Madison, or with me.

"Stop lying," Shuman said.

Okay, so it was me he was upset with.

"We got the complete lab report on Claudia's death," he said. "She was poisoned with a lethal cocktail of cleaning and beauty products dumped onto that fruit bouquet. They came from inside the RV the models were using."

A flicker of hope flared in me.

"Maybe it was an accident?" I said. "Maybe somebody spilled something, or splashed something—"

"Whoever did this wanted Claudia dead. They threw everything they could get their hands on into the mix." Shuman's expression hardened. "And until you start telling me the truth, Haley, there's no way I can protect you."

It hadn't occurred to me that I might need protection. And I wasn't sure who it would be from: Detective Madison or Claudia's killer. Plus, Shuman seemed so irritated with me I didn't know if he'd provide it, even if he could.

The one thing I did know for sure, as I got out of the shower the next morning, was that Debbie's disappearance was weird and probably not coincidental.

Did she know something about the murder she hadn't mentioned? Was the clue she'd given me about two women arguing at the Holt's luncheon just a lie to throw suspicion off herself?

I got a little chill thinking about that because it would mean that Debbie had murdered Claudia—provided she had a motive, of course.

Something else to add to my list of leads and suspects that I intended to work on today. I'd stayed up late last night and come up with a plan for solving Claudia's murder. And, as with all great plans, it started with the right look.

I styled my hair in an efficient yet trendy updo, and went a little conservative on the makeup, then took up my usual position in front of my closet. I needed the perfect thing to wear for today's fact-finding mission.

Even though Debbie was missing and presumed—by Detective Madison, anyway—dead, I had to focus on solving Claudia's murder. Rebecca had given me a good lead, so it was at the top of my list.

That made it a Marc Jacobs day. Definitely a Marc Jacobs day. I picked a green croc clutch from the shelf, then matched it with a chic Dior suit I hadn't worn in a while, and left my apartment. Something fluttered to the ground as I opened the door.

I figured it was a pizza delivery ad or an offer for a discount oil change at the Jiffy Lube; my apartment complex was huge, so those sort of things were always being stuck in the doors. But this was an envelope, the kind greeting cards came in.

Okay, this was weird. It wasn't my birthday, or any other special day.

I looked up and down the walkway in both directions, thinking I might see who'd left it. Nobody was there.

I tucked my clutch under my arm and checked out the envelope. My name was written on the front. I didn't recognize the handwriting. Since I'm not big on suspense, I ripped it open and pulled out the card.

A picture of two cuddly puppies was on the front. Inside, there was no preprinted message, just a line written in the same hand that read "I've got my eye on you."

I froze for a second, thinking. Then it came to me. Oh my God. Ty. It had to be Ty. In the Holt's parking lot he'd promised me I would see a different side of him and—wow—was this ever a different side!

The whole scenario flashed in my head. Ty pushing aside all of his important work, postponing meetings, using all his mental energy to come up with something special to do for me. Then rushing to a store, sorting through dozens of cards, deciding none were good enough for me. Him dreaming up just the right message to write, then sneaking over here to put it in my door before I got up.

My insides felt all gooey as I got into my car and drove toward the freeway. I fished my cell phone out of my clutch and called him. His voice mail picked up, so I left him a message, thanking him for getting my day off to such a great start.

Then, for some reason, Doug Eisner popped into my head. After the detectives left last night, Doug had mumbled something about an early morning meeting and taken off. I figured I'd seen the last of him—not that I blamed him, of course.

I headed for Sherman Oaks via the 405 freeway. Traffic was always a nightmare through this stretch, but especially during the morning and evening rush hour. Still, I managed to weave in and out, and cut off a couple of cars.

I exited the freeway on Ventura Boulevard and parked in a garage off Sepulveda. This was a fantastic area. Lots of huge, modern office buildings, a great mall with terrific shops, wonderful restaurants and apartments. Just the sort of place I figured Claudia would work.

I took the elevator up to the third floor where L.A. Affairs was located. Mom had never used this particular event planning company, but she'd been to parties they'd staged. Mom, who once met First Lady Nancy Regan and declared her dull, wasn't easily impressed, but she raved about L.A. Affairs.

Claudia had worked there for a while, according to Rebecca, so I figured it was a good place to find some new info on her.

Things were different on a job. Because of the endless, mind-numbing hours spent there, coworkers seemed more like family—only better. You could tell them most anything and not worry about it being passed on to relatives at the next holiday gathering.

I hoped Claudia had felt that way about L.A. Affairs.

The elevator stopped on three and I got out. Double doors at the end of the corridor had L.A. AFFAIRS written on the glass in gold letters. I pushed my way inside and came face-to-face with the receptionist, a woman in her forties with blond hair, wearing a suit that probably fit great seven years and twenty-five pounds ago.

She popped up from behind her desk and exclaimed, "Are you ready to party?"

"I'm always ready to party," I said. It's an automatic response of mine.

The receptionist giggled nervously and clasped her hands together.

"They make me say that," she confided, then glanced around as if to see if anyone was watching.

No one was, unless they happened to stick their head out of the cube farm off to the left. From the buzz of conversation in the office, I doubted anyone had time to monitor the receptionist's greeting.

"I'm Mindy. I'm new here," she said quietly, as if that explained something. "My husband left me. Just up and left. Out of the blue. I had no idea."

"Sorry to hear that," I said.

"But I'm working here now. So, everything is fine. Really. Just fine." She pulled in a deep breath, straightened her shoulders, and forced a smile. "So, are you ready to party?"

"Actually, I'm here about Claudia," I said.

Her shoulders sagged again. "Oh yes. You and several others—"

The phone rang. It was one of those big console models that appeared to be tied into America's Missile Defense Network. Red and yellow lights flashed frantically.

The receptionist stared at it, wringing her hands. "Oh, jimminy, now let me see . . ."

She pushed a button, taking us to Def Con 4, I think, and three more lights flashed.

I could be here all day, at this rate.

"If I could just speak with someone about—" I began.

"Here," she said, and thrust a sheet of paper at me while still staring at the ringing phone.

"I just need to talk to—"

"Someone will talk to you," she said, then pointed down the hallway. Finally, she started pushing buttons. "Are you ready to—hello?—oh yes, are you ready—hello, hello?—are you ready—"

I walked away.

Several small offices were off to my left, rooms apparently used by L.A. Affair's upscale clientele during the event-planning process. They were all well decorated so that the wealthy felt at home, and filled with books and catalogs of party theme ideas.

I glanced down at the paper the receptionist had given me and saw that it was an employment application.

Oh my God. She thought I was here to apply for Claudia's job. Gross. Somebody would have to be totally desperate to take the job of someone who'd been murdered.

Suddenly, my job at Holt's didn't seem so bad.

Then it occurred to me that this might be my best chance of actually talking to someone about Claudia. I slipped behind the desk in one of the offices and dug a pen from my clutch.

Of course, total honesty on an employment application

wasn't required. Everyone knew that. It's expected, really. So for my current position I put "college student"—no need to mention that I was taking only two classes, even though they were both really hard—and indicated that I worked part-time to supplement my scholarships—which I didn't really have, but oh well, no need getting into this thing too deep. I rounded out my job history with my positions as lifeguard, receptionist, file clerk, and two weeks at a pet store; I didn't include the whole Pike Warner law firm thing.

I stood in the doorway of the little office and looked down the hallway until I saw someone headed my way, then jumped out in front of her. I figured her for a few years older than me, blond, wearing a terrific YSL suit.

"Hi," I said, thrusting the employment application at her. "I think I'm supposed to see you."

It was a total lie, but I didn't have all day.

"Mindy," she muttered, and rolled her eyes toward the receptionist.

"She said her husband left her."

"Six months ago," she said, then huffed and took the application from me. "The person who does the hiring isn't here. I'm Theresa. I'll make sure she gets this."

I knew she was trying to blow me off—which is exactly what I would have done—but I couldn't let that happen.

"Actually, I was hoping I could talk to someone about Claudia. She was a friend of mine," I said—again, not a complete lie—"and I feel kind of strange applying for her job."

Theresa paused and gave me and my Dior suit a quick once-over. I shifted my Marc Jacobs clutch higher so she could see it and be properly impressed.

I guess she deemed me worthy of her time because she shrugged and said, "Claudia and I were pretty close. She wasn't crazy about this job, so I don't think she'd have cared one way or the other."

"Really? I thought she loved it here," I said. "But I guess she'd been under a lot of pressure lately, with all the problems she was having."

"Boyfriend problems," Theresa said. "Who doesn't have those?"

My heart jumped. Was she talking about Ty? Did she know that Ty was trying to get back together with Claudia before she died? Did absolutely everybody in L.A. know that but me?

I was dying to ask her, but Rebecca's face popped into my head, and I knew I had to stick to my planned investigation.

I hate it when I have to do the right thing.

"I heard that the mom of one of the models she coached was giving her a hard time," I said.

Theresa shook her head. "She never mentioned it."

"Claudia had a stalker," I said.

She gasped. "You're kidding. That's awful—just awful."

"Do you have any idea who it might have been?" I asked.

Theresa frowned and I could see by the twin furrows in her carefully made up forehead that she was thinking hard.

"I have no idea. Claudia never talked about the men in her life. Except for an old boyfriend, but she only mentioned him once, and—" Theresa gasped and her eyes widened. "Do you think maybe the old boyfriend was stalking her?"

Theresa kept talking, but a buzzing noise in my head blocked out her words.

The only old boyfriend of Claudia's that I knew about, or that anyone had ever mentioned, was Ty. Did that mean Ty was Claudia's stalker?

Oh, crap.

# Chapter 17

I was totally freaked out after talking to Theresa at L.A. Affairs. I couldn't even call Marcie—that's how weirded-out I was. To calm myself, I raced to the Judith Leiber store and spent some quality time with the evening bag I wanted. Even that couldn't rid my mind of the notion that Ty might be Claudia's stalker.

But he was my boyfriend. Sort of. I should know enough about him that a crazy idea like that wouldn't even occur to me. Yet it did. Which was totally *his* fault, of course.

Since I was already in the mall, and had on my really sharp Dior suit and carried my awesome green croc Marc Jacobs clutch, I decided to check out a few of the stores. Some really great school supplies might be waiting on the racks for me.

My cell phone rang as I stood at the entrance of Nordstrom. It was Marcie. I almost didn't answer—I wasn't up to telling the whole Ty-might-be-a-stalker story yet—but hearing Marcie's voice might make me feel better. Best friends can do that.

"I've got a great purse party lined up for us," she said, when I answered.

The vision of a huge purse party bloomed in my head, a party bigger than anything Rita and Tiffany had ever done, one that I could rub in Rita's face until the end of time.

My day suddenly got better.

"Yeah? Who's hosting?" I asked as I strolled through the mall.

"We'll sell tons of bags," Marcie said.

"Good. Who's hosting?" I asked again.

"It's a terrific location. We'll get lots of referrals," she told me.

I sensed a pattern here. And not just because Marcie was my best friend and I knew her well.

I didn't say anything, just kept the phone pressed to my ear, and finally Marcie gave it up.

"Holly," she told me. "Holly is hosting the party."

*"Holly?"*

I didn't like Holly, which was all *her* fault.

Holly had hung out with Marcie, me, and a bunch of our friends—I'm not sure who let her into our group—but she was totally not cut out for the party scene. She was no good at bars or clubs, yet she insisted on coming.

All sorts of things can happen there, and you just have to roll with them. Such as, a girl I know drank too much and passed out cold on the dance floor, so an ambulance hauled her to the emergency room. The guy she was with went with her, after he got another beer—the bartender had announced last call so, really, you couldn't blame him—took pictures of her with his cell phone while she was passed out on the gurney with tubes stuck in her, and sent them to all his friends. She went home in hospital booties because she lost a shoe, but the ER doctor wrote it up as a "fainting spell" so her insurance covered it.

See? Cool stuff.

Holly wouldn't roll with anything. And as if that weren't bad enough, one time she asked the waitress for light alcohol in her drink. Light alcohol. And I was sitting right next to her. How embarrassing.

Holly ignores all the established rules of partying. She wouldn't eat before hitting a club, which is a must—if you don't want to end up on a gurney in the ER wearing one shoe while your date e-mails your picture to everyone. The drive-through at Taco Bell is perfect. Just grab a bag of tacos and eat them in the car on the way over. They coat the stomach perfectly and you don't lose any partying time.

I tried to give Holly some of the other tips I've picked up over the years, such as, always step onto a chair before trying to dance on a tabletop. Don't just throw your leg up there and think you can do it, because you can't. Always check for stability first. Holly looked at me like I was crazy.

That wasn't why I didn't like her, though. It's because she was a crier.

At a club, all Holly wanted to do is scam for men. She never wanted to hang out with the girls and just have fun. Guys sense desperation, of course, so none of them ever approached her. This caused her to drink too much—and it is, after all, full-strength alcohol—so she always ended up drunk and crying.

It really spoiled the party mood.

"I know you don't like Holly," Marcie said, "but this is business. Rita and Tiffany wouldn't turn down a party just because they didn't like the person hosting."

"That's because they have no standards," I told her.

Which was true. I'd only met Tiffany once, and just for a couple of minutes, but I saw immediately why she and Rita were such good friends. Tiffany had on jeweled Wal-Mart sandals and a T-shirt with "workin' it" across the front that, I'm sure, made her the envy of her trailer park. She'd just moved here from Alabama or Arkansas—I don't know, one of the *A* states—because her boyfriend had lost his job at the Piggly Wiggly. But that was okay with Tiffany because he had a good personal injury case going.

"So we're doing the party. Right?" Marcie said.

I huffed, annoyed that there was no good reason not to.

"Yeah, we'll do the party," I said. "But if we go out afterward, Holly is *not* coming with us."

"Deal," Marcie said, and hung up.

I turned around and headed back toward Nordstrom, and my phone rang again. I figured it was Marcie calling back, but the name of Bradley Olsen from the Golden State Bank & Trust appeared on the caller ID screen.

A little wave of guilt hit me because I'd promised Evelyn and Christine that I'd check further into Cecil's disappearance, and I hadn't done it yet. Maybe Mr. Olsen was calling to say he'd turned up something that would put an end to this thing once and for all. I could really use a break.

"Miss Randolph, something's come up," Mr. Olsen said in his concerned-banker voice. "I'm afraid I might have been hasty in my earlier assessment of this Cecil Hartley's intentions toward Ms. Croft."

So much for the break I needed.

"I took another look at Hartley's credit bureau report and noted a recent inquiry from a mortgage company," Mr. Olsen said. "I happen to know one of the loan officers there, so I phoned and asked a few questions, discreetly, of course. Seems Hartley is in the process of refinancing his house, cashing out some of the equity."

I didn't know much about mortgages or equity, or the banker lingo that went with it, but I did know what "cashing out" meant.

"How much?" I asked.

"One hundred fifty thousand dollars."

"Wow, that's a lot of cash," I said.

"It is," Mr. Olsen said, though he didn't sound particularly impressed. He was, after all, VP of the GSB & T, where some of his customers spend that much on lunch.

"But that's not what concerns me," Mr. Olsen went on. "It seems that, with this refinance, a woman will be added to the deed."

I already knew who it was, but I asked anyway.

Mr. Olsen paused for a moment, and I pictured him flipping through the file. "A Ms. Barbara Ingalls. But simply adding another person on the title of the property isn't what concerns me. This woman intends to execute the loan documents using Cecil Hartley's power of attorney."

"She can do that?" I asked.

"Oh yes, it's perfectly legal," Mr. Olsen said. "But after what you told me about Hartley's investment advice to Ms. Croft and him being, perhaps, a gigolo of sorts, I'm concerned that he may be running some type of scam on this Ingalls woman. Frankly, this new turn of events seems suspect to me."

It seemed suspect to me, too. But I wasn't sure what it really meant. Cecil, according to his daughter, was crazy about Barb and willing to do anything to keep her in his life, so putting her on the deed to his house wouldn't be out of line. Unless, of course, Barb had gotten Cecil's power of attorney, then murdered him, as Evelyn suspected, so she could cash out his equity and pocket it herself.

"I'll stay on this," Mr. Olsen promised, and hung up.

I knew what I had to do. I scrolled through my address book and made a call to Detective Shuman, figuring I'd get a pretty cold reception. I did, especially after I said, "I need to talk to you about a murder. No, not Claudia's. Another murder."

For once, I was glad to start my shift at Holt's. That whole thing with Cecil and Barb had irked me, and even after I'd called Detective Shuman, I hadn't felt any better. Probably because Shuman wasn't the least bit interested in checking into a murder that may not really have happened, when he already had a real murder to solve and suspected I was withholding information.

When I arrived at the employee break room, the usual line had formed at the time clock. Rita glowered at me, which wasn't unusual, but so did everyone else, which was.

"Thanks a lot, Haley," someone groused.

"Way to go," another person complained.

Did I miss a memo? A meeting?

Everyone glared at me as the line moved forward.

"What's going on?" I asked.

"One of those damn cats of yours attacked Shannon in the stockroom," the heavyset guy from menswear said. "So now all of us employees might have to get rabies shots."

*"What?"*

Colleen, that sort-of retarded girl, glanced back at me. "The cat is possessed with the evil spirit of the person who murdered that girl. I heard that Jeanette's going to have a priest come in and bless the stockroom."

Okay, well, I guess that couldn't hurt anything.

Rita glared at me as I punched in, and I was tempted to fling it in her face that Marcie had landed us a huge purse party. But I decided to spring it on her afterward, when I could pummel her with the astronomical number of bags we'd sold. I checked the work schedule, and left the break room.

For some reason, I was assigned to the sewing department again tonight. That squirrelly old lady Marlene must have requested me, because I usually worked in a different department every night; I got passed around like a Saturday night sweetheart, which was okay with me. The good news was that I'd noted on the schedule that Bella was working in housewares tonight, next to sewing.

When I got to the department, there was no sign of

Marlene, but Bella was there. She'd really hit her stride with her famous landmarks hairstyle. Tonight the St. Louis Arch spanned her head.

"Look at this," she said, flipping through a pattern book. "Right here. Patterns for headbands, scarves, all kinds of head gear."

I joined her at the table and opened one of the books. Wow, there were all kinds of patterns for making just about anything. Place mats, curtains, teddy bears, handbags—*handbags?*

"I'm thinking I ought to start my new business now," Bella said, "so I'll be ready when I graduate from beauty school."

There were patterns for *handbags?* You could *make* a handbag?

This revelation startled me. I felt a tingle race up my spine—then realized it was my cell phone in my back pocket that I'd put on vibrate.

We were not supposed to have cell phones on the sales floor, so I slipped over to the housewares department, crouched down behind a display of vacuum cleaners, and saw that I'd received a voice mail. It was from Doug.

Doug? That was a surprise. I figured I'd never hear from him again after last night in the Holt's parking lot.

I listened to his message.

"Hello, Haley. This is Doug. I'll meet you tonight for coffee, as planned. I'm counting the hours until I see you again."

Counting the hours? Okay, that was weird. Anyway, I had to hand it to him for sticking with our date after being accosted by Detective Madison.

As I tucked my phone away, I noticed a man hanging around the cookware. Not your typical pots and pans customer. Thirty, or maybe a year or two younger, kind of tall, with brown hair that needed a trim, wearing slightly rumpled khakis and a polo shirt. Handsome, in an off-the-rack sort of way.

Working in a department store, you see all sorts of people. Young, old, smart, stupid, rich, poor. Most are pleasant enough. They say thank you when you help them find something, or make small talk at checkout.

I practiced being just pleasant enough that customers didn't complain about me; even that was a stretch—especially with the difficult customers, the ones you couldn't make happy, no matter what.

Since starting work at Holt's, I'd gotten pretty good at spotting a potential shoplifter. I recognized a customer in a foul mood so, when I saw them, I could *just happen* to need something from the stockroom and take off. Employees from other stores "shopped" us, and I'd gotten good at their tactics.

But this guy standing by the cookware wasn't like anyone else I'd ever seen before. He didn't belong here.

He looked at me across the vacuum cleaners, and we made eye contact. A little jolt went through me. Wow, blue eyes—great blue eyes. Then he grinned, one of those half-boyish, half-come-hither grins.

"What can you tell me about this cookware?" he asked.

I rounded the vacuums. Too bad we weren't in lingerie. *That* I could explain.

"It can be used for cooking, I understand," I told him.

He raised an eyebrow. "You don't cook?"

"I dial."

"Come on, you must cook something," he said.

"My favorite recipe is 'open bag, serve at room temperature,'" I told him.

He nodded, and we both studied the cookware display for a moment. Then he turned to me again.

"You're Haley Randolph. Right?" he said. "I'm Ben Oliver."

My mind raced as I tried to place the name. Nothing came to me.

"I'm a reporter with the *L.A. Daily Courier*," he said. "I'd like to talk to you."

Oh, crap.

# Chapter 18

"**N**o comment," I said, and walked away.

"Give me a break, will you?" Ben said, catching up with me. "I'm on deadline."

"I don't know anything about the murder," I told him.

"Who said anything about murder?" Ben asked.

I stopped. "Aren't you here about Claudia's death?"

He eyed me sharply. "So you *do* know something about her murder."

"No, I don't," I insisted, but it came out sounding a little weak.

No way was I going to talk to a newspaper reporter about Claudia's death. I'd seen what the media had done to the Missing Server. I sure as heck didn't want to become known as the Surprise Witness and end up with my face plastered all over the front page, the Internet, and the network news broadcasts.

Ben gave me a disarming grin and shrugged. "I'm just here for the cat story."

Okay, this was worse. Way worse. I didn't want to be the Surprise Witness, but I definitely did not want to be the Cat Lady of Holt's.

Ben pulled a little notebook out of his pants pocket and flipped a page.

"According to a source," he said, "you've just been elected president of a pet rescue."

"*What?*" I all but screamed. "Who told you that?"

He glanced at the notebook again. "A coworker of yours named Sandy."

Oh my God. *Oh my God.* Sandy had told me her mom was involved with some sort of pet rescue. They'd elected me president? Was this nightmare never going to end?

"This is a lame-ass story," I said. "Why are you wasting your time on it?"

"My editor's idea," Ben said. He shook his head. "His idea of punishment, that is."

"You must have screwed up big time," I said.

"So give me something on Claudia Gray's murder," he told me, "so I can redeem myself."

"I don't know anything."

"I think you do."

I'm really going to have to brush up on my lying skills.

"Look, I don't want to be in the newspaper. Okay?" I said. "My life is kind of complicated right now, so just leave me out of the story."

"All I need is a quote. One sentence," Ben said, pulling an ink pen from his pocket.

I huffed, making sure he knew this didn't suit me, then somehow channeled my mom and said, "I'm thankful to everyone who has lent their support to caring for these cats, and grateful for the opportunity to make life better for them."

I almost added that I wished for world peace, but stopped myself.

Ben jotted it down.

"There. You have your quote," I said. "Now will you leave me alone?"

He studied me for a moment, then shook his head. "No. I think I'll keep my eye on you."

Oh, crap.

\* \* \*

The possibility of mass rabies shots had dampened everyone's altruistic spirit, luckily, so I had no bags or cases of cat food to haul out to my car after my shift ended. Which was good, because I had something important to take care of tonight.

I pulled out my cell phone and called Jack Bishop, the Adonis of private investigators, as I fed my time card into the clock and left the break room. Employees glared at me again, but I ignored them. I was getting good at that.

Jack picked up on the first ring.

"Hey, Jack," I said, "I'm in need of your services."

It was a leading statement, but Jack brings that out in me, somehow.

"Are we talking about what I think we're talking about?" he asked, in his best Barry White voice.

A warm chill swept over me, and I was on the edge of agreeing to most anything he suggested. But things weren't that simple with Jack.

"I believe we are," I told him. "Surveillance."

"Not exactly what I had in mind," he said.

"I'm serious," I said. "I want to hire you. I'll pay."

"You bet your sweet little ass you will," Jack said.

I got an even warmer chill this time, but fought it off and gave him the time and place to meet tonight. I hung up and crossed the parking lot, only to stop still in my tracks.

Doug stood beside my car.

Oh my God. Doug. We were supposed to go out for coffee tonight. I'd forgotten all about it. But I'd just told Jack I'd meet him.

Jeez, I couldn't cancel Doug—not with him standing right in front of me. He'd remembered our date and he'd showed up on time—even after the incident with Detective Madison.

"Good evening, Haley," he said. "You look nice tonight."

I looked like crap, but it was sweet that he'd made the comment.

We decided to have coffee at the Starbucks down the street. I told him I didn't want to leave my car in the Holt's parking lot after closing, but really, he drove a white Kia, which was beyond embarrassing, and besides, I wanted to be able to make a quick getaway and meet Jack. We drove our own cars.

Doug ordered the same drink as me, a mocha Frappuccino, and we sat at one of the little tables near the window. He paid, which was nice.

"So, Haley, how was your day?" he asked.

Okay, that was weird. A date who asked how your day was? I'd have to tell Marcie about this.

Since I didn't want to mention the two murder and one missing persons investigations I'd been involved with today, or the rabies shots everyone at Holt's was destined for, or the newspaper reporter who'd threatened to splash my name all over the front page, I didn't have much to talk about. So I told Doug about Bella's headgear business idea and how I'd learned that all sorts of things—even handbags—could actually be made with a pattern and a sewing machine.

"Are you two going into business together?" Doug asked.

The idea took me by surprise. The notion of designing my own handbags had occurred to me, but I'd never considered the possibility of going into business with anyone, especially Bella.

"Maybe I'll talk to her about it," I said.

Doug glanced down at my sweater—I'm sure it was my sweater he was looking at—and said, "You have very nice clothing. I think you'd be good at it."

I asked Doug about his day, which I wasn't the least bit interested in, but thought I should ask. He started telling me about his job and my eyes glazed over, but he didn't seem to notice.

Ty popped into my head. I'd phoned him this morning

to thank him for the note he'd left on my door, but he hadn't called back. Even when he was super busy, he called me back . . . usually . . . sometimes . . . well, occasionally. I wondered why I hadn't heard from him.

Maybe the "new him" wasn't so new after all.

Doug was still talking and I was buzzing pretty good from the chocolate and caffeine in my Frappuccino, and I was anxious to meet Jack. Finally, Doug said he had to go.

He walked me to my car and opened the door for me. For a minute, I thought he was going to kiss me, but I guess he lost his nerve because he backed away and just said good night. I waved as I swung out of the parking lot, heading for Altadena.

When I pulled into the industrial park, there was no sign of Jack's Range Rover. No sign of anything, really. The painting contractor and the auto parts place near Edible Elegance were closed for the night. A couple of security lights lit the empty parking lot.

I whipped into a space and killed the engine, surprised—and a little disappointed—that Jack wasn't there yet. But I was late. Maybe he'd been there, then left. I decided I'd wait awhile, even though the place was kind of creepy at night.

About forty-five seconds ticked by and I went for my phone. I'd call Jack, see what was up. I didn't want to—

A thud hit my passenger window. I jumped and saw Jack's face staring in at me.

"Jeez, you scared me to death!" I said as I threw my door open and got out.

Jack sauntered around the car. "Here's a tip, Nancy Drew. If you're doing surveillance work, don't park under the security light."

"This isn't exactly a surveillance job," I admitted. "More like breaking and entering. Sort of."

"Sort of?" Jack echoed, giving me the evil eye that was, really, sort of sexy.

"My mom's business," I said, nodding toward the Edi-

ble Elegance sign on the door. "I only have to break in because I don't have a key."

Jack continued with the evil eye, which I was starting to
really like, then disappeared behind the building, where I
guessed he'd parked, and came back with a set of lock picks.
He had the door open in a flash. We went inside and I
flipped on the lights.

"Not very covert," Jack said, squinting at the sudden
brightness.

The office looked just as it had the other day when I'd
been here to talk to Debbie. Nothing out of place. The
cops hadn't been by, apparently, because the place hadn't
been trashed. I figured they hadn't gotten a search warrant
yet, or maybe had better leads to follow up on.

"What are we looking for?" Jack asked.

I gave him a quick rundown on Mom's business—I left
out the parts that made her look stupid, mostly because it
was a bad reflection on me—and how Debbie, the manager, had disappeared.

"The homicide detectives investigating Claudia's murder are looking for her," I said. "I want to see if there's
anything here that might tell me where to find her."

I'd called Debbie's cell phone a couple of times already,
but didn't reach her. I'd also left messages on the business
line. On the phone atop the desk, the light flashed indicating
messages were waiting. I figured mine were among them.

Though I didn't tell Jack, I intended to give anything I
learned about Debbie's whereabouts to Shuman. I figured
I owed him that much; plus, it might compel him to check
into Cecil Hartley's possible murder for me. My version of
a trade-off.

Jack sat in front of the computer and I pulled open a file
drawer.

"How are things going for you?" he asked.

Wow, two men on the same day had asked me how I
was doing. Was that weird, or what?

"College, work. The usual," I said.

"Has Kirk Keegan showed his face yet?" Jack asked.

This was the second time he'd asked me about Kirk lately. Maybe I should be worried.

I didn't want to think about that right now, so I changed the subject.

"I keep thinking about dying," I said. "Claudia was so young, and, well, I've been thinking I should make preparations, or something."

"You're buying a burial plot?" Jack asked.

That creeped me out big time.

"No, more like what I should leave behind," I said. Then something else occurred to me. "Oh, and by the way, if I'm severely injured in a crash, or something horrific like that, and some scientist wants to make me bionic, don't hesitate. Tell my mom to do it."

"Got it," Jack said. He scrolled through a few more screens, then asked, "Aren't you doing some modeling?"

I stopped and looked back at him. "No way. My sister models. Not me."

I saw him give me the once-over, and I knew what he was thinking. "We look absolutely nothing alike," I told him.

Jack turned back to the computer and I pulled out another file. In it were hard copies of invoices, dating back to last year when Mom had started the business and put Debbie in charge of running it.

I recognized most of the names of the Edible Elegance customers. Some were family friends and acquaintances of my parents, others were well-to-do clients, and a few were celebrities.

I noted that, as time went on, the price of the Edible Elegance bouquets had increased. A good business practice, I guessed, since they were obviously in demand.

As I flipped through the invoices, I realized that apparently not everyone thought that raising the price of the fruit bouquets was a good idea. I found correspondence from customers complaining that the final price was higher than the original quote. Some of them threatened—

Hang on a minute.

I stood up straighter and read a message sent to Debbie a few weeks ago. It was from Cynthia Gray. Claudia's mother.

"Found something," Jack said.

He rolled back from the computer and pointed to the screen. I looked over his shoulder, but didn't see what I had expected. I thought he was searching the files for a clue to Debbie's whereabouts, but instead he'd found an e-mail message regarding the chocolate name tags used on the fruit bouquets at the Holt's luncheon the day Claudia was killed.

Attached was a list of the names of the VIPs who would get a personalized bouquet. Claudia's name was there, along with the rest.

"Who sent this list?" I asked.

Jack scrolled down. The e-mail had been sent by Ada Cameron. Ty's grandmother.

I felt a little dizzy. Ty's grandmother had ordered the fruit bouquets from Edible Elegance? She'd specifically asked for name tags? Provided a list of VIPs?

Oh my God. *Oh my God.*

Had Ada murdered Claudia?

# Chapter 19

Except for the fact that she'd end up in prison, it would be really cool if Ty's grandmother had actually murdered Claudia.

I'd met Ada last fall, and I'd run into her a couple of times since, and we'd always hit it off. She thought I had "spirit," which I took as a compliment. Ty had told me that his grandmother liked me.

Maybe Ada had been glad that Ty and Claudia had broken up, and didn't want them to get back together. Maybe she'd done away with superficial Claudia to protect the Cameron/Holt bloodline, ensure its survival for five more generations by breeding in strong women, like me.

That was my fantasy, anyway, and I was sticking to it until some other theory came along.

"Debbie told me the name tags for the VIP table were my mom's idea," I suddenly remembered. "Why would she lie?"

"Maybe she was trying to make your mom look good? Make her appear involved in the business?" Jack shrugged. "Or maybe she just forgot."

I figured that all of those reasons were a possibility. From the number of invoices I'd just looked through, business was booming. Debbie couldn't remember every detail. And since her boss was my mom, she'd probably wanted to say something nice about her—and that's not always easy to do.

I remembered then that I had the note from Claudia's mother in my hands. I showed it to Jack.

"Could mean something," he said. "Could mean nothing."

"Enough to cause Debbie to murder Claudia?" I wondered.

A squabble over the cost of fruit bouquets at a luncheon wasn't, on the surface, a big deal. But since I'd worked at Holt's I'd seen customers—people who were probably loving, kind, considerate people in their real lives—go ballistic if they didn't get the refund they expected on returned merchandise, or if they missed a sale by a day and the store refused to honor their coupon.

"We're done here," Jack said.

"Hang on a second," I said. "Pull up the calendar, will you? Print it out."

While Jack did that, I checked Debbie's address book and found the name of the woman who supervised the workers that actually created the fruit bouquets in the workroom that adjoined the office. It was too late to call her now, so I copied her phone number and tucked it inside my purse, along with the deliveries that had been scheduled. If Debbie didn't show up soon, I'd have to make sure these orders were filled—Mom sure wasn't going to do it, which was probably for the best.

Jack shut down the computer and rose from the chair. I shoved the folder of invoices and correspondence back into the file cabinet. When I'd arrived, I decided to give Shuman any info I found. Now I wasn't so sure.

If I gave him a heads-up on the pricing dispute between Claudia and Debbie, he'd have to come into the office, check it out for himself. And then he'd find the list of names for the VIP fruit bouquets that Ada had sent over.

Naming his grandmother as a murder suspect might put a damper on my relationship with Ty.

I flipped out the lights and we left the office, locking the door behind us. Jack walked me to my car. A breeze had come up and it was kind of chilly. Jack gave off a lot of heat and I thought about snuggling closer—just to get warm, of course. I think Jack might have been thinking the same because he eased a little closer.

"So you've really never done any modeling?" Jack asked.

Why did he keep asking me that?

"No," I told him.

"Never?"

"Never, ever," I said.

"Not even for pictures that were a little ... naughty, maybe?"

"I'm naughty in private," I told him.

Jack's gaze gave off that smoldering look that made me think naughty thoughts. I was pretty sure he was thinking the same.

"I owe you for tonight," I said.

"You sure as hell do," he told me.

The air between us had superheated. The office or the backseat of his Range Rover flashed in my mind—which is really awful of me, I know, but really, it was *his* fault for being so hot—when Jack stepped back.

"I'll let you know what I want," he told me. "And when I want it."

He opened my car door. I got in and drove away, wondering what in the world was wrong with me. Did I have bad breath? BO? Was I giving off some sort of don't-have-sex-with-me vibe?

Ty didn't want to have sex with me, and now Jack had just blown a perfect opportunity. What was wrong with me?

I drove home contemplating calling Marcie, but this

wasn't the kind of thing I could ask even a best friend. Not yet, anyway. Maybe after we'd had a few beers, or binged on Snickers bars.

I parked my car and went to my apartment, fumbling for my keys. It was late and nobody else was around. Few lights shone in the windows around mine. When I got to my door I found a envelope sticking out of the frame.

Another card from Ty.

I felt a little guilty because I'd had coffee with Doug tonight; plus, I'd just been with Jack, contemplating naughty deeds, while Ty had been picking out a card, writing a special note, sneaking up here to surprise me with it.

And I felt *really* guilty because the idea that Ty had been Claudia's stalker had taken up a ton of space in my head. Plus, I'd wondered if his grandmother was a cold-blooded murderer.

I ripped open the envelope. In it was a card with a picture of the same cuddly dogs as before. On the inside was written "I'm still watching." Beside it, Ty had drawn a happy face. Only, apparently the MBA program he'd completed didn't include art classes because the happy face looked more like a skull. It was kind of creepy, really.

I glanced around, thinking suddenly that somebody was watching. I saw no one. Still, I rushed into my apartment and slammed the door.

The next morning when I opened my apartment door, I checked in both directions to see if anybody was lurking. Nobody was there. No note, either.

Then I felt bad about being paranoid for no reason, and for thinking ill of Ty just because he couldn't draw a decent smiley face on a greeting card.

I got in my car and took the surface streets toward Valencia. For a second it popped into my head that maybe I'd been too quick in refusing Ty's invitation to go to Europe with him. It would have been terribly romantic, of course, and I could have done some fantastic shopping. Plus, we'd have definitely had sex.

But the more I thought about it, the more I realized that I'd been right in the first place. If I'd gone, it would have signaled to Ty that I was okay with our relationship as it was. I'd have started to believe it myself.

I deserved better, and so did Ty, really.

Still, we would have had sex.

I circled the mall and drove into the great little area nearby where Wallace Inc. was located. Lots of shops, restaurants, and galleries were there, making it a favorite spot of mine.

Ty still hadn't returned my phone calls, so I hoped I'd find him here today. Wallace Inc. was scheduled to open soon, so I figured he'd be here checking on things, taking care of last-minute details.

I nosed in at the curb, just down the block from the store. Brown paper covered the display windows and an OPEN-ING SOON sign sat discreetly in the lower corner. The front door stood open and workmen wearing tool belts went in and out.

No sign of Ty's Porche or BMW, so—unless he'd bought another new car that I didn't know about—he wasn't here.

But I didn't want to give up on him yet; plus, I wanted to see the store. I got out of my car and headed up the sidewalk. The day was gorgeous, lots of sunshine, and a mild temperature. Moms pushed baby strollers amid the other shoppers.

That made me think of Christine and little Annie, and how I still hadn't heard anything back from Detective Shuman about Cecil Hartley. I needed to call him, but I didn't want to do it without offering him some info in trade. Something that might help with Claudia's murder.

Since the weather was so nice and I wanted to think a bit about what I could tell Shuman, I crossed the street and headed away from Wallace Inc.

So what info could I give the detective that would induce him to abandon his real investigation and help with mine?

I mentally reviewed my suspect list. The pageant mom was way down my list; I hadn't been able to find out anything about her. Nor had I gotten any info about the person Claudia was seen arguing with at the luncheon.

After last night, though, I was thinking that maybe that person was Debbie. She might have claimed she'd overheard Claudia arguing with someone else just to throw suspicion off herself. And, since she'd disappeared so suddenly, I had to wonder if anything she'd said was true.

Whoever Claudia's stalker was might be a viable suspect, except that since I'd thought maybe it was Ty, I didn't feel so great about investigating the possibility. Maybe Shuman should handle that one.

I got a queasy feeling, thinking that Ada might have killed Claudia. She hardly seemed the type—she was a grandmother, after all. But she surely had strong feelings about the Holt's Department Stores, the family business that had endured for five generations. If she didn't like Claudia, or didn't think she'd make a good match for Ty, or didn't believe their marriage was in the best interest of the stores, she wouldn't have stood back and done nothing. Although I'd only seen Ada a few times, I could tell she wasn't the kind of woman to settle for whatever.

I'd walked a few blocks, so I crossed the street again and headed back toward Wallace Inc. I still hadn't come up with anything I could give Shuman that would induce him to help me, so I pulled out my cell phone and punched up Jamie Kirkwood's number.

Since exchanging phone numbers with her that day in front of her apartment building, I hadn't heard from her. I kind of thought I might. When I'd seen Rebecca at the dress store later that same day and explained how sometimes a witness would remember something important later, I'd thought that maybe Jamie would be just that sort of person. She was smart, studied hard, maintained good enough grades to keep her scholarship, so chances were her memory was excellent. If anybody could come up with an important recollection from that day, I knew it would be Jamie.

She didn't answer her phone, but that didn't surprise me. I figured she had class, working or studying. I left a message and hung up.

Jamie hung in my thoughts for a minute and, for some reason, I thought maybe I'd forgotten something important about that day at Holt's myself. Nothing came to me, though, so I placed another phone call, this one to Claudia's sister—my last hope of finding info to pass on to Shuman.

To my surprise, Rebecca answered. We made small talk for a minute, then got down to business.

"I'm still investigating," I said.

"You are?" Rebecca asked, sounding surprised.

"I told you I wouldn't quit," I reminded her.

"Listen, Haley," she said, "just stop. Okay? I mean, you have a lot on you already, and I don't expect you to—"

"No," I told her. "I'm not quitting. I made you a promise and I'm going to stick to it."

Yeah, yeah, I also wanted to clear my mom and myself of murder charges, but I really wanted to help Claudia's family, too.

"Do you know anything about your mom being upset about the fruit bouquets she had at one of her luncheons?" I asked. "There was a discrepancy over the price."

"Are you saying Claudia was killed over an incorrect invoice?" Rebecca asked.

She sounded relieved, but I didn't want to give her false hope.

"It's just something I'm checking into," I said.

"Who told you this?" she demanded. "Was it that Jamie

Kirkwood girl? That Missing Server? Did she see something?"

"This isn't about the Holt's luncheon," I explained. "It was a luncheon at your house for the models that Claudia coached. Jamie was there, but she didn't have anything to do with the pricing."

"She was there? At my house?" Rebecca asked, sounding panicked.

I guess it freaked her out that Jamie, who'd been at the scene of Claudia's murder, had also been at her house, in her home, the place where we all think we're safe. I didn't blame her. I knew how weirded-out I felt receiving that note on my door with the creepy smiley face/skull on it, and it was supposed to be something nice from Ty.

Then I regretted that I'd called Rebecca at all. I shouldn't have involved her. Obviously, she was still too upset to deal rationally with the investigation.

"Never mind, okay?" I said, trying to sound casual. "It wasn't a big deal, anyway. I'll talk to you later."

We hung up and I continued down the street toward Wallace Inc. I still didn't see Ty's car parked outside, but I didn't want to wait around forever. I slipped inside.

Chaos reigned, but I could see the store's potential. Hardwood floors, bright colors, tons of racks and display tables. Workmen moved around and from farther back into the shop, I heard saws and drills running. Several girls—new hires, I guessed—moved merchandise around.

"Are you here to fill out an application?" someone asked.

A woman stepped in front of me. She looked to be in her mid-thirties, casually dressed in jeans and a sweater. I figured her for the store manager Ty had told me he'd hired, and apparently she thought I was there to apply for a job.

"No," I said. "I wanted to see if—"

"Haley!" she exclaimed. "I'm Tina Mitchell, the store manager. You are Haley, right?"

"Well, yeah," I said. My mind raced, but I couldn't place her name or her face.

She must have realized my dilemma because she smiled and said, "I recognized you from your pictures. In Ty's office."

I froze. Ty had my photo up in his office?

I'd already have known this, if I'd ever been to his office. And it was totally *his* fault that I hadn't.

But I'd never given him a picture of me.

"What a fabulous idea for photos. So much better than those stuffy studio portraits," Tina declared. "The one of you behind the counter at the Holt's Customer Service Booth is terrific. So is the one where you're working at the register. But my favorite is the one where you're in the stockroom, sitting on a bed-in-a-bag set."

Those pictures were taken from the Holt's security surveillance.

Tina threw her head back and laughed. "That one is Ty's favorite, too, because it's sitting right on the corner of his desk."

Ty lifted pics of me from the surveillance tapes, had them framed, and put them in his office?

"I've got to go," I said, and headed toward the door.

"Did you need something?" Tina asked.

"No, nothing," I said, and hurried outside and down the block.

Okay, that was totally weird. Did it mean that Ty was so crazy about me that he'd gone to all that trouble just to have pictures of me in his office? Or did it mean that Ty was . . . well, just crazy?

I got to my car and saw a paper stuck under the windshield wiper. Great, just what I needed, a flyer about a discount nail shop.

But it wasn't a flyer. It was an envelope.

I whirled left, then right, looking up and down the block, trying to spot Ty. I didn't see him.

I opened the envelope and inside was the same style of card with the puppies on the front. Inside was written "You can't hide from me." Underneath, was the same skull/happy face.

Oh, crap.

# Chapter 20

Okay, so maybe the cards weren't from Ty.

The idea popped into my mind as I left Wallace Inc. and headed for the freeway.

Maybe they were from—well, I had no idea who they might be from. They'd started out sweet, but that drawing— the one I hoped was a poor rendition of a smiley face— was starting to look more like a skull, and the message had seemed sort of threatening.

Ty didn't seem like the kind of guy who'd leave creepy notes, but what about those pictures of me from the Holt's video surveillance tapes that he had in his office? That was kind of weird. And I *had* wondered if he'd been Claudia's stalker.

Maybe the skull/happy face thing was Ty's idea of a joke.

I'd know that if he'd ever left me a card before—one he'd signed his name to. So here I was wondering what was up with Ty, not knowing what my sort-of boyfriend was really like—which was totally *his* fault.

Then another thought bloomed in my head. If the cards were meant to be threatening, and they weren't from Ty, that would mean—

I didn't want to think about what that would mean. Not right now, anyway. Because right now, I had to go see my mom. I wasn't really up for seeing Mom, but I didn't have a choice. I had to get things handled with Edible Elegance.

When I got to the house Juanita pointed me toward the patio. Mom sat under an umbrella table beside the pool wearing a Liz Claiborne shirt, four-inch heels, and Gucci sunglasses, and working the phone. Her day planner was open in front of her.

She gave me a little wave, talked for another minute, then hung up and sighed heavily.

"Everything is arranged," Mom declared, as if she'd just organized the Normandy invasion.

I didn't ask what she was talking about. I didn't have that kind of time—or patience, at the moment. That didn't stop her, though.

"Hair and makeup are handled," she said, consulting the list in her planner. "Gowns, shoes, and jewelry, of course."

"Mom, I need to talk to you about Debbie," I said.

She stared at her list, then picked up an ink pen. "I'm missing something."

"Have you heard from her?" I asked.

Mom tapped the pen against the list. "It's something . . . I just can't quite recall."

"Mom, this is really important," I said. "Has Debbie contacted you?"

She looked up at me then. "Who?"

"Debbie. The woman who runs Edible Elegance for you."

Mom sat back in her chair and frowned. "Why on earth would she call *me*?"

I took that to mean that Mom hadn't heard from Debbie, which didn't surprise me. Mom wasn't the kind of person you'd rush to for anything but a fashion emergency.

"You need to call your accountant," I said. "I think something fishy is going on with the billing for Edible Elegance bouquets. He needs to check into it."

Mom gazed skyward for a moment, then suddenly brightened. "Oh yes, of course. The limo," she said, and added something to her list.

"Never mind, Mom. I'll call the accountant myself," I said.

I should have just done that in the first place. I don't know why I always thought Mom was going to be different, why I kept hoping that someday things would change.

"I saw the gown you selected at Chez March," Mom said. "Lilliana showed me. Excellent choice."

Warmth glowed in my belly, the same feeling I always got whenever she paid me a compliment, just like when I was four years old.

"I saw Rebecca Gray at Chez March," I said. "I was surprised her family was still going to the charity gala."

"Well, of course Rebecca is going," Mom said. "She's receiving one of the awards."

The annual gala at the Biltmore was mostly an occasion to get together and show off gowns and jewelry, to see and be seen. But to make the evening seem less superficial than it actually was, money from the overpriced tickets was donated to charity, and the Westbrook Crystal Recognition of Achievement Award, named after some old geezer who died back in the '40s, or something, was presented to a select few sons and daughters for their achievements, academic or otherwise.

Really, it was just an excuse to brag about your child and force other parents to sit and listen, something parents—well, most parents—seem to like to do.

I'd never been given one of the awards, but my older brother had, upon his appointment to the Air Force Academy; I was still holding my breath over my younger sister.

"I didn't know Rebecca was getting an award," I said.

So now it all made sense. No wonder she and her family were attending the charity gala, on the heels of Claudia's death.

"I don't know who her date will be. She's rather a plain-looking little thing," Mom said. Then she turned to me, and I saw that gleam in her eye that I'd learned to recognize—and run from—long ago.

"I've got class," I announced, and dashed into the house.

No way was I hanging around for Mom to ask me who I was going to the charity gala with. Ty had insisted he'd come back from Europe in time, but since he hadn't even returned my phone calls, I wasn't about to give Mom that little chunk of info.

I got in my car and headed for the freeway. I absolutely could not show up at the gala without a date, so I would have to come up with somebody.

My cell phone rang and my heart jumped; I was thinking that finally Ty had returned my call. But when I looked at the caller ID I saw that it was Doug, and he'd left me a voice message. I merged onto the freeway, watching traffic with one eye as I listened.

"Hello, Haley, this is Doug," he said. "I just wanted you to know that I was thinking about you. And, by the way, I forgot to ask what your favorite color is. Hope your day goes well."

I looked down at the phone, then put it to my ear and played the message again.

He wanted to know my favorite color? What was with this guy?

Okay, it was weird, but it was kind of nice, too. Ty had never asked what my favorite color was. Of course, I'd never asked Ty that question, either, but that's not the point.

I pulled into the Holt's parking lot and got to the employee break room two long minutes before my shift started. Everyone waiting in line glared at me—I guess they were still miffed about the whole rabies shot thing—so I gazed across the room, as if I was thinking about something important.

Standing at the microwave was someone I'd never seen before. A new employee, probably. She looked really good—

Oh my God. That wasn't a new employee. It was that girl who'd lost about forty pounds. Only now she looked like she'd lost even more weight; plus, she didn't have on those black-frame glasses she always wore. I guessed she'd gotten contact lenses. She looked really good.

I started to go over and tell her—and not just because she, unlike every other person in the room, would be compelled to speak to me—but the time clock *thunked* and the line moved forward. I punched in, checked the work schedule, and headed to the sales floor.

I'd only gotten a few feet when I saw Jeanette. The dress she had on—a Holt's original, obviously—was a gray, brown, and black swirl pattern. From behind, it looked like two groundhogs in a logrolling contest.

She stopped suddenly and spun around, watching as everyone exited the break room and headed for their assigned department.

"Haley, could I see you for a moment?" she called.

Okay, this must be something good. The store manager had better things to do than hang around outside the break room to speak with a lowly minimum-wage peon like me. Besides, if she had bad news, she'd ask me to come to her office—I knew this from personal experience.

"You received this here at the store." Jeanette pulled an envelope from her pocket and held it out.

I froze. Was there a card with cute little dogs on it inside? Along with a kind of weird, sort of creepy drawing? Was it from Ty? Or some psycho whack job who'd somehow tracked me down?

When I didn't reach for the envelope right away, Jeanette apparently felt she had to explain further. She held it out and squinted.

"It's from the Cuddly Creatures," she said, "whatever that is."

I ripped open the envelope as headed across the store, and immediately my blood started to boil.

The Cuddly Creatures wanted me on their Web site, according to the note inside. Bad enough that the pet rescue Sandy's mother worked with had elected me their president; now another one wanted to plaster my face all over their site.

Great. Just great. My worst fear come true. I was now, officially, the Cat Lady of Holt's.

And all because my name and face had been splashed all over the television and newspaper, courtesy of those reporters.

Well, I wasn't taking this. No way.

I spun around and went back into the employee break room, grabbed my cell phone out of my purse, and stomped back to the stockroom—the only place in the store I could have an uninterrupted personal conversation on company time.

I had called 4-1-1 and gotten the number of the television station that had interviewed me, ready to blast that reporter for putting me in this situation, when it occurred to me that they might record all of their incoming calls, and that my hysterical voice—with most words bleeped out—might headline tonight's eleven o'clock news.

I hung up, punched 4-1-1 again, and called the *L.A. Daily Courier*. It took a while for Ben Oliver to come on the line, so I had a little time to calm down and come up with a plan, in case the newspaper recorded its incoming calls as well.

"Oliver," he said, sounding bored.

"This is Haley Randolph, remember me?"

"Yeah, the cats," he said, and I'm pretty sure he yawned.

"How about murder?" I suggested.

"How about it?" he echoed.

I pictured him sitting forward at his desk, grabbing up a pen to take notes.

"Come to the store," I told him. "If you want info, be here in fifteen minutes."

I hung up.

Okay, okay, I know the whole thing was sort of cloak-and-dagger, and I had no intention of telling him anything about Claudia's murder. But he was responsible—partially, any-way—for this weird turn my life had taken, and he needed to hear about it.

Instead of going to my assigned department, I hung out in the Junior's section by the front door—careful to avoid all customers, of course—and watched the parking lot. When I saw Ben headed toward the building—in only sev-enteen minutes from the time of my call—I went outside and intercepted him.

"Over here," I said, and led him to the corner of the building where no one would see us.

He glanced back and forth, and said, "What have you got for me?"

"Are you recording this?" I asked.

Ben shook his head. "No."

I nodded toward the parking lot. "Is your photographer friend out there, snapping pictures of us?"

He frowned, as if he thought I'd watched too many movies.

"It's just you and me," he said.

"Good, here's something I want you to see."

I pulled the envelope from Cuddly Creatures out of my back pocket.

"Look at this! Look at what you've done!" I shouted. I slammed it against his chest—he didn't flinch or even fall back a step, which was sort of hot—and shouted, "I told you I didn't want to be in your story! I told you not to write about me! But you did! And look what you've turned me into—the Cat Lady of Holt's!"

Ben took the envelope from me, opened it, and read the note inside. He studied it for a minute, then shook his head.

"I don't understand what this has to do with me," he said.

Was this guy an idiot, or what? No wonder his editor had him doing fluff pieces.

"This is a pet rescue," I said, jabbing my finger at the note. "They want to put me on their Web site. I'm going to end up with every pet rescue wanting to—"

Ben snickered. He pressed his lips together, but a giggle slipped out, which just made me madder.

"This isn't funny!" I shouted. "You've—"

"This isn't a pet rescue," he said, still trying hard not to smile. "Cuddly Creatures is a porn site."

I just stood there. I couldn't move, couldn't speak, couldn't even process what he'd said.

"It's a—" I tried to say the words, but couldn't.

"Porn site." Ben shook his head. "Not that I go in for that sort of thing myself, but word gets around."

Oh my God. *Oh my God.* A porn site wanted me? This could *not* be happening.

"This is a mistake," I said, shaking my head really hard to demonstrate that I was correct. "Why would they contact me?"

"You tell me." Ben pulled a notebook from his pocket and opened it.

Oh my God, he intended to write about this for the newspaper?

"No!" I shouted, and grabbed for the notebook. He was quicker, though, and pulled it away.

"You called me out here for a story, and believe me, this is a big one," he said, grinning.

The image of the Biltmore charity gala flashed in my head, and all my mother's uppity, snooty, beauty-queen cult friends whispering and pointing when I walked in. My dad at work. My brother in the Middle East. What would they say when friends showed them the story? Doug would never speak to me—and I'd started to like him a little. And what about

Ty? What about his grandmother? If she'd killed Claudia because she wasn't good enough for Ty, what would she do to me if I were linked to a porn site?

"If you write this story—if you even think about writing it—I'll sue you, your editor, the newspaper—everybody," I told him. "My family will *own* your newspaper."

"Sounds like a good lead." Ben jotted on his notepad. " 'Heiress threatens reporter to keep porn life secret.' "

"Don't you dare write that," I told him.

"Then give me a better story," he said. His expression hardened, and he moved a little closer. "Give me something on Claudia Gray's murder."

I gasped and stared up at him, too stunned to speak.

"I've got a four o'clock deadline tomorrow," Ben said. "If I don't hear from you before then, I'll know which story to run."

Oh, crap.

# Chapter 21

Istood outside the store watching as Ben drove away, frozen
in horror, too numb to move.

A porn site wanted me? How could that be? None of it
made sense.

Yeah, okay, I could understand a pet rescue site wanting
me, after all the publicity over the supposed cats in the
Holt's stockroom. But a porn site?

Jack Bishop and his question about me modeling popped
into my head. Then Troy and the other guys from menswear
who'd been staring at me for days came to mind, and that
brought recollections of the Pike Warner attorney the day
of Claudia's death, the men sitting across from Jack and me
at lunch, the painting contractors outside Edible Elegance.

What was going on?

I pulled my phone from my pocket and called Jack as I
paced up and down the side of the Holt's building, so as
not to be spotted by anyone. He answered on the first ring.

"Am I in a porn magazine, or something?" I blurted out.

"Best centerfold I've seen in a while," Jack said.

"It's not me!" I exclaimed.

He chuckled. "Sure looks like you."

"Well, it isn't," I told him.

"You look a lot like this Randi Rushmore," Jack said.

Suddenly, "Mount" Rushmore took on a whole new meaning.

"At least tell me she's a top-rated porn star," I said.

"One of the best," Jack said.

"I don't do porn—and I never will."

Although, now that I thought about it, porn stars probably made a lot of money and definitely didn't need a college degree.

"Do you have a birthmark?" Jack asked. "Randi Rushmore has a rather distinctive birthmark in a . . . memorable spot."

"No," I said, and gasped in relief. "Then that proves it isn't me."

"Doesn't prove anything, unless it's verified," Jack pointed out. "So, just say the word and I'll confirm your claim, then go online, and put the word out that it's not you."

Jack's method of "confirming" my claim flashed through my mind—what a hot evening that would be—but not exactly the circumstances I wanted.

"I'll let you know," I told him, and hung up.

It was a Fossill evening. Definitely a Fossill evening.

After enduring another shift in the Holt's sewing department and surviving Marlene's instructions to the students who'd signed up for her class on basic garment construction, I'd left the store, ready for this day to end. But Doug had called on my drive home and asked if I'd like to have a late dinner with him. Since nobody else was asking me out these days, I said yes.

I pulled on jeans and a red sweater, then transferred my essentials—about five pounds' worth—into my Fossill tote, and was ready to leave when my doorbell rang. I told Doug not to come to my place, I'd meet him at the restaurant. I didn't want him here in case there was another note waiting for me. Doug was the closest thing to a normal relationship I'd had in a while, which wasn't saying much given the circumstances of my life lately, but still, I didn't want to scare him off.

I looked through the peephole in the front door and saw Detective Shuman waiting outside.

This couldn't be good.

For a minute, I was tempted to stand still, hold my breath, and pretend I wasn't home. But that would only postpone whatever Shuman had come here to talk about, and since I wasn't big on suspense, I opened the door.

He was alone, no sign of Detective Madison, and I realized that it was after ten at night, way past Shuman's normal duty hours. Maybe this was a social call.

"How's it going?" I asked, closing the door behind him. "Want something to drink?"

"No, thanks," Shuman said.

I invited him to sit down, but he remained on his feet. He frowned his cop-frown. Not a good sign.

When will I learn not to invite a homicide detective into my home?

"Have you found out anything about Cecil Hartley's disappearance?" I asked, hoping to hold off the inevitable.

Shuman shook his head. "I'm here about the Claudia Gray investigation."

"I haven't heard from Debbie," I said, figuring it better if I just put that out there right away.

Shuman looked at me as if he was tired, as if he expected something more but didn't want to have to go to the trouble of asking for it.

"There was some sort of dispute between Claudia's mom and Debbie over the price of the fruit bouquets she ordered," I said. "I don't know, maybe the two of them got into it at the Holt's luncheon."

"Everything goes back to Edible Elegance—your mom's company," Shuman said. He made it sound as if Mom and my arrests were imminent, which ticked me off a little.

"Not everything," I insisted. "What about Claudia's stalker?"

Jeez, I really hoped Ty wasn't Claudia's stalker and I hadn't just thrown him in front of the bus.

"What about it?" Shuman asked, looking harder at me.

I flung both arms out, indicating it should be obvious.

"She had a stalker. Did you find out who he is? Why he was stalking her?" I asked.

Shuman uttered a bitter laugh and turned away. "Damn, Haley, is there a lie that you won't tell?"

Stunned, I just looked at him for a second, then said, "I'm not making this up. Rebecca told me all about it."

"Is that so?" Shuman demanded. "Then how come she didn't tell us about this supposed stalker?"

"She didn't tell you?" I asked, surprised.

"She had nothing to tell us," Shuman said, sounding a little angry. "And now, suddenly, you come up with this wild idea of a stalker?"

"I'm just repeating what Rebecca told me," I said, feeling a little angry myself. "Maybe she figured someone else in the family had already told you—"

"Jamie Kirkwood's dead."

Breath went out of me. My knees felt a little weak. I sank onto the sofa.

Shuman dropped next to me, his anger gone, replaced by despair. Not something you often saw in a homicide detective.

"What . . . what happened?" I managed to ask.

He pushed both hands through his hair, then took another moment before he answered.

"Hit-and-run," he said quietly. "Earlier today . . . in front of her apartment building."

A weight seemed to grow inside my chest, holding me down, keeping me from breathing easily. I'd only talked to Jamie twice, but she'd gotten to me, somehow. Her life was hard, yet she kept pushing forward. If anyone deserved a break, it was Jamie, but now . . .

Shuman loosened his necktie and opened the top button of his shirt. "This could be connected to Claudia's murder."

That got my attention.

"Jamie was being threatened," Shuman said. "According to her roommate she'd received numerous threats."

"And she didn't tell you?" I asked, surprised.

Then I realized I shouldn't have been surprised at all. Jamie had no parents, no family, and was so focused on her classes she probably had no close friends. She'd been handling her problems by herself for a long time. Turning to someone else for help wasn't something she'd think to do.

"Witnesses at the scene reported that when Jamie stepped into the street, a car pulled out from the curb and hit her," Shuman said. "Didn't stop. Just kept going."

"Someone had been waiting, watching for her," I murmured, mostly to myself.

"I think Jamie saw something at the Holt's luncheon. I think she saw the person who put the poison on Claudia's fruit bouquet," Shuman said.

Suspects ran through my head: the model seen arguing with Claudia, the pageant mom, Debbie, the stalker, Ty's grandmother Ada.

Then I realized something else: Jamie had been sick that day. Had she maybe sneaked a bite of one of the fruit bouquets, the one meant for Claudia? Had she, as Shuman suspected, seen who'd administered the poison? And had that person found her, run her down to silence her?

"We're following some leads," Shuman said.

"Anything promising?"

He nodded. "Maybe you can explain why the last phone call Jamie received was from you."

"Me?" The word came out kind of squeaky, so I know I

sounded guilty. But I couldn't help it. My heart rate picked up and my stomach felt queasy. I swallowed hard to try and calm myself—and sound innocent.

"I ran into Jamie outside her apartment—"

"So you know where she lived?" Shuman asked, in his best tough-cop voice.

"Well, yeah," I said, and rushed on before he could ask how I learned her address. "We exchanged phone numbers—just to be friendly—and so I called her to see if she wanted to hang out, or something."

Yeah, okay, I know most of that was semitruthful, but how would it sound if I told Shuman I'd deliberately sought Jamie out, then called her just to try and get more info?

"Where were you today between five and six o'clock?" he asked.

In television crime dramas, this is the point where the suspect refuses to answer and asks for an attorney. But there was no reason for me to do that—I was innocent; plus, I had an airtight alibi.

"At work," I told him.

"Did somebody see you there?"

"Sure," I said, then realized that maybe my alibi wasn't so airtight after all.

During those hours I hadn't been in my assigned area. I'd been hiding out in the stockroom phoning the television station and newspaper; then I'd gone outside and stayed out of sight along the side of the Holt's building talking to Ben Oliver, then Jack Bishop.

I was absolutely, positively never inviting Detective Shuman into my home again.

Even though I had no evidence or alibi, I told him, "I had nothing to do with Jamie's death. You have to believe me."

"I wish I could, Haley," Shuman said, and it sounded as if he meant it. "But I can't believe anything you tell me anymore."

PURSES AND POISON   207

He left without another word and I just stood there in my living room, not feeling so great.

I didn't like that Shuman wouldn't believe me. I mean, jeez, we'd gone shopping together just a couple of months ago and bonded over a really great Burberry scarf for his girlfriend. And now he thought—actually believed—that I was involved with not one, but two murders?

Then another thought came to me, one that didn't make me feel any better: if I hadn't lied to Shuman and Madison about substituting for Jamie at the luncheon—even though, technically, it was an omission, not an actual lie—I wouldn't be in this spot right now.

Definitely not a great feeling.

I dropped onto the sofa, thinking maybe I would—

Oh my God. Doug.

I shot straight up, grabbed my Fossill tote, and ran out the door to the parking lot, only to find Doug walking toward me.

"I'm so sorry," I said.

He was a nice guy—boring but nice—and it was really crappy of me to keep him waiting. I wished I could tell him the reason, but explaining that I'd been delayed by a homicide detective who'd accused me of yet another murder might send the wrong message.

"I was concerned when you didn't arrive at the restaurant on time," Doug said, looking genuinely troubled. "Are you all right? Do you need a few minutes?"

It was nice that he picked up on the fact that I was a little frazzled, and was willing to postpone our date a bit, but I waved away his concern.

"Just hungry," I said.

"Let's take my car," Doug said, and rested his hand on my lower back as he guided me across the parking lot toward his tiny Kia.

"Hey, wait." I stopped and looked up at him. "How did you know where I lived?"

"I found it on the Internet," he explained.

My cell phone rang and my heart did a little flip-flop at the thought that it was Ty calling, finally—leave it to him to call at the most inopportune moment—but it wasn't Ty. It was Jack.

"I just need a quick minute, okay?" I said to Doug.

"Sure," he said.

I walked a few feet away and answered the phone.

"You owe me," Jack said. "I've decided what I want. And I want it now."

Oh, crap.

# Chapter 22

I looked like a hooker. No, actually, I looked like a porn star, which is exactly what Jack wanted.

Streetlight flashed into the Lexus as he drove through L.A. I wasn't sure where we were.

I had on a tight, ultrashort, strapless red dress that Jack had picked out for me, a mega push-up bra, thigh-high boots with zippers up the back—they were part of a Halloween costume, I swear—glitter eye shadows, a dozen layers of cherry-red lipstick, and that was about it.

Jack looked good. Tonight he had on charcoal slacks and a sport coat, a black turtleneck, and sunglasses, even though it was after midnight.

"You're clear on this?" he asked.

"I know what you want," I told him. "Just get out fast, okay?"

He glanced at me. "I usually take my time, but I'll make an exception tonight."

We were headed to a club I never heard of, an exclusive place frequented by celebrities, stars, and high rollers that offered privacy and very personalized services. Jack had gotten a tip that a guy he'd been trying to serve court papers on was there tonight.

"So who are we looking for?" I asked.

"A real dirtbag," Jack said. "Shawn Dorsey."

"The date-rape guy from last summer? Gross," I said. "I thought he was in jail."

Jack shook his head. "No such luck. Dorsey's family is loaded. They managed to shut down the media and hired an army of attorneys that got the criminal charges dismissed."

"Bastards," I said.

"Civil lawsuits have been filed, but Shawn, being the slimy worm that he is, is good at eluding the process server."

"So now it's up to you to get him served," I said.

"And you." Jack glanced over. "I owe you for this one."

"I'll tell you what I want," I said, "and when I want it."

While my life wasn't exactly on the line tonight, there was a slight possibility of danger. Jack had been clear about that up front. I was the bait, but he'd taken more than the usual precautions to ensure that nothing went sideways.

We pulled up to the curb in front of the Fisher Club, marked only by a small, purple neon sign. A line formed behind velvet ropes, and a couple of hulking men in suits kept watch on the crowd.

Jack left the Lexus and spoke with one of the men. Apparently, a lot of wrangling was required to get into a club like this. He had connections everywhere.

Once I was inside, under the guise that I was porn star Randi Rushmore, word would be passed along that I wanted that sleazeball Shawn Dorsey to join me; then Jack would serve him the court summons, and we'd leave.

That was the plan, anyway.

When Jack opened the car door I got out—carefully, so as not to be mistaken for Britney—and caught my reflection in the glass doors of club. I hardly recognized myself, so I figured I'd pass for Randi Rushmore—as long as nobody wanted a peek at the infamous birthmark.

Inside the club, the floor throbbed with the beat of the music, and lights flashed over the packed dance floor. Lots of men looked my way—maybe this porn star thing wouldn't be so bad—as I was shown to the private room Jack had arranged for. A big purple circular sofa sat in the center, surrounded by thin purple curtains that veiled the view of the rest of the club.

I sat down and crossed my legs—not a full-on Sharon Stone leg cross, but close—and waited. A waitress brought me a drink, which I didn't touch, and a few minutes later Shawn Dorsey came inside.

What a pig. Plump and soft, he looked like a used car salesman, complete with the pinky ring. No wonder he had to drug women to have sex.

Dorsey leered at me, which made me want to throw up, and approached the sofa. As soon as he sat down, Jack walked in and tossed the bundle of court papers at him.

Oh my God. This was too cool—just like being an undercover cop, or something. Did they need a college degree?

On reflex, Dorsey caught the court documents, then realized what had happened. He turned to me with murder in his eye. He knew he'd been set up.

Okay, so maybe undercover work wasn't that cool.

I rolled away, but he caught my arm—only for a second. Jack shoved Dorsey, sending him tumbling over the back of the sofa, then grabbed my hand and we headed for the door.

My heart raced, my legs shook. I could hardly keep up with Jack as we made our way through the crowd, then out to the street. The Lexus still sat at the curb. He put me inside, jumped behind the wheel, and peeled out.

"You're buying me something—and I don't want some stupid toaster or rug shampooer," I told him. "I want a handbag—and you're getting it for me."

Jack grinned as we turned the corner. "Whatever you want."

I love the smell of the purse department in the morning.

The display case at Nordstrom was filled with the latest styles from Dooney & Bourke, Coach, Kate Spade, and many of my favorites, and all of them whispered to me as I stood caressing the glass. But I ignored their sirens call— I can be really strong when I need to.

I headed through the mall and spotted Ben Oliver seated in Starbucks. He had on the same khaki pants I'd seen him in yesterday—I recognized the wrinkles—and he looked a little disheveled. Guess he wasn't a morning person.

Good. I hoped I inconvenienced him big time. Since I had to get up early to deal with his threat to expose me as a porn star, so could he—and on my turf, too.

I got a mocha Frappuccino—just to be sociable, of course—and sat down across the table from him.

"Are you ready to talk murder?" Ben asked, pulling out his notepad.

"Not so fast, newsboy," I said. "If I give you this info, I want some assurance that you won't ever write about me— no matter what."

Since I wasn't likely to win the Nobel Peace Prize, or anything even close, I didn't think there was much chance I could be in the newspaper again. But still, you never knew.

"You have my word of honor," Ben told me.

Lots of newspaper reporters have honor; I just wasn't sure if Ben was one of them.

"That's the best you can offer?" I asked.

He didn't look offended, which told me how highly he rated his own honor, and said, "That's it."

"So tell me the reason your editor stuck you with that stupid cat story," I said. I figured any sort of dirt I could get on him would do.

"Old news," Ben told me, and flipped to a fresh page in his notepad. "What do you know about Claudia Gray's murder?"

"Nothing," I said. "I've got another murder for you."

"Exactly how many murders are you involved with?" he asked.

No way was I getting into that thing that had happened at Holt's last fall. And I sure as heck wasn't giving up any info on Claudia; if I wouldn't tell Shuman what I knew, I wasn't going to tell this guy.

But Shuman had all but told me to my face that the supposedly missing, maybe dead Cecil Hartley was way down his list, and Evelyn, Christine, and little Annie needed answers.

I gave Ben a rundown on what I knew, what I had learned from the GSB & T—no names, of course—and what I suspected. I figured that even if Ben didn't believe me, he'd be so desperate to get back to doing news stories that he'd take on most anything.

He looked dubious. "I'd better not find out this Hartley guy is some old boyfriend of yours and you're trying to set up the new girlfriend."

Was absolutely everybody questioning my credibility these days?

"Okay, look," I told him. "I've got another tip for you. If it doesn't check out, you can do whatever you want with the Cecil Hartley thing."

Ben just looked at me, waiting.

"That creep Shawn Dorsey?" I asked.

He perked up.

"He was served with court papers last night at the Fisher Club, so the civil suits are a go," I said. "Plus, he was seen in the company of a porn star—a top-rated porn star—named Randi Rushmore."

"How do you know—"

"Get on it," I told him as I rose from my chair. "And get back to me on Cecil."

I thought Ben might follow, but he started writing and went for his phone.

I won.

In my next life, I want to come back as me.

Feeling pretty good about myself, I strolled through the mall. Ty popped into my head. He still hadn't returned my calls, so, not being one to stand by and wait for things, I called his cell phone. His voice mail came on again, so I left another message, and hung up.

"Hey, wild thing," somebody said from behind.

I turned and saw Jack. He looked really hot today, dressed in jeans and a black leather jacket.

"Are you okay?" he asked.

"Next time," I told him, "*you* can be the porn star and *I'll* be the process server."

Jack chuckled. "Are you ready to do this?"

We'd set up today's meeting when he dropped me off at my apartment last night. I'd been a little shaken at the Fisher Club—although it was kind of cool that people thought I could pass for a porn star, a top-rated porn star—but now that I'd calmed down I had a change of heart.

"Forget it," I said.

"No," he told me. "I promised you a handbag."

"My purses are kind of expensive," I told him.

He gestured to my Tommy Hilfiger bucket bag and shrugged. "Get whatever you want. You earned it."

We walked to the Judith Leiber store. I paused in the doorway in humble reverence, as always when in the presence of genius. I glided to the display case, slowly, solemnly, and pointed to the bag of my dreams.

"That's it?" Jack asked. "Don't you want something bigger?"

"It's a Judith Lieber," I said softly.

He shrugged. "It's just a little evening bag."

Oh my God. How could he not know?

"It's a *Judith Leiber*," I said again, and managed not to shout.

The salesclerk came over, an older woman in a stark black dress, with conservative hair, makeup, and shoes. From the look on her face, she remembered me from all the times I'd been here to spend a few quiet moments with the evening bag, and seemed happy that my boyfriend—or sugar daddy—had finally come to buy it for me.

"Would you like to see this?" she asked quietly.

"Yes, please," I whispered.

I bounced on my toes as she ever so slowly opened the case. From the corner of my eye, I saw Jack's gaze wandering. He checked his watch.

What's the matter with him?

The clerk laid the bag in my hands—I'd never actually touched it before—and light suddenly beamed down from above, I swear, and I heard angels singing.

Oh my God. *Oh my God.*

I absolutely *had* to have that bag. I was here, this close, the moment was upon us, and I simply could not leave the store without it. It would be like stopping in the middle of sex. Sort of.

"Isn't it beautiful?" I said, cradling the bag in my palms.

Jack glanced at it, then at the clerk. "We'll take it."

"Of course, sir," she replied, dipping her lashes at him in deference, and taking the bag from me. "That will be two thousand dollars, plus tax."

Jack stilled.

I gasped. Oh no. No, no, no. He couldn't back out now.

"Austrian crystals," I said—actually, I think I moaned—"elegantly handcrafted."

He didn't say anything.

"It's got a satin lining," I offered.

Jack raised his right eyebrow.

"And comes in a gorgeous box," I added.

He didn't move, didn't blink.

"With a keepsake bag!"

I'm pretty sure I shouted that.

My heart raced. My palms sweated. Time stood still. World peace hung in the balance.

Finally, Jack reached for his wallet. "Wrap it up," he said to the clerk. She batted her lashes at him again, and moved away.

I collapsed against the display case.

# Chapter 23

It was impossible to top a Judith Leiber purchase, even at some of the most upscale stores in the world, but that didn't stop me from taking a turn around the mall after Jack left. I was too wound up to drive home, and besides, if I walked around the mall everyone would see my shopping bag and be jealous.

I couldn't wait to show Marcie my new evening bag. As a confirmed handbag aficionado—our nice way of saying handbag whore—she would truly appreciate it.

Maybe I would call her.

I stopped—making sure I was in the center of the walkway where everyone would see me—pulled out my cell phone, and saw that I had received a message from Doug. I'd been so completely caught up in my Judith Leiber moment, I hadn't heard it ring.

I listened to his message.

"Hello, Haley, this is Doug. I'm making plans for our big date and wanted to discuss a few ideas with you. Give me a call."

I froze. My mind scrambled back to last night when I'd had dinner with him.

Big date? We had a big date coming up?

Yeah, okay, I'd kind of rushed through dinner with him

because I had to meet Jack, and I'd had Ty on my mind, but I'd have remembered agreeing to a big date, wouldn't I?

Not being big on suspense, I called Doug. He picked up immediately.

"Haley, it's so good to hear from you," he said. "How's your day going?"

I didn't want to get into the whole I-just-got-the-world's-greatest-handbag-because-I-was-mistaken-for-a-porn-star thing, so I replied, "Great. How about you?"

"It's been a very gratifying morning," he responded. "As I mentioned in my message, I have some ideas for our special date and I wanted your opinion."

What the hell was he talking about?

"Our special date, huh? Wow, is it that time already?" I asked. My mind raced, trying to dredge up some clue as to what this was all about. Nothing came to me.

Doug chuckled. "Hard to believe, isn't it? But it's been a week since we met."

Our big date was the one-week anniversary of the day we met? Doug remembered? *I* didn't even remember. And not only had Doug known the date, he was already making plans.

Ty couldn't even remember to show up on time for one of our dates.

Doug started yammering about a Web search he'd done, or something, but I wasn't listening.

Ty flashed in my head. I hadn't heard from him in days. He never made any big plans for us, never mentioned our special date—okay, okay, I couldn't remember the day we'd met, either, but still—he hadn't done any of the things Doug had done, even after we'd almost had sex at his apartment last fall.

"Just pick a place. Surprise me. Whatever you choose, I'll like it," I told Doug.

Then another thought came to me, and it just seemed like the right thing to do.

"Listen, I was wondering if you'd like to go to this charity gala at the Biltmore with me and my family?" I asked.

Doug didn't answer right away, and I wondered if he'd drifted off or gotten distracted by something shiny on his desk. Finally he said, "I'm flattered by your invitation. Very flattered."

"So you'll go?" I asked.

"I would be honored to accompany you, Haley," Doug said. "And honored to be a part of your evening with your family."

I gave him the details and I could tell he was diligently writing them down. He asked a few questions, then promised to get back to me with more info on our big date—which I'd forgotten about already—and we hung up.

All in all, I knew Doug would make an acceptable date for the charity gala at the Biltmore. He would look good in a tux, which was way up on my list. Even though he wasn't part of our usual family social circle, my mom would be okay with him being there since he had a degree and a job she could brag about. Also, my dad would finally have someone he could to talk to.

But instead of feeling pleased with myself for choosing a date who would impress my parents, I was still thinking about Ty and growing angrier by the minute.

I would call Ty and tell him not to bother to come back early from Europe to take me to the gala—not that I ever believed he'd actually do that, but still—because I already had a date.

Of course, it would be easier to slam him with my decision if he would return one of the many calls I made to him.

Okay, that was it, I decided, anger boiling in my stomach. I wasn't putting up with him as my sort-of boyfriend any longer.

Instead of wasting time with his personal cell phone, I called the Holt's corporate office and asked to speak with him.

The scene bloomed in my mind: Ty, heading up a huge meeting, a conference room packed with the captains of industry; his secretary rushes in, tells him there's a call from me—she's been informed to put through all calls from me, *regardless*—so he stops the entire meeting, rushes to the phone to—

"Sarah Covington," she said in my ear.

What was she doing on the line? I had specifically asked for Ty.

"I'm calling for Ty," I told her.

"I'm covering his calls," she said.

I heard her shuffling papers in the background, like she was *so* important.

That ticked me off, so I channeled my mom with little effort and used my I'm-better-than-you voice.

"This is Haley," I announced. "I'll hold for Ty."

Sarah snickered—it was muffled, but I heard it—and said, "You'd better get comfortable because he'll be a while. He's in Europe."

"Already?" I asked, too stunned to sound even slighty snooty.

Mom would be so disappointed in me.

"He left on the red-eye Tuesday night."

Sarah kept talking but I didn't hear anything she said.

Ty left in the middle of the night? On Tuesday? He left early, and hadn't told me? And he hadn't even called to tell me good-bye?

My blood boiled as I hung up the phone and headed out of the mall. Like an idiot, I'd phoned him a bunch of times and he'd not returned my call once—okay, so maybe he didn't have an international calling plan, but still.

Wait a minute.

I had talked to Ty in the Holt's parking lot Tuesday night, when he claimed I would see a different side of him. According to Sarah, he left that night.

I got a chill up my back.

That meant Ty had left *before* those notes started showing up at my apartment, then on my windshield. Now I knew for sure—without any doubt—that they couldn't possibly have been from him.

I stopped dead still and clutched my Judith Leiber shopping bag to my chest. I had to face the truth: the sender was Claudia's murderer.

Whoever that person was must think that I was close to finding him or her.

And now that person was after me.

Where had it all gone so wrong?

I stood in the Holt's stockroom staring at the big rig with PURINA PET FOODS emblazoned across the side, backed up to the loading dock.

Was there a time, a specific moment, when my life had taken this weird turn? When it had spun completely out of control? There must have been.

Jeanette and the driver were standing near the truck, engaged in a slightly heated discussion. I should probably have joined them, but I couldn't move.

When was it? I wondered.

Only a few weeks ago I'd been a dedicated college student, pulling down solid B-minus grades, focused on getting my degree, and looking forward to a bright future somewhere, doing something. I had a boyfriend, sort of. People liked me.

Now I hadn't been to class in I didn't know how long, and I'd lost track of how many homework assignments I'd missed. I'd been mistaken for a porn star—a top-rated porn star, but still. I was a suspect in two murders and a disappearance. I'd been elected president of a pet rescue I'd never heard of; most of the Holt's employees had turned against me; my sort-of boyfriend had left the country without telling me good-bye; some psycho stalker had left creepy notes on my door and windshield. And now—

*now*—I'd somehow caused an entire tractor trailer load of cat food to be delivered to the store.

The meeting between Jeanette and the truck driver broke up. She wasn't happy; her expression kind of looked like a jack-o'-lantern three days after Halloween.

"The driver is refusing to take this load back to the Purina warehouse," Jeanette told me in a tight voice. "He says if we don't want it, it's up to us to ship it elsewhere."

"I had no idea Purina was going to make a donation," I told her, for about the millionth time. "I never heard a word from them. Not a single word. I swear."

Jeanette was not impressed with my explanation.

"Get this stuff out of here," she demanded. "I want it out of my stockroom immediately. And those cats, too. Find them and get rid of them—today."

"I'll spend my entire shift back here, if that's what it takes," I told her.

Jeanette huffed out of the stockroom and I sank onto the stairs, as case after case of cat food was unloaded from the truck. I distracted myself with thoughts of the lunch hour purse party Marcie and I had thrown today in an office building on Wilshire. Lots of oohs, aahs, gasps, some giggles, a little pushing and shoving—sort of like a handbag orgy. We sold dozens of purses and made bank, and it would be cool to throw our success in Rita's face, but even that didn't cheer me up.

My mind drifted back to trying to figure out how my life had gotten so crazy, in such a short time, and finally I pinpointed the moment.

It was when I didn't speak up, didn't tell anybody that I'd substituted for Jamie at the luncheon.

At the time, it seemed like the right thing to do—anybody in my place would have done the same thing. I'd told myself it was an omission, not an outright lie.

But if I'd handled things differently, Detective Shuman

wouldn't doubt every word I said, and maybe he wouldn't consider me a murder suspect.

Maybe Jamie wouldn't have been killed.

Maybe I wouldn't feel so icky about myself.

The only thing for sure was that I'd brought most of my troubles on myself.

Not a great feeling.

I wished I could get a do-over, but since Doc Brown wasn't going to show up, all I could do was go forward.

Maybe I wasn't supposed to be a college student. Maybe my future lay elsewhere.

That thought roamed around in my head for a few minutes. I considered several possibilities, some kind of cool, some just weird, but I couldn't come up with anything definite. Not yet, anyway.

There was only one thing I knew for certain: I couldn't decide what was next in my life until I solved Claudia's murder.

# Chapter 24

Juanita took my duffel bag from me as I walked into my parents' house. Her smile seemed a little brighter than usual, and who could blame her? Tonight was the charity gala at the Biltmore, which meant my mom would be gone and Juanita would get an extra night off.

After she got Mom ready, of course.

"She's upstairs," Juanita said.

Occasionally, I was okay with living in my mom's world. Today was one of those times.

Mom, my sister, and I had done the girl thing for years, pampering ourselves with a day of beauty in preparation for the annual charity gala. Mom arranged for a mani, pedi, and massage for each of us here at the house, along with a hairstylist, of course. Juanita bought food for us and kept the wine flowing.

I took the wide staircase up to the second floor. The house was built in the '30's, or something, and had a classic, old-world feel to it, with dark woods and high ceilings.

Several years ago, Mom had knocked out a few walls at the rear of the house and created a huge master suite, with giant walk-in closets—one for each season, plus a smaller one that my dad was allowed to use—an expansive bath area, and a retreat with a fireplace. She decorated it in a dozen shades of beige and white. It suited her.

I spotted her reclining on the chaise on the balcony that overlooked the garden, wrapped in a thick white terry robe with a towel around her hair. A heavy facial mask covered her cheeks, chin, and forehead, and cucumber slices rested on her eyelids.

"Hi, Mom," I called, stepping outside. "Where's—"

"Aspen," she said. When I pulled up, I hadn't seen my sister's car in the driveway. She always—always—got here before I did.

"She's not going tonight?" I asked, stunned.

"Skiing with her new boyfriend," Mom said. "He's French."

My heart jumped, sending my stomach for a quick lurch. My sister wasn't here? She was in Aspen? I'd have Mom all to myself tonight?

The idea whipped through my mind—which was majorly childish, I know—but it zinged me pretty good. For once, I wouldn't have to see the two of them with their heads together, whispering about something or someone they figured I wouldn't understand or care about. Wow, how cool was this?

"Your father and I are flying up to meet him," Mom said.

The little zing in my stomach morphed into a painful zap. I whirled and saw two open suitcases in the bedroom.

Oh my God. Mom and Dad weren't going to the charity gala tonight, after all? They'd made other plans and hadn't told me?

Or did Mom not want to go to the Biltmore because my sister wouldn't be there?

Yeah, okay, I knew Mom and I hadn't had the closest of relationships, but it worked for us—at least, I thought it had.

First Ty had blown me off, now my parents?

"So we're . . . we're canceling for the gala tonight?" I

asked. I tried not to sound hurt or, worse, childish, but didn't quite pull it off.

Mom raised her head slightly, lifted a cucumber slice, and opened one eye.

"Of course not, sweetie. We're flying up tomorrow." She replaced the cucumber slice and reclined on the chaise once more. "Have Juanita bring us more wine, would you? Then sit with me. I want to hear all about Doug."

Over the next few hours Mom and I were massaged, polished, buffed, plucked, powdered, and styled from almost every conceivable angle. We talked about absolutely everyone and everything imaginable. We had wine. We giggled. And finally, we were ready to leave for the Biltmore.

Mom looked chic in a champagne-colored, draped, vintage Halston gown. The diamond bracelet and earrings she wore—passed down to her by her grandmother—completed the look to perfection.

I wore a sleek, chocolate-brown Dior gown with a sweetheart bodice that required a strapless bra—it wasn't really a special occasion without uncomfortable underwear. My hair was styled in a simple, carefree updo that had taken the stylist ninety minutes to create, and was held in place with enough spray to stop a bird in flight.

Mom and I gave ourselves one final check in the mirror.

"You look stunning, Haley," she said, covering me with her critical gaze. "Absolutely—"

She gasped and her eyes widened, sending me into panic mode.

Oh my God. Had she seen a loose thread? A speck of lint? Was I wearing something *wrong*?

Then her features settled into humble reverence and she whispered, "Is that a *Judith Leiber* you're carrying?"

Raw admiration shone in her eyes as I lifted the bag and held it between us.

"Austrian crystals," I said—actually, I think I moaned— "elegantly handcrafted."

"With a satin lining," Mom responded.

"It came in a gorgeous box," I whispered; then in unison we said, "With a keepsake bag."

Mom looked at me as if I were onstage at the Biltmore, receiving a coveted Westbrook Crystal Recognition of Achievement Award.

I had never felt so proud in my life.

Dressed in tuxedos, my dad and Doug waited at the foot of the stairs as we descended. They'd probably gotten ready in less than fifteen minutes.

Dad came forward, told Mom how elegant she looked, and offered his arm; he knew better than to kiss her and risk damaging her makeup.

Honestly, I never understood the attraction between my mom and dad. He was an aerospace engineer and my mom was—well, to be generous, I'll just say that she wasn't like him. They seemed to have nothing in common.

But he loved her. You could see it in the way he looked at her, the way he touched her, the way he indulged her. Mom, I think, loved him for those same reasons.

I didn't understand their relationship, but hey, I didn't have to. It worked for them.

"You look beautiful tonight," Doug said to me, and seemed to be a bit breathless.

"You look very handsome yourself," I told him, and it was true. For a guy who probably seldom—if ever—wore a tux, he filled it out nicely.

The limousine Mom had arranged for waited in the driveway, and whisked us away.

Why hadn't Ty called?

The thought bounced around in my mind as the limo glided onto the freeway.

He had promised he would leave Europe, come home so we could go to the Biltmore together tonight. He had sworn I would see a different side of him.

For all he knew, I was standing by, waiting for him to arrive. And not only was he not here, he hadn't even called.

I glanced at Doug. He and my dad were talking about airplanes, or something. Doug was a nice enough guy, but jeez, why wasn't Ty here instead?

The Biltmore Hotel—it was officially named the Millennium Biltmore, but almost no one called it that—was located in the heart of downtown Los Angeles on Grand Avenue. Its Italian-Renaissance architecture offered historic grandeur with modern convenience. The Academy Award Ceremony was held there back in the '30s and '40s; celebrities, presidents, and dignitaries visited regularly.

I just thought it was a cool place to go.

Mom filled Doug in on the hotel's eighty-some-year history as our limo swung into line behind the other limos and expensive cars at the hotel's entrance. He soaked it up—I think he was actually interested in the details, which was kind of weird—as the uniform valet opened the limo doors for us.

Entering the Biltmore on a night like this was beyond awesome. The lobby was huge, with a mural behind the front desk, a fountain, hardwood floors, ornate carpets, and a soft lighting from the huge fixture overhead.

Dozens of couples, all dressed in gorgeous gowns and terrific tuxedos, moved along with us. Everyone spoke in quiet voices, exchanging pleasant greetings, or simply nodding. Classical piano music played from somewhere. I held my Judith Leiber evening bag so that everyone would see it and be envious.

We turned right into the main galleria, our heels clicking on the expensive floor, above us a dramatic coffered ceiling.

Mom sidled up next to me.

"Do you see what Maxine Davis is wearing?" she whispered, managing to speak without actually moving her lips or allowing her composed demeanor to slip, thanks to her beauty pageant training.

I waited the required four seconds before glancing Maxine's way and, thanks to my fifty percent beauty queen genes, refrained from shrieking in horror at the Marge-hair blue gown she had on.

"What is that woman thinking?" Mom demanded.

I love it when Mom talks smack about people.

We moved with the crowd up the stairs and into the Crystal Ballroom, an elegant space filled with golds, bronzes, mirrors, columns, and heavy drapes.

Two crystal chandeliers and dozens of candle wall sconces lit the grand room with soft light. The ceiling was painted with images of angels, cherubs, and urns; the carpet was woven with an intricate pattern of greens and reds.

The round tables were set with elegant gold china and treated with white linens and rich orange and red floral centerpieces. At the front of the room sat the stage where the awards would be handed out, along with the dance floor that would be utilized after the presentations. Along each side of the room were balconies where additional tables were set.

We found our table. I figured Mom would want to sit boy-girl-boy-girl, as usual, which would put me between Dad and Doug. Being seated between two aerospace engineers was great if you were taking a written test, but not so hot if you were hoping for lively conversation to get you through a long evening.

Just as Doug pulled out my chair, Mom said, "Haley, sweetie, sit next to me."

At first I thought I hadn't heard her right, but she patted the chair next to her as she allowed Dad to seat her.

Oh my God. *Oh my God.* My mom wanted me to sit next to her? Mom was breaking the boy-girl-boy-girl rule—for *me*?

I settled into my chair between Mom and Doug and placed my evening bag prominently on the table. It was tough to make women in this crowd jealous, but a Judith Leiber evening bag would do it.

Lots of people stopped at our table. Greetings were exchanged and Doug was introduced. He did okay, but I figured he must be a little overwhelmed.

I know I was. But not from the elegant surrounds or the wealthy company—I'd been attending these kinds of things for years—it was because of Mom.

I'd never sat next to her before. If anyone did—other than my dad—it was my sister. They were alike. They belonged together.

But there I was, sitting beside Mom, the two of us whispering back and forth, admiring—or verbally trashing—the gowns, hairstyle, jewelry, and dates of everyone around us. For once, I had Mom all to myself.

Yeah, okay, I know it sounds silly, and I should have outgrown that feeling long ago, but it was great.

This is what it would always be like, if my sister weren't around. Not that I wished her any harm, of course, but her Aspen ski trip with her new French boyfriend couldn't have worked out better—for me.

The other people who rounded out our table for ten joined us and the room settled down as dinner was served. Over the hushed voices and the clink of silver against china, I spotted the Cameron family seated at a table nearby.

Ty flashed in my head.

Discreetly, I checked my cell phone in my purse. I'd put it on vibrate just in case he called—not that I'd speak to him if he did, but still.

My heart jumped. I had a message waiting.

I checked the caller ID, formulating in my head how I'd blast him for not calling, not arriving, not coming through on his promise—for, essentially, being himself—and saw that the call wasn't from Ty. I didn't recognize the name and, really, if it wasn't Ty, I didn't care who had called. I put my phone away.

My stomach felt a little queasy at the thought of how the evening would have turned out if I'd taken him at his word, if I hadn't invited Doug.

An empty chair beside me; all of Mom's friends stopping by, asking who we were expecting; everybody staring, wondering who had stood me up.

How embarrassing would that have been?

Mom sure as heck wouldn't have wanted me sitting next to her.

Mom leaned over and commented about the fine line between daring and slutty in making a gown selection, just as my gaze landed on Rebecca Gray. She sat with her parents at a table near the front of the room, along with the other recipients of the Crystal Recognition of Achievement Award.

Rebecca seemed to be trying to make the best of the evening, her dad resembled a zombie, and her mom looked ready to bolt for the door.

I felt kind of guilty for thinking how glad I was that my sister wasn't here tonight.

"Rebecca's parents look like they don't even want to be here," I said to Mom.

Discreetly, she glanced their way, then turned up her nose, ever so slightly.

"Cynthia wouldn't be here, if it weren't for Claudia's death," Mom said, then added, "You'd think she could make an effort, for appearance's sake."

I looked at Cynthia, then at Mom again, sure I'd misunderstood.

"Cynthia wasn't supposed to be here tonight?" I asked.

"Of course not," Mom said. "She was going with Claudia to Europe."

I still thought I hadn't heard right.

"Cynthia hadn't intended to be here? Tonight? When Rebecca got her award?" I asked.

"She always traveled with Claudia," Mom said.

Oh my God. I could only imagine how proud Rebecca must have been when she learned she was receiving an award, then how hurt when her own mother told her she wouldn't attend the presentation. If it hadn't been for Claudia's murder, Cynthia would be in Europe tonight and—

Hang on a minute.

A big picture of Rebecca bloomed in my head, a picture of the day I went by the Gray house and talked to Rebecca in the study. She seemed devastated that Claudia had died. She told me it wasn't supposed to be like that, or something. I thought she meant that someone as young, talented, and beautiful as Claudia wasn't supposed to die, but now I wasn't so sure.

Rebecca had given me that list of suspects. The list that led nowhere.

Nobody had heard about the stalker Rebecca claimed was terrorizing Claudia.

Nobody knew about the pageant mom Rebecca claimed was angry with Claudia, the woman I assumed was arguing with her at the luncheon. When I asked around, everyone said they saw someone arguing with Claudia. Someone young, one of the models, they thought, not a mom.

Rebecca was there that day, at the luncheon. She dropped by to bring Claudia's passport.

Rebecca was young and small. She could easily be mistaken for a model.

Maybe Debbie had told me the truth. Maybe the argument she overheard was between Claudia and Rebecca.

If all that were true, it would mean—

"I'll be right back," I whispered to Mom, and left the table.

I hurried out of the Crystal Ballroom, down the stairs, and headed left through the main galleria. Ahead were big glass doors that led to the smoking area. It was the nearest place I could go for a private conversation.

Luckily, there was no wind—not that my hair would move, anyway—and only one guy was out there. I fished my cell phone from my purse and called Detective Shuman. I got his voice mail, so I left a message and went back inside.

The dessert course was being served as I sat down at the table again. My insides were jiggly, thinking that across the room, only a few feet away sat Rebecca, who had murdered her sister.

I drew a breath. I had to relax. I didn't want to give anything away by my expression. I absolutely, positively had to remain calm. I couldn't let anything rattle me.

"Good evening," someone said from behind me.

I turned in my chair. Ty stood beside our table.

Oh, crap.

# Chapter 25

Oh my God. Ty looked handsome—beyond handsome, actually. He wore a fantastic Armani tux, his hair shimmered, his eyes sparkled; the lighting in here was really working for him.

My heart fluttered as he gazed down at me with that special look that could only mean—

Wait a minute.

Ty's special look seemed, well, sort of angry. His gaze swept the table. No empty chair for him. Another man beside me, obviously my date.

Okay, this was uncomfortable.

Ty spoke to everyone at the table—except me—shook hands with all the men, then left.

Oh my God. *Oh my God.* He hadn't contacted me once while he was gone, he hadn't called to confirm he'd be here, he showed up late—and he had the nerve to be angry *at me?*

"Excuse me," I said, and left the table.

I caught sight of Ty in the main galleria, heading for the Fifth Street exit. I raced after him—as fast as I could in a tight gown, strapless bra, and three-inch heels.

"Ty?" I called.

He whirled around. The pleasant expression he'd maintained in the ballroom had vanished, anger in its place—and I didn't need to be his sort-of girlfriend to see it.

"What the hell is going on?" he demanded, gesturing toward the ballroom. "I've been working twenty-four-seven, busting my ass to get here tonight, and you're with some other man?"

"I didn't think you'd make it," I explained.

"I told you I'd be here!"

"And why should I have believed you?" I shouted back. "You're totally, completely unreliable. You never show up on time—and tonight proves it!"

Ty glared at me, more angry than ever because I was right and there was nothing he could say to refute it.

He tried another tactic. "You could have had a little faith in me, Haley. A little faith in *us*."

Okay, now I was really angry.

"I didn't hear a word from you while you were gone—not one word," I told him.

"What are you talking about?" he demanded.

I ignored his question.

"I didn't know if you were going to show up or not," I told him. "Did you expect me to miss out on being here tonight? Or sit here with no date?"

Ty shook his head. "I don't understand what you're talking—"

"It's simple, Ty. You don't have time for me. I'm going to spend this evening with someone who does."

I spun around and marched back to the Crystal Ballroom. Ty didn't follow, but I didn't think he would—and I was glad he didn't. Anger and hurt rumbled inside me, and if he came after me and apologized or something, I would have cried—and totally ruined my makeup.

I paused at the entrance to the ballroom and drew in a cleansing breath. Inside were people who cared about me, who wanted to be with me tonight. My parents. Friends. Doug—especially Doug.

Yeah, okay, he was kind of boring and I never listened to much of what he had to say, but he'd been nice to me, really nice.

Inside the ballroom, people were milling around as the dessert service concluded. The award presentations would start in a few minutes. I spotted Doug striding toward me, looking concerned.

See? *That's* how a date is supposed to act.

"Haley, could I speak with you for a moment?" he asked.

Doug touched my elbow and guided me to a corner of the room. He paused for a moment and cleared his throat.

"Well, Haley," he said. "We've been at this for a while now and, frankly, it's not working."

I just stared at him.

"We've given it a try—a good try," Doug said. "I think we need to admit to ourselves that it's over."

"You're . . . you're dumping me?"

"I believe this is for the best," he said.

"You're *dumping me*?"

Heads turned at the closest table. A waiter with a tray of dirty dishes stopped and stared.

Doug nodded. "In time, I know you'll get over me."

"*What?*"

"You're hurt now," he said. "But you're strong. You'll find someone."

Doug patted my shoulder, then left.

Oh my God. *Oh my God.* I couldn't believe this. *Doug* just broke up with *me?* Doug, with his junior high jacket, his wimpy white Kia, his you-make-me-want-to-slit-my-wrists conversation skills? *He'd* broken up with *me?*

Everyone around me stared. The waiter shook his head in sympathy. Two women at a nearby table bent their heads together and whispered.

*Stop!* I wanted to scream. I'm not some loser. I have a Judith Leiber purse, for God's sake.

I squared my shoulders, put my nose in the air, and walked back to my table.

"Where's Doug?" Mom asked as I sat down.

I was tempted to say he'd wet his pants, but didn't.

"Family emergency," I said.

The award presentations got under way with their droning introductions, long-winded acceptance speeches, and polite applause. I didn't hear any of it, my thoughts bouncing back and forth between Ty and Doug.

Ty wasn't willing to give me the kind of relationship I wanted, the kind I thought I deserved. I didn't think of myself as demanding—jeez, asking someone to show up on time for a date wasn't reaching for the moon—but he couldn't manage it. He had something else in mind for our relationship. I knew I'd done the right thing with him tonight.

Doug? I guess I hadn't provided the kind of relationship he was looking for—although just what that might be, I hadn't a clue. Not that I really wanted to date him, but still.

I snapped out of my relationship dilemma as Rebecca Gray took the stage to accept her Westbrook Crystal Recognition of Achievement Award. She got an exceptionally loud round of applause, but I knew it was mostly because everyone knew her sister had been murdered.

Her acceptance speech was brief. She came off the stage and into the waiting arms of her dad, who gave her a big hug, and her mom, who managed to look her in the eye and smile with something that approached pride. Everyone in the room was thinking the same thing: if only Claudia could be here tonight to share this.

Rebecca sat down with her parents as the presentations continued, and I saw her showing the crystal statuette to her mom. They whispered back and forth for a few seconds, and that was it.

While her mom watched the next person receive her award, Rebecca studied her mom. Her smile dimmed, faded, then disappeared. Rebecca glanced at her dad. He gave her a nod, then turned away. She left the table.

I figured Rebecca was heading for the ladies' room, but I wanted to make sure. If Detective Shuman received the voice mail I left earlier, he might show up. I didn't want to have to tell him I had no idea where she was. I followed her.

The south galleria was a very long, very wide corridor with a gorgeous ceiling and thick red and green carpet that led from the hotel's main galleria, past the Heinsbergen Room, the stairs to the Biltmore Bowl and the Regency Room, to the doors that exited onto Grand Avenue. I expected Rebecca to hang a right toward the ladies' room, but she didn't. She kept going.

I went after her. She picked up her pace. So did I—not easy, given the way both of us were dressed. She teetered down the staircase positioned halfway through the south galleria. I followed. Rebecca glanced back, saw me, then started to run.

I yanked my dress up past my knees with one hand and turned on the speed.

"Rebecca, wait!" I called. "It's okay! I understand!"

She looked back again and I saw tears in her eyes. But she kept running. I caught up, grabbed her elbow, and spun her around. She offered little resistance.

"It's okay," I said again, in the most calming voice I could muster, considering I'd been running in a strapless bra. "I know what happened. With Claudia."

Rebecca just stared at me for a few seconds, then burst out crying.

"I didn't mean it! She wasn't supposed to die!" Rebecca wailed.

Detective Shuman had told me that whoever murdered Claudia had thrown every beauty and cleaning product they could get their hands on in the RV that day into the mix, to make sure she died. I saw it differently.

"You just wanted to make her sick, didn't you?" I asked.

Rebecca sobbed louder. "Yes! I just wanted her to stay home. Not go to Europe. So Mom wouldn't leave."

"So she'd come here tonight and see you get your award," I said.

"I worked so hard to get good grades, get into a good school, get the award, but it was never enough!" Rebecca said. "Everything was always about Claudia!"

She cried harder. I didn't try to console her. Better to get her emotions out. We were alone in the corridor, not disturbing anyone.

"It was Mom's fault," Rebecca declared. Her tears stopped and her expression turned angry. "That day. The day of that stupid luncheon at that stupid store. I was studying—studying—for a big test, and Mom made me quit. She made me drive all the way over there to give Claudia her passport."

"So that's when you got the idea to . . . make Claudia sick?" I asked.

Rebecca swiped at her tears with the backs of her hands, and her expression morphed from angry to creepy.

"I told you not to get involved with this," she said. "I told you I was watching."

The notes at my apartment and on my car windshield. Rebecca had sent them.

A wave of fear swamped me. The rooms along the south galleria weren't in use tonight. I heard no one else in the corridor behind us. Through the glass doors ahead I saw Grand Avenue. One car went past. This time of night, few people came to this part of town.

My thoughts skipped ahead and I gasped aloud.

"Jamie," I whispered. "The Missing Server. You killed her, too."

"What else could I do?" Rebecca exclaimed, flinging out both hands. "She saw me around those fruit bouquets. Then she got sick. She must have known I'd poured that stuff onto Claudia's food. I thought she'd keep her mouth shut! She was nobody—*nobody*—just some scholarship kid scrabbling for money! She'd even served at our house for one of Claudia's stupid modeling things!"

"Did Jamie call you? Threaten to tell?" I asked.

Rebecca shook her head. "I knew she'd figure out what I'd done. I couldn't take a chance. I asked around campus, found out where she lived. I *had* to do it."

Poisoning her sister—or just trying to make her sick—on the spur of the moment was one thing. Understandable, maybe. But hunting down Jamie Kirkwood, lying in wait, then running her down?

I realized I was standing in front of a cold-blooded killer—and I wasn't feeling so great about it. If she attacked me, I figured my intricate updo and the multiple layers of spray would protect me from any long-term brain damage, but other than that, I was vulnerable.

Where was Shuman?

I ended up here tonight with two—count them: two—dates and neither of them was here when I might need him.

Then suddenly, without warning, one of my mom's crisis management techniques popped into my head and I knew exactly what to do.

"You need to fix your makeup," I said to Rebecca. "Let's just slip into the restroom."

The ladies' room would be full of women. I didn't want to throw anyone else into harm's way, but I figured Rebecca had enough of her own mother in her not to make a big scene—or kill me—in front of people who mattered.

She didn't move. Her eyes narrowed.

"You're going to tell, aren't you," Rebecca said.

It wasn't a question. She already knew the answer, so I didn't lie to her.

"You need to tell your mom," I said. "Explain it to her so she'll know you didn't mean to really hurt Claudia. It would be better coming from you."

Rebecca shook her head frantically and her eyes got wide. "No. No, I can't. She'll—"

Her gaze lurched to the corridor behind me. She broke for the door.

I glanced back and saw Detectives Madison and Shuman ambling toward us. Rebecca must have remembered them from their visits to her parents' house.

I took off after Rebecca. Shuman dashed past me—I could have run that fast if I had on his outfit—caught Rebecca's arms, and wrenched them behind her. Rebecca collapsed against him, sobbing, and confessed everything.

Detective Madison trotted up a moment later, huffing and puffing. He gave me a smug smile, and said, "So you two were in on this together, huh?"

# Chapter 26

Detective Madison insisted I not leave the scene, so I stayed in the south galleria. I don't know how long I stood there, exactly, but I had on three-hour shoes and my toes had been screaming for a while now.

Someone on the hotel's manage staff had discreetly gotten Rebecca's parents from the ballroom and brought them here. At the sight of their daughter in handcuffs, Cynthia fainted. After hearing the story, her dad staggered outside and threw up. Paramedics came. Both were transported to the hospital, leaving Rebecca in the back of an LAPD squad car parked at the curb.

The one saving grace was that no one in the Crystal Ballroom had learned what was happening, so the Gray family was spared from being a spectacle in front of their friends and colleagues. That would happen tomorrow when the reporters who'd gathered on the sidewalk along Grand Avenue blasted the story to every imaginable media outlet.

I sent a message to my parents in the ballroom telling them to go home without me, I'd arranged for a ride with a friend. It was a total lie, of course, but I didn't want either of them anywhere near this mess.

I gave a statement to Madison and Shuman and, luckily, Rebecca backed me up by chanting that she didn't mean to kill Claudia, only Jamie. Madison was definitely disappointed I wasn't involved.

Detective Shuman walked over. It was just the two of us. Everyone else had gone. Madison was outside the door on his cell phone.

Shuman looked as if he wanted to say something. Thank me, maybe, for solving the murder, or blast me for all the secrets I kept from him. I thought about apologizing, but didn't. This was our relationship now. We could be friendly, but we couldn't be friends.

I didn't like it, but there it was.

"We found Debbie Humphrey, the woman who runs your mom's fruit bouquet business," Shuman said.

A jolt went through me. I really hoped he wasn't about to tell me she was dead, and Madison was outside on the phone calling for a squad car to come and pick me up.

"She's got a sheet a mile long," Shuman said. "Fraud, embezzlement, mostly. You should get an accountant to look at your mom's books."

So Mom had hired a criminal to run Edible Elegance. Not surprising. No wonder Debbie had disappeared after I stopped by the office and mentioned that the police would want to question her in connection with Claudia's death. She wasn't guilty of murder, but dozens of other crimes— including robbing Mom's business of every cent, probably— and didn't want to be there when the cops came around.

"Honestly, I've about had it with that business. I'm sure I won't have any trouble getting Mom to close it," I said. I didn't add that she probably wouldn't even notice.

Shuman and I just looked at each other for a minute. Neither of us liked the way things had turned out between us, but there was nothing to be done. He joined Madison outside. I headed back through the hotel.

I glanced inside the Crystal Ballroom. Staff was in there cleaning, everyone else gone. I decided my evening definitely needed a boost. The liquid kind.

The Gallery Bar off the main galleria boasted a rich wood interior and elegant furniture. A long polished granite bar served signature martinis, fine wines, and exclusive liqueurs.

I just wanted a beer.

The bar was dimly lit, nearly deserted when I walked in. Two guys sat at the bar, one watching a basketball game on the wall-mounted TV, the other huddled over a drink. In the back of the deep room, I saw a couple cozied up together on one of the leather benches.

I slid onto a stool at one of the high tables near the adjacent Cognac Room, a sultry-looking lounge with soft couches and wooden cabinets stuffed with Biltmore memorabilia, and ordered a beer from the waitress. I desperately wanted to kick off my shoes, but was afraid I wouldn't be able to get them on again.

So, this was what my life had become, I realized, sipping my beer. Drinking alone. Zero-for-two for the night in the date department. No clear idea of where my life was headed.

I glanced at my reflection in the mirror behind the bar. At least my hair had held up.

A face, other than my own, stared back at me from the mirror.

Ty.

I whirled on the stool as he walked out of the Cognac Room. He looked impeccable. Bow tie perfectly straight, shirt crisp, not a hair on his head out of place.

Obviously, he hadn't fallen to pieces after our confrontation in the main galleria earlier this evening.

He placed the drink he carried on my table.

"I heard about Rebecca," he said.

"I know that was tough for you, since you'd been close to the family," I said. "Especially since you wanted to get back together with Claudia."

Ty frowned. "Who told you that?"

I shrugged. "It's understandable. You and Claudia dated for a long time. She was really beautiful and—"

"Who told you that?" Ty asked again, a little more forcefully, which was kind of hot.

"Detective Madison."

Ty snorted a bitter laugh and looked away.

My hopes rose. I'd wondered if Madison had made the whole thing up just to rattle me—which he'd succeeded in doing.

"I don't know where he got the idea, but—"

"I told him," Ty said.

Oh my God. It was true. Ty had wanted to get back together with Claudia all along. My heart sank.

"Well, I guess that explains why you never wanted to have sex with me," I said.

Ty looked confused—I got that from him a lot—and said, "I told Detective Madison about my relationship with Claudia at the store, the day she was killed. He asked. He was investigating her murder. I had nothing to hide, so I told him."

"Okay, okay, slow down," I said. I know it sounded crappy, but I was sick of hearing about Claudia. "You can date whoever you want. It's not like we—"

"You've got it wrong," Ty said. "I'm not the one who wanted us to hook up again. It was Claudia. She wanted to get back together with me."

I sat up straighter on the stool, stunned. I hadn't even considered that it had been Claudia's idea.

"She came to me a few weeks before she died," Ty said. "I told her no. I wasn't interested."

I let that sink in for a minute. I'd been living with the certainty that Ty wanted to get back together with Claudia for so long now, the idea wasn't easy to shake.

Then I realized that, even if I accepted it, it wouldn't change anything between us.

"I had one of my assistants phone you, let you know I'd meet you here tonight," Ty said. "Didn't you get the message?"

Oh, crap.

The message I'd seen on my cell phone when I'd gone to call Shuman. I hadn't recognize the name, so I didn't listen to it.

"I sent you flowers," Ty said. "You didn't get those, either?"

"No," I said, stunned that he'd gone to the effort.

"Damn it," he muttered. "I made arrangements before I left. Sarah promised me she'd take care of it."

I perked up. "Sarah Covington? She was supposed to handle it?"

Okay, this was kind of cool. Not getting the flowers would be worth it if it got Sarah in trouble with Ty.

But, really, I knew that a phone call or floral bouquets wouldn't change anything.

"Flowers would have been nice, and so would the phone call," I said. "But face it. We're still not right for each other."

"What the hell are you talking about?" he asked.

"What's my favorite color?" I asked.

Ty just looked at me.

"What day did we first meet?"

He kept staring.

"What's my favorite sports team?" I asked.

He said nothing.

"Why do you want to date me?" I asked.

He opened his mouth, but nothing came out.

"Tell me one thing we have in common," I said.

Ty looked annoyed.

"If I'd known I was going to take a test," he said, "I would have studied."

"But you shouldn't have to study. That's my point. You should know these things about me," I said.

Ty stewed for a few minutes. I couldn't tell if he was angry, or hurt. Maybe a little of both.

"So that's it? You're saying we're through?" he asked.

A little lump rose in my throat, making it tough to talk, but I managed a quiet, "That's what I'm saying."

Ty walked out of the bar.

My eyes burned and I wanted to cry. It was late in the evening, too late to worry about my makeup, but I still needed to get a ride home somehow and I didn't want to look like a raccoon if I had to take a cab.

So I sniffed and tipped up my glass, finishing off my beer in a couple of big gulps.

"That was quite a scene," someone said.

The guy at the bar had turned on his stool and was looking at me.

"Real tender," he said sarcastically. "I missed tonight's deadline, but it will look great in Monday's edition. Probably get me front page, above the fold."

Oh my God. Ben Oliver. The reporter from the *Daily Courier*.

"What are you doing here?" I blurted out.

"Guess you didn't recognize me in this rig, huh?" he said, and touched his lapels.

He had on a tuxedo, sort of. The bow tie dangled around his neck, the top button of his shirt collar was open. The sleeves were a little short. He looked rumpled and shaggy.

"Twenty-bucks-a-night rental at Wal-Mart," he said. "Nothing but the best for a night like this."

"You were in the Crystal Ballroom? For the award presentations?" I asked. It came out sounding kind of shocked because, really, I was shocked.

Ben picked up his drink and rose from his stool. He strolled over, swirling his glass.

"I wanted to thank you for the tip," he said. "Cecil Hartley?"

Oh my God. I'd forgotten all about the definitely missing, supposedly dead Cecil Hartley.

"Did you find him?" I asked, desperate to hear some good news tonight.

Ben studied his glass for a moment, then nodded. "My editor loved it. Ran with it. Flew me to Arizona. Called in favors from every law enforcement agency from here to the New Mexico border. Had forensic experts and criminal lawyers lined up for quotes, television news teams standing by, a helicopter ready to lift off. My editor spared no expense, exhausted every resource imaginable."

Another death. I didn't think I could take any more tonight, after listening to Rebecca, knowing what she'd done to her sister and Jamie. I didn't want to hear the details of Cecil's demise.

"At least the truth is out," I said, "and you're back in your editor's good graces."

"Not exactly."

Ben studied his drink for a moment, swirled it a few times, then took a sip and looked up at me.

"Cecil Hartley is alive and well, enjoying his new life with his new girlfriend."

"*What?*"

"Seems old Cecil was fed up with that daughter of his sticking her nose in his business, sick of neighbors spying on him, tired of living in the same house, on the same street, in the same town, doing what everybody else thought he ought to do," Ben said. "So he packed up the new girlfriend in the new RV and left."

"But Evelyn saw the RV at the house. Barb was there, but not Cecil."

Ben nodded. "Cecil needed some things from the house but didn't want to show his face, afraid some of the neighbors might be watching. Imagine that."

I squirmed on the stool.

"I guess your editor isn't so happy with you," I said. I left "because of the tip I gave you" unspoken. "But, hey, you must have made major points with him tonight for being on the scene when Claudia's murderer was arrested."

Ben took another sip of his drink. "I was in the ballroom, covering the award presentations, when that went down."

"Oh."

"Tomorrow I'm covering a fishing derby. After that, the Little Miss Community pageant. And later this week, I'm interviewing a grandma who self-published a book on how to make your own brown sugar."

Ben drained his glass and placed it on my table, then walked away. At the door, he turned back.

"So thanks for the tip," he called. "I'll remember it . . . Randi."

Oh, crap.

# Chapter 27

Two blocks from Evelyn's house, I phoned her. I figured she'd be up, even though it was barely past eight on a Sunday morning. Her voice was muffled, like I'd awakened her, but she told me to come on over.

I wasn't really up for her tea and brick cookie service at this early hour, but I had to talk to her and I couldn't wait. I might chicken out, if I did.

For a while now I'd been thinking that my life needed to take a different direction. Standing alone in the main galleria at the Biltmore last night, wondering how I'd get home, I figured out some of it.

I called Marcie—what are best friends for?—and she came immediately. We sat on my sofa for a couple of hours talking things out. She said I was crazy, and while Marcie is almost always right about things, I had to go with my gut on this one.

I swung around the corner onto Evelyn's street just as a Mercedes pulled away from her house. It shot past me in a blur, but I caught a glimpse of the driver's face.

Was that Bradley Olsen? From the GSB & T?

I craned my neck looking in my rearview mirror, my side mirror, trying for another angle. The Mercedes disappeared around the corner.

Okay, that was weird. Was that really Mr. Olsen? What the heck would he be doing at Evelyn's house? At this hour of the—

*Oh my God.*

I nearly ran my car up on the curb.

Evelyn and Mr. Olsen? Together?

Well, at least somebody had a hot night.

I parked, rang the bell, shouted my name, and Evelyn let me in. She looked immaculate, as always, wearing khaki pants, a peach blouse, and an unusually wide smile.

"Good morning, Haley," Evelyn said. "Come in. Let me get us some tea."

"No, thanks," I said, following her into the living room. "Listen, I'll make this quick. I need you to go see Bradley Olsen with me tomorrow morning."

Evelyn froze. "At the Golden State Bank and Trust office?"

"I need to talk to Mr. Olsen about the money you're holding in your account for me," I said.

Her brows drew together. "Did you need to buy new school books? Something for your classes?"

"Not exactly," I said. "I want to talk to Mr. Olsen about something."

I'd said Bradley Olsen's name three times now, but Evelyn hadn't broken down and confessed anything. In fact, she barely blinked an eye, which was kind of disappointing. Maybe I'd been wrong.

"Well, Haley, you know I gave my word I wouldn't let you spend this money on anything except school supplies or medical emergencies, or things like that," Evelyn pointed out.

"I want to set up a scholarship fund," I told her. "In memory of Jamie Kirkwood."

With scholarships to students who didn't have rich parents, a trust fund, or a college account, maybe they wouldn't have to work every menial job they could get to make ends meet. Maybe they wouldn't end up witnessing a murder. Maybe they wouldn't end up dead.

It bugged me that during Jamie's short stay on this earth, so few people had known her, loved her, helped her. No parents, few friends, just another face in a sea of students. I wanted the world to remember she'd been here.

"All of your money?" Evelyn asked.

"Yeah," I said. "The whole eighty grand."

Marcie had told me last night that I should keep a little for myself, but I didn't want to. I wasn't so sure college was right for me anymore, and I could always make more money somewhere, doing something.

Evelyn smiled. "That sounds like a wonderful idea."

"Oh, and Cecil Hartley? He's fine. Living in Arizona with the new girlfriend," I told her.

Evelyn looked stunned. "But why hasn't he come back? Why hasn't he contacted anyone?"

I thought the truth would hurt Christine and, probably, Evelyn, so I just said, "I think it's part of his grieving process."

Evelyn looked as if she understood.

I waited another few seconds, but Evelyn still didn't say anything about her and Bradley Olsen, so I left.

Of course, there were a zillion things I could do right now, I thought as I hit the freeway. Shopping, of course. A new purse. Yeah, that would boost my spirits.

But I couldn't quite bring myself to hit the mall right now, not when my entire future hung in the balance. I figured I'd go home, surf the Net, see what other opportunities I could come up with.

I got a mocha Frappuccino at the Starbucks drive-through—just to energize my brain cells—and headed home.

On the way I called Sandy. She didn't answer, so I left a message saying that I had to resign as president of her mom's pet rescue, but as a parting gift I was giving them a truckload of Purina cat food.

The sewing machine that I won in the Holt's raffle still sat in my living room when I walked in. Maybe I would start my own clothing company, or something. That sounded cool. Maybe I could design my own line of handbags. Cooler still.

I grabbed a bag of Snickers bars from the kitchen and my laptop, ready to forge my future, when my doorbell rang. I looked out the peephole and saw a guy holding a floral arrangement.

Okay, this was weird.

I opened the door.

"Delivery for Haley Randolph," he said, and handed me a vase filled with red roses.

They were gorgeous. I placed them on the end table beside my sofa and opened the card. My heart jumped.

Ty.

"Where do you want these?" the deliveryman asked.

I turned and saw him holding a vase of yellow roses.

"More flowers?" I blurted out, my eyes wide.

The guy chuckled and gave me a crooked smile. "You must have given somebody one hell of a wild night."

Actually, I hadn't given anyone a wild night in a really long time, which made this all the more weird.

He stepped outside and brought in vase after vase of flowers. Spectacular arrangements in every color imaginable. I plucked off the cards.

Oh my God. They were all from Ty.

"Sign here," the deliveryman said.

I scribbled my name on his clipboard and handed it back.

He squinted at me. "You look familiar. I've seen you somewhere before."

"I look like a porn star—a top-rated porn star—but I'm not," I told him.

He looked me up and down once more, then left.

I stood in the center of my living room and counted the

floral arrangements. One for every day Ty had been in Europe.

It cheered me up a little to think that he had reamed Sarah Covington for not sending the flowers, as instructed. Nice to know that something good had come out of our breakup.

The doorbell rang again.

"Did you forget one?" I asked.

I thought I would see the delivery guy standing there. I didn't. It was Ty.

My heart swelled. I wished it would quit doing that every time I saw him. Breaking up would be so much easier.

Ty didn't wait for an invitation. He strode inside, jaw set, expression grim.

"Blue," he said.

I just looked at him.

"Monday."

"What are you talking about?" I asked.

"Blue," he said again. "Blue's your favorite color."

I gasped, too stunned to say anything.

"Monday," he said. "We met on a Monday. In the break room at the store. You were reading *People* magazine and jacked up on chocolate."

"You . . . you remembered?"

"You don't have a favorite sports team because you don't have enough patience to sit through a game," Ty said. "And you don't get to decide when it's over between us. We're in this relationship together. That means we decide things together. I get a vote, and I vote that we stay together."

"But things have always been so weird between us," I said. "We never had sex."

"We're fixing that before I leave here today. But right now we have to get this relationship worked out."

"Look, Ty, I appreciate the flowers, and you coming

here," I said. "But nothing's changed. We still don't belong together. I asked you last night to name one thing we have in common and you couldn't."

Ty looked at me for a minute and his expression softened. I figured he didn't have an answer, just like last night.

"You're right. I can't recite a list of all the reasons I like you, or why we should be together, or everything we have in common," he said. "I have advisers for everything. I read memos, reports, charts, and graphs. I analyze data to determine the best possible course of action."

He stopped and took a breath. My heart skipped a beat.

"But when it comes to you, Haley, I don't have to analyze anything. I don't have to *think*. I just *know*," Ty said. "And I *know* I'm crazy about you."

"Really?" I asked, my heart thundering in my chest.

Ty came closer. He took both my hands and held them in his.

"We can figure this out. We can find a way to make things work," he said. "We just need to decide how to get started."

"You can make the big decisions," I told Ty. "And I'll make the small decisions."

He frowned. "Are you sure?"

"Of course," I said. "But *I'll* decide which decisions are big, and which decisions are small."

Ty grinned. "Sounds good to me."

He drew me into his arms and kissed me. Wow, what a kiss. My knees went weak.

He pulled away. "Come with me to Europe tonight."

"You have to go back? Tonight?" I asked, surprised.

"I have to work but I'll make sure I have every evening, every weekend free. I'll take off as many afternoons as I can. We'll see the sights together. It will be a great way for us to get back on track."

"I—I don't know," I stammered.

"I'll call my travel agent." He pulled out his cell phone.

My head spun. Europe? With Ty? Oh my God. He seemed different, and Europe was totally awesome, but—

My cell phone rang. I flipped it open.

"Are you ready to party?" a woman screeched in my ear.

"Who is this?" I asked.

"They make me say that," she said, with a nervous laugh. "Haley, this is Mindy from L.A. Affairs. I was supposed to call you last week, but oh my goodness, that phone in the office. Gracious, it's a real pill to work with. Listen, we need you to start work first thing in the morning."

I looked down at the phone, then put it to my ear again.

"What are you talking about?" I asked.

"The job of event planner you applied for, remember?" she said.

I'd filled out an application as an excuse to talk to some-one about Claudia. I'd forgotten all about it.

"We're in a real fix here," Mindy said. She giggled. "Some-thing kind of fell through the cracks, since we've been shorthanded. It's a big deal. A really big deal, actually. That's why we need you in the morning."

I glanced across the room at Ty, still talking to his travel agent.

"It's a huge bash honoring the legacy of a handbag de-signer," Mindy said.

I perked up. "Handbags?"

"All the designers will be there. Marc Jacobs, Kate Spade, and—oh, there are lots more," Mindy said. "Oh, you should see the gift bags."

"Gift bags?" My breathing got heavy. "Who's being hon-ored?"

Mindy giggled. "Oh, goodness, now, let me think. It's, oh, it's somebody who's dead—or maybe still alive. I don't know. The name is—oh yes, it's Judith Leiber."

*"Judith Leiber?"*

"Have you heard of her?" Mindy asked.

"Yeah, I've heard of her," I said—actually, I think I moaned.

"Then you're just the person we need!" Mindy declared.

My doorbell rang. The way my luck was running, I expected to see the Prize Patrol waiting.

"Can you be here first thing in the morning?" Mindy asked.

I opened the door. No one was there. An envelope stuck out from under my welcome mat.

"Haley?" Ty called. "I've got a seat for you."

I picked up the envelope and pulled out a slip of paper.

"Haley?" Mindy asked in my ear. "Tomorrow morning?"

"Haley?" Ty said again. "What's it going to be?"

On the paper, someone had scrawled, "You've been warned."

Oh, crap.